W9-AEE-510

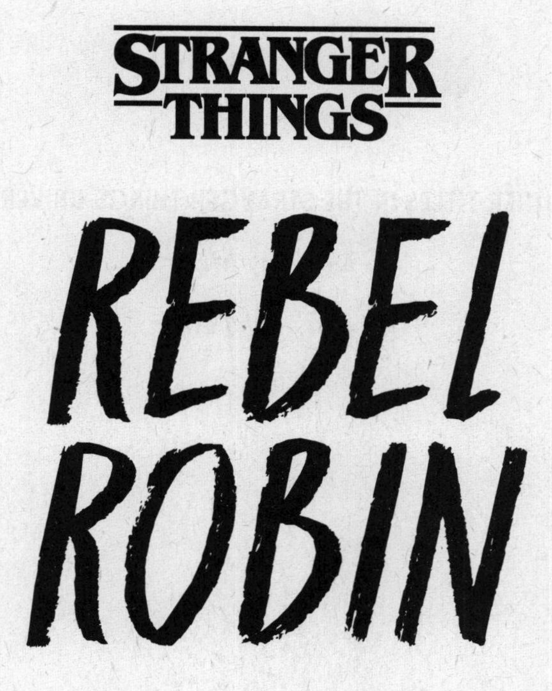
STRANGER
THINGS
REBEL
ROBIN

OTHER TITLES IN THE STRANGER THINGS UNIVERSE

Runaway Max

Lucas on the Line

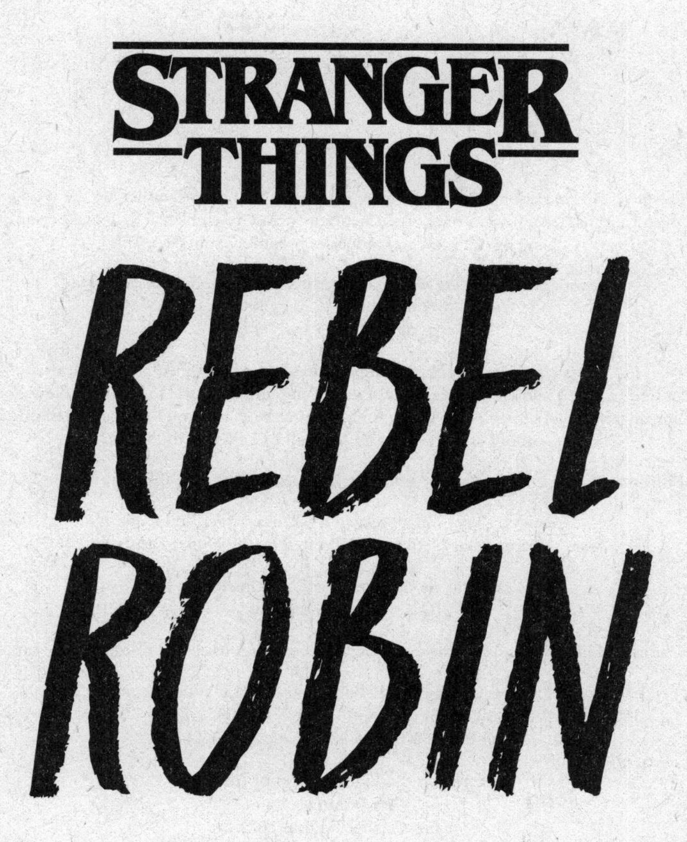

A. R. CAPETTA

EMBER

 Published in the United States by Ember, an imprint of Random House Children's Books, a division of Penguin Random House LLC, New York. Originally published in hardcover in the United States by Random House Children's Books, a division of Penguin Random House LLC, New York, in 2021.

Ember and the E colophon are registered trademarks of Penguin Random House LLC.

Stranger Things and all related titles, characters, and logos are trademarks of Netflix, Inc. Created by the Duffer Brothers.

Visit us on the Web! GetUnderlined.com
ReadStrangerThings.com

Educators and librarians, for a variety of teaching tools, visit us at RHTeachersLibrarians.com

Library of Congress Cataloging-in-Publication Data is available upon request.
ISBN 978-0-593-37556-3 (trade) — ISBN 978-0-593-37558-7 (ebook) —
ISBN 978-0-593-37559-4 (paperback)

Printed in the United States of America
4th Printing
First Ember Edition 2022

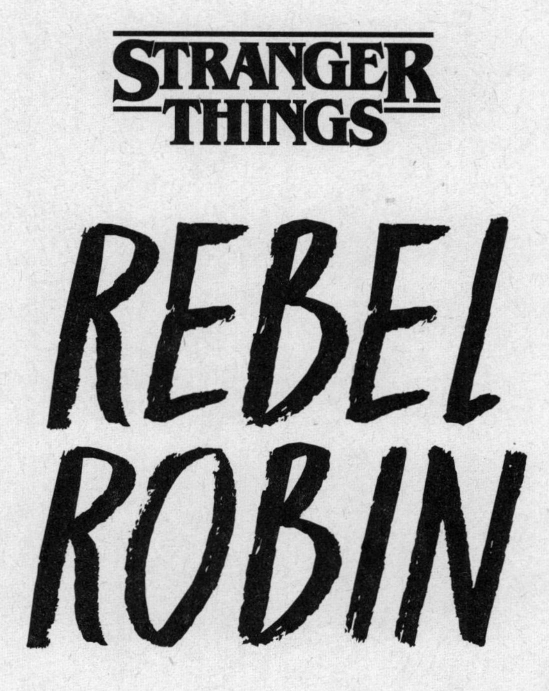
STRANGER THINGS
REBEL ROBIN

HIGH SCHOOL

PROLOGUE

JUNE 8, 1984

I run so fast the lockers blur. Stitches in my abruptly altered dress pop as I pass couples who've cut out of the festivities in favor of making out in the darkened senior hallway. Their egregious kissing would usually be enough to get me to turn around and seek an alternate route, but right now it's just gross background noise.

This feels like a nightmare I've had a thousand times—running through the halls of Hawkins High School. But even in my most extreme dream scenarios, I've never had this little hair. I've never been wearing this much makeup. And prom night has *never* been thrown into the mix by my subconscious.

I'm nearly at the end of senior hall. No turning back now.

I'm headed into the belly of the high school beast—which is the weirdest part of all, because in my dreams I'm always trying to break out of this place. I would never, ever voluntarily break *in*.

"Stop right there, Miss Buckley!" shouts a voice, pinched and petty and adult-sounding. One of the incensed mom chaperones.

"Hey! Back here! Now!" That gravelly command was definitely issued by Chief Hopper.

It's not a real rebellion unless you're in trouble with authority—right?

I wonder how much trouble I could get in for crashing prom and causing some moderate property damage on the way in. Suspension? Expulsion? Would the irate parents of Hawkins High students press charges for what I just did in the parking lot?

I run faster.

Rounding the corner, I pass the concessions that line the hallway outside the gym. About a dozen people are mingling and grazing on platters of cookies and chips and trying to figure out exactly how spiked the punch is.

"Robin!" The sound of my name echoes down the hall. Dash is the one shouting it now. Dash, who I used to think was my friend.

I need to slow him—and all of my detractors—down. So I make a *tiny* detour, barreling into the table that holds about seventy gallons of (judging by the smell, extremely spiked) punch. It pours out in a cascade and I leap forward, avoiding the worst of the spill as everyone else screams and gets their prom attire coated in sticky chemical sugar.

The big double doors of the gym are in sight now. From inside, I can hear the hard-driving heartbeat of a New Wave hit. Is Tammy Thompson already dancing? What will she think when she sees me burst in, wild and reckless and trailed by local law enforcement?

What will she say when I tell her how I feel?

No more time for hypotheticals.

I throw the double doors open. The prom greets me with wild synthesizers and the smells of sweat and AquaNet.

"Hey, Tam," I whisper, practicing for the big moment of terrifying honesty when I show her how I've felt all year, and in doing so simultaneously turn this rebellion all the way up to eleven. "Do you want to dance?"

HAWKINS
HIGH SCHOOL

PART ONE

HAWKINS
HIGH SCHOOL

CHAPTER ONE

SEPTEMBER 6, 1983

The first history class of the year hasn't even started, and I know exactly how it's going to unfold, minute by minute, period by period. I have the entire academic year pegged. At least, I swear I do, until Tammy Thompson walks in.

Something about her is different.

Maybe it's her hair. It used to be pin-straight and red. Now it's short, tousled, and redder. It could be her smile. In freshman year, she was semi-popular and at least semi-fine-with-it, but now we're sophomores and she's got a grin that says she's determined to win friends and influence prom queen elections. (Not that we can go to prom as sophomores, unless an upperclassman invites us, an event so rare and special that people in this school talk about it like it's a meteor sighting.)

Maybe it's the fact that when I see her, music infiltrates my brain.

Soft, obnoxious music.

Wait. My brain would *never* play Hall and Oates. I twist around in my seat and realize that Ned Wright is in the back of the room with a boombox perched on his shoulder. He's turned it down so Miss Click—sitting at her desk, ignoring us like a pro, acting like we don't exist until the bell rings—won't confiscate it. When class starts, he'll slide it under his desk and use it as a footrest. (He's been doing this since eighth grade. He's also a pro.) But for right now, Tammy Thompson is strolling across the room on a cloud of "Kiss on My List" and raspberry-scented . . . something. Lotion? Shampoo? Whatever it is, it reminds me of the scratch-and-sniff stickers I collected with a fervor back in middle school.

She slides into a seat, and her friends greet her in high-pitched flutters.

"Oh my gosh, your hair."

"How was the beach, Tam?"

Tam?

Maybe that's the difference—she's got a new nickname to go with her fresh haircut and enhanced smiling capabilities. "Tam," I whisper, quietly enough that nobody can hear me under the how-was-your-summer uproar.

Miss Click looks up. Ominously.

One minute until class starts. If I was a run-of-the-mill

nerd, like I'm pretending to be, I would have a stack of pristine, unsullied white notebook pages ready to go. I would have already done a few chapters of the reading to get a jump start. My pencils would all have perfect, identical, weapons-grade points.

As it is, I plunge down at the last minute and rummage in my bag, looking for my history textbook and anything that will leave a mark on paper. There's a graveyard of gum on the underside of the desk. And the perm I let Kate talk me into right at the end of summer—the perm that made my scalp tingle for a week and still makes my head smell perpetually like overcooked eggs—means my hair is big enough that I have to be extra careful how much space I leave for clearance.

I almost hit my head on the underside of the desk when I hear her start to sing.

Tammy's voice rises over . . . Hall's? Oates's? It's bold and sweet and, yes, she uses vibrato as generously as I peanut butter my sandwiches, but the point is she's not afraid. Everyone can hear her. I come back up from my deep dive into my backpack and look around at our classmates, but nobody seems to care that Tam is now singing her heart out in the middle of the room with thirty seconds to go until class starts. And she doesn't seem to care if anyone is watching.

What does *that* feel like?

I spin my pencil, feeling every one of the six edges on my finger.

Then the bell rings, Miss Click stands up, and everything slides back into place, exactly the way I thought it would be.

Including when Steve Harrington shows up three and a half minutes late, looking lost, probably because his hair flopped into his eyes and he couldn't see any of the classroom numbers. How does he get anywhere with that hair? It looks even bigger than it did last year.

"Hey, people," he says.

Everyone laughs like the part in a sitcom where the audience guffaws at the main character's not-particularly-funny motto. They know they don't have to do that in real life, right? Even Miss Click beams at him like his hair somehow cured cancer. That's an extreme and rarefied level of popularity, where even the teachers don't glare at you because you're simply too socially precious.

Steve jams himself into the desk next to Tam.

She turns the color of a fresh raspberry.

This whole thing is so ridiculous that my brain glitches and my fingers stop working and my pencil drops to the linoleum with a hard clatter. When I go to pick it up, it's just out of reach. I duck, I grasp, but I can't quite get it. When I finally do, I feel so triumphant that I come up way too fast and knock my head on the underside of the desk. Aka the gum graveyard. My head clangs hard, and my frizzed-out perm touches a dozen ancient pieces of gum at once. They're so hardened that they don't stick to me.

Which is good. And also horrifying.

"Robin, do you need to go to the nurse's office?" Miss Click asks with a pitying look as I resurface. Her concern is touching.

"Unless the nurse has a time machine that will take me back exactly one class period, no."

"All right, then," she says, launching into her first-class-of-the-year monologue.

At least the attention of my classmates doesn't last long. And Tam doesn't even seem to notice my disgrace. (Not that I want her to.) But it bothers me, just a tiny bit, that the reason she *doesn't* notice me is that she's too busy humming "Kiss on My List" while she stares at Steve Harrington.

HAWKINS
HIGH SCHOOL

CHAPTER TWO

SEPTEMBER 7, 1983

I wanted to make it through my entire schedule before declaring this outright, but I am truly not impressed with sophomore year.

"It's like all of the teachers just gave up," I say. "Like they collectively decided that this year is the dead zone of our education." I'm one of those weird people who like to actually *learn* while they're in school. At least, I was. Now that I have the creeping, cold, cynical sense that none of our teachers actually want to be here, it's getting harder to care by the minute.

Milton, Kate, and Dash are into school in the intense high-achiever way that they are into everything. At the beginning of our first band practice, when I suggest that sophomore year doesn't really count, they seem taken aback. Milton actually gasps.

Kate frowns and shuffles through her music and drill charts (which she doesn't need, because she's had everything memorized for months). She's shorter than I am—well, most of the girls in our grade are shorter than I am, so I'm not sure if that's a helpful description. Kate is five foot zero and zero-tenths, although she likes to say that her perm adds at least two inches. "If our teachers don't care about our education, we're going to have to care twice as hard."

That's Kate. She fights for everything, including battling her way to first chair of the trumpet section as a sophomore.

"We're all reaching the point where we're pretty much smarter than our teachers, anyway," Dash adds with a smirk.

Dash doesn't work nearly as hard as Kate. Dash—short for Dashiell James Montague, Jr.—sits in the front row of every class but doesn't take notes, claiming that he retains everything. Then he skips showering on the day of the test, shoves everything into his head, and gets an A. He says he's enamored of learning, but he only has eyes for his GPA. Plus, he doesn't seem to notice that his lack of showering on test day throws off everyone in a ten-foot radius, which really isn't fair to the people around him who are trying to write coherent five-paragraph essays.

You know the type.

“Seriously, though, I think all four of us are smarter than ninety percent of the teachers in this school,” Dash asserts.

“You’re not smart enough to realize that I can hear you,” Miss Genovese declares without looking up from her sheet music.

“She’s got scary-good hearing,” Milton whispers.

“Yes. Yes, I do,” Miss Genovese agrees. “That’s why I’m the band teacher. I can hear every wrong note you play, too,” she announces to the group in general. “And it pains me. Your reedy squeaks haunt my dreams.”

She goes over to help Ryan Miller in the percussion section with his quads. Dash waves at us all to come closer. I sniff cautiously. His auburn hair looks clean, and he’s giving off the scent of pine soap. No tests imminent. I scooch my chair closer. “Teachers are just scary in general,” he whispers. “I don’t think they’re here to teach us. I think they’re here to feed off our innate potential.”

“Like vampires?” Milton asks. He’s taking this way too seriously. But Milton is very, very serious. And nervous. I’d worry about him, but he worries so much it’s probably redundant.

“Think about it. They’re not really that bright, they move slowly through the halls, they need our brains to survive. They’re clearly zombies.”

Milton and I groan. Kate gives a nervous giggle.

Dash has been on a horror movie kick since fifth grade, when he realized it set him apart from kids who still slept with night-lights. The gleeful sense of superiority never quite faded. If it eats flesh, drinks blood, or lurks in the shadows, Dash is on board. This year we watched *The Evil Dead* over the summer. A lot. He got a top-of-the-line VCR for his last birthday—yes, his *own* VCR, which is ridiculous even by rich-people standards—and he kept inviting everyone over for viewing parties, but no matter what tape he boasted about having, we always ended up watching *The Evil Dead*.

I stopped going sometime in August, pretending that my parents needed me to help out more at home. The truth was, I couldn't handle watching Kate and Dash inch closer and closer to each other on the couch, the whole time acting like they didn't know their thighs were on a collision course.

That's another thing about sophomore year.

In middle school, crushes were talked about exclusively on the bus and during sleepovers, and dating was a novelty. In freshman year, relationships became inevitable. This year, things have ramped up to a complete frenzy. We're less than a week in, and there have already been a slew of hallway make-outs, dramatic breakups, and declarations of undying love. The situation is amped up in marching band because we start practices halfway through the summer.

I give the room a quick scan. At least half of the girls in the band room are wearing jewelry inscribed with the names of their boyfriends, who are also in band. (Band nerds date band nerds: it's the law of the land.) When a couple makes it official, the boy gives the girl a gold anklet with both of their names on a gold nameplate charm. But most of the girls don't think that anyone can see the evidence of their boyfriends' devotion, so they buy longer gold chains and wear the name-plate charms around their necks.

I've been waiting for the day when Dash finally gives one to Kate. (Really, Kate's been waiting for that day, and I've been waiting by proxy.) Even right now, at this very moment, Kate and Dash are sending each other looks in some kind of Morse code.

Dash's eyelashes: *Let's make out later.*

Kate's eyelashes: *Maybe!*

Dash's eyelashes: *Really?!?!*

Kate's eyelashes: *I already said maybe. I'm first chair, practice is about to start, you're distracting me.*

Dash's eyelashes: *But you're so pretty.*

Kate's eyelashes: *Really?!?!*

I don't know how much of this I can tolerate.

All Kate wants to talk about now is boys in general, and Dash specifically. It's bad enough when popular girls like Tammy Thompson completely lose track of their own brains over hapless hair piles like Steve Harrington.

Which brings me back around to the zombie conversation. "If our teachers are undead, they're also undernourished. Have you noticed how hungry they look? Our brains aren't giving them much sustenance. Maybe we aren't as smart as we think we are. Maybe it's because everyone's too obsessed with *dating stuff* all of a sudden."

Hint. Hint.

Kate just gives another nervous laugh and turns back to

her trumpet, practicing her fingering for one of the many John Philip Sousa marches Miss Genovese is always inflicting on us.

I scared her off, but I don't feel better about it.

"All right," Miss Genovese says. "Time to get your squads for the 1983 marching band season in order! You have three minutes to name yourselves, and not a second longer. Please don't ask me how long it's been. There is a clock above the door."

Groups of four huddle together—except for ours, which is already gathered. I'm the only French horn in marching band. Well, technically I only play the French horn in concert band. In marching band it's a mellophone, which is played in exactly the same way but is slightly flattened instead of round, so I can carry it around for months on end. Freshman year, Miss Genovese tacked me onto a squad with three trumpet players, which makes sense, I guess, because the mellophone looks like a trumpet with bonus squiggles in the middle section. Since that moment, the four of us have been socially fused. Kate likes to say we're an atom, because that's the kind of endearingly nerdy metaphor she goes in for.

But the truth is, even with all of the time we've spent together in the band room and on the field, on the bus and at games, I'm not *quite* as fused as the rest of the group. On some level—the subatomic one, I guess—I get the sense that I don't quite fit in with most of the band kids. That no matter how much time I spend with them, I'll never be *one* of them.

And that can be scary because at Hawkins High, standing out is pretty much a death sentence unless you're popular.

"All right," Dash says, snapping me back into the moment. "Sophomore year squad name. Go."

"We're going to be Odd Squad again, right?" Milton asks. "We already voted on it last year. I think we should keep it that way, for continuity, and also because coming up with a new name is going to be an ordeal." Milton is the only junior in our group, and while his quiet, nervous nature keeps him from acting like the de facto leader, Kate and Dash tend to listen when he speaks up like this.

"I love Odd Squad!" Kate says.

"Odd Squad it is," Dash adds.

I nod. Not that they were waiting for my vote.

We spend the next two minutes in silence. Kate and Dash have moved on from eye-flirting to ankle-flirting. (I've seen Dash's feet: gross.) I concentrate on getting ready to play for the first official practice of the year. I have the pieces memorized, but that's only half the battle with my instrument. Let's be honest: it's murder compared to most of the instruments in this room. It's an elaborate contraption of metal tubes that seems to exist solely to bleat out a squeak at exactly the wrong moment. I chose it back in elementary school because no one else wanted to play it. I don't exactly regret my choice—but I wish someone had told me how much time I'd spend emptying a spit valve.

We figured out our squad name too fast. We still have two

minutes left. Two minutes of nothing. Now, thanks to Miss Genovese's little reminder about the existence of the clock, all I can seem to do is listen to it. It's one of those big, round black-and-white ones with a second hand that audibly clicks the moments of your life away.

Click. Click. Click.

Three more seconds gone.

I catch Miss Genovese staring at the exit door in the back. I've seen her run for the teachers' parking lot the second school ends to light up one of her beloved menthols. I've smelled the smoke stubbornly clinging to her hair after lunch. She leaves the room like there's a fire at her heels—just enough time for a quick one.

Our teachers don't want to be here. My classmates only care about rubbing up against each other. I'm supposed to get through three more years of this, how?

Right when I'm thinking about standing up and strolling out the door, Sheena Rollins, who plays oboe, does that exact thing. Or at least she tries. When she gets close, one of the jerkwads in the percussion section bars her way.

If I'm worried about not quite belonging, Sheena Rollins is the poster child for aggressively not fitting in. She's in the class ahead of me, so it feels like I've had a front-row seat for the year-by-year increase in bullying as she got overtly stranger. Her wardrobe is part of it. She wears white from head to toe: sometimes it's white overalls and a white tiara, and sometimes it's a puffy white miniskirt and an oversize flowing shirt. None of it follows the unspoken code of what everybody else is wearing. And most of the time, it looks like Sheena sewed at least part of the outfit herself. (Another point of bullying for my brand-obsessed peers.) Today she's in a white fifties-style dress with tiny black dots, and a white cloth headband.

"Hey, Sheena," someone says. "What do you think you're doing? Teacher's not here to give out passes. Sit your polka-dotted ass down."

Sheena pushes her lips together, but she doesn't sling a comeback. She doesn't say a word.

Here's the other thing about Sheena Rollins: I remember her from elementary school as a soft-spoken kid, but I haven't heard her speak a word since seventh grade. She even plays the oboe so quietly that Miss Genovese is constantly telling her to "blow harder." (Which doesn't exactly help when it comes to vulgar joke time.)

"Where are you going?" Craig Whitestone asks, a grin as shitty as cafeteria meat loaf on his face.

Sheena shrugs.

"She's lying," Dash pipes up.

"Dash," I whisper, with an elbow to his side that misses and collides painfully with his trumpet.

"She spends the whole period in the bathroom," Kate informs me, as if that makes it okay that she's been policed by her fellow band members.

"So?" I ask. "Who cares?"

"Band kids don't ditch," Milton reminds us.

"Miss Genovese just ditched," I remind him.

"She's the *teacher,*" Kate breathes in a sacred tone. Teachers can do no wrong in her book.

Sheena tries to walk around Craig, but he blocks her. She tries again, head ducked, walking with a little more determination, but Craig grabs her by the ponytail, tugging her back into the room. A few of his fellow jerkwads laugh.

"Hey," I say. "Let her go, you walking spit valve."

"It's their mess," Kate hisses. "Don't get involved."

I know that I shouldn't, on a pure survival level. Which is perhaps the grossest thing of all.

"Hey, Sheena," Craig says. "You're all dressed up with nowhere to go. Do you want to dance?"

He nods at his friends, and a few of the band kids start playing sloppily. Sheena jumps on a chair to avoid playing into his stupid joke. Craig just gets down on his knee like he's serenading her, which makes her blush—in a furious way. She jumps off the chair and makes another break for the door, but Craig catches her arm and spins her in a travesty of a dance move. A couple of the big, beefy guys on percussion decide to back Craig up, too. They circle around in front of the double doors so that Sheena really can't leave the music room. They dance in front of her, turning and waggling their butts, and then turning back around and thrusting their hips forward to waggle their . . . other bits.

In case you didn't know this: band kids can be surprisingly lewd. By the time Miss Genovese comes back in, it's like a barnyard crossed with a burlesque, and she can barely rein us in.

“All right.” She crosses her skinny little arms. “Who started it?”

I go to point at Craig Whitestone, but Kate grabs my finger. At least half of the class points at Sheena.

“Miss Rollins,” Miss Genovese says with a few dry clucks. “That’s detention. On the first day. Impressive, really.”

Sheena flops back into her chair, looking ready to snap her oboe into pieces and walk out. But she doesn’t. She stays because she has to, and everyone makes her life hell because . . . well, because they do.

A few years ago, most of Sheena’s torment came exclusively from the popular kids. But in high school, I’ve noticed this kind of behavior spreading through the student body, everybody collectively getting better and better at making life miserable for the students who don’t fit in.

Maybe I’ve watched too many of Dash’s horror movies, but the truth seems pretty clear.

High school is a monster, and it’s eating everyone I know.

HIGH SCHOOL

CHAPTER THREE

SEPTEMBER 9, 1983

The more I look, the more I see the monstrous nature of high school. Specifically, Hawkins High. Here's the paradoxical problem: either you fall into the deadly trap of trying to be like everybody else, or you get devoured for being different.

Two days after Sheena tries to leave the band room, I catch her at her locker. Every few days, it cascades with items that people have shoved in through the slits in the metal: white glitter, nasty notes, condoms.

Today, she's blinking at her textbooks, shaking her head. She tries to open one of them, but she can't. Some bottom-dweller took them to the woodshop, cut them in half, and glued them back together.

"Who even has time to do things like that?" I mutter.

Then I rush forward to help her. "Sheena . . . ," I say, but she either doesn't hear me or doesn't want my pity. She's already moving fast, toward the far end of the hallway, where she dumps the textbooks into the trash.

A teacher catches her and gives her detention for ruining school property.

That teacher, Miss Garvey, escorts her to the principal's office, putting a hand on Sheena's shoulder and saying in her gentlest voice, "Things like this wouldn't happen if you made it just a *smidgen* easier for people to understand you, Sheena."

I am a smidgen away from throwing up on Miss Garvey's shoes.

I think about going straight to the principal and telling him everything I just saw. But would he care? Or would I just end up in detention with Sheena for pointing out that this school is rife with delinquents? The answer is self-evident, so instead of fighting the many-headed monster that is Hawkins High, I leave.

There's no field practice on Fridays, and our first game of the season isn't until next week. The second after the last bell rings, I grab my bike out of the rack. It used to belong to my mom. It's covered in her old flower decals, and the handlebars end in the sad, stubby remains of streamers that I pulled out when I was thirteen. It has a single speed, and every day it has to rub shoulders with a bunch of shiny ten-speed Huffys and Schwinns. I climb on the banana seat (ouch. every time.) and fly away.

Riding around by myself is the best feeling in the world. As a bonus, the breeze makes my hair wing out behind me and I can't smell my perm anymore. The sidewalk ticks beneath my tires, square after square. The trees are thickly green, the houses starched white.

As I bike down a smooth stretch of sidewalk, I reach for my Walkman and turn it on. I don't have to check what's in there—it's always loaded with my language tapes.

French tape 2, side 1, "Weather" clicks on.

"Le temps," a woman says in her very soothing, very French voice.

"Le temps," I mutter.

"La tempête."

"La tempête."

"La brise."

"La brise."

I'm getting into a good rhythm when a car speeds by, away from the high school, honking at me so I jolt out of the moment and nearly eat pavement. I put a hand to my Walkman. It's fine. But it easily could have dropped and shattered, and I would have no way to listen to the language tapes that I begged my parents to buy me in eighth grade (from an infomercial, no less).

I ride expertly, no hands on the handlebars, both middle fingers raised—with a smile.

"Choke on diesel!" I shout.

"Die, loser!" someone shouts back.

"So nonspecific." I push down on my pedals and stand up

to shout, before they're out of range, "You need a comeback coach!"

I don't know who's driving. They probably didn't see who I was either—the mere fact that they're in a car and I'm on an ancient bike is enough. Power dynamic, established. Loser, apparent. But it's not really about winners and losers. We *all* live in small-town Indiana. There's nothing big or shiny to win. I think people know that, even if they don't want to admit it. Which means spitting on people (literally or metaphorically) is just another way to pass the time. I fully believe that if we lived in a place where we had things to do, things that mattered, my middle fingers would get less of a workout. But I live in Hawkins. If I stay long enough, I'm going to become the Jane Fonda of middle fingers.

My hands wrap around the handlebars again. I add a few dings from my metal bell just in case the jerk who passed me is still paying attention.

I keep riding to the outskirts of town, where there are more clouds than cars. The day is pristine, but taking the long way—past the fields and around the quarry—is starting to turn on me. It gives me time to think about how the horror show of a popular kid in that car is just one of the monster's many claws. Its reach goes way beyond the school itself. Which means I'll never be able to escape it. Not while I live here.

But there's nothing I can do about that. I'm stuck in a town so normal that it actually hurts. A town where *normal* has grown teeth.

By the time I get home, I'm ready to let some of this frustration out. I pull the spare house key out from its hiding place under a planter, and as I let myself in I'm already yelling, "I can't believe you voluntarily chose to live here!"

Mom is dancing around the living room in a crocheted sweater that cuts off around her belly button, worn tight over a long flowing dress. She's got her eyes closed, fingers snapping. Most of the time when I get home she's still at work and I just let myself into an empty house, but today she's home early.

"You can't believe what, honey?"

A record is turning on its carved wooden stand, letting out the predictable sounds of a plaintive voice insisting that if someone doesn't love them now, they never will again. Mom is stoned at four p.m. and listening to Fleetwood Mac.

"I can't believe that you *chose* to live *here,*" I say.

"Those words are so pointed, Robin," she says in a whisper-tone. "Can you start again from a place of peace?"

When she starts speaking in mantras, I know I'm not getting an answer.

Usually, I'd drop this topic on the shag carpet, find myself a snack, and go to my room to get my homework out of the way so I could work on what I actually like: languages. I'm up to four so far (English, Spanish, French, Italian), and I want to be fully fluent in each of them before I start adding more.

But something about staring down the rest of sophomore year is starting to mess with my head, and the normal routine just won't do. I go over to the record player and turn the volume down. Mom flicks her eyes open—she doesn't like it when anyone disrupts her records. She worries about scratching them as much as other people would worry about hurting a friend's feelings.

"Did you know that they created this song by splicing together pieces of other songs?" she asks in a hyper-impressed, dreamy sort of state. You'd think Fleetwood Mac single-handedly (quintuple-handedly?) brought about world peace.

"Did you know they've had two new albums since *Rumours* came out?"

"Neither of those is nearly as good," she says. "Robin, baby, you know how I feel about this. People are obsessed with *new.*"

I really do know what she means. Everyone at school gobbles up new fashions, new fads, new technology. Milton obsessively collects anything that can play New Wave—from keytars to eight-tracks. Dash owns a dozen gray V-neck sweaters that he swears are different brands, even though they look exactly the same on his skinny frame, and he's got a pair of prep-tastic Sperry Top-Siders for every day of the week. Kate is only allowed to own things she can wear to church, which means she's blown five years' worth of allowance on a secret wardrobe that she keeps stuffed in her gym locker at school. Right now she's collecting overpriced lace headbands because she wants to look like some new pop singer with a severely Catholic name.

The Odd Squad are pretty tame examples, actually. Tam and her friends seem to have a new tube of lipstick or shade of eyeliner every day. And don't give me a megaphone and ask how much Steve Harrington must spend on hair product and chunky, unflattering sunglasses, because people will hear about it all the way in Michigan.

Everything in our lives is supposed to be shiny, store-bought, or sickeningly expensive. All three is the holy trinity. Another thing the high school monster is good at: constant, ever-faster consumption. I'm not even trying to keep up. I love the flaking paperbacks that I find at the library book sale. The only pieces of technology I own are an off-brand Walkman for my language tapes and a Polaroid camera that Kate gave me for my birthday last spring (which I suspect was her old model, because she had a newer, shinier 8mm). Most of my clothes are vintage or hand-me-downs from various "cousins." (Not actual cousins, but the kids of Mom and Dad's hippie friends. And they have a lot of kids.)

I happen to agree with my mom on this.

But there's another side to the argument. "You and Dad are a little too invested in *old* stuff. If it was made in the sixties, you immediately think it's sacred. You know you can't actually worship macramé and lava lamps, right?"

Mom crosses her arms and squints at me, her groovy state grinding to a halt.

"Seriously, how did two complete flower children end up stranded in Hawkins, Indiana?" I ask, plopping down on the carpet and tucking my feet under me. It's progeny vs. parent, and I'm going to stay right here until she coughs up the truth.

"You really need to know?" Mom asks.

"I really do."

I don't ask Mom and Dad a lot of questions, or if I do, they're usually rhetorical. I don't demand answers. I've always been an "easy child," as Mom calls me, going along with things, never kicking up trouble. Maybe it's the novelty of this moment that makes her suspicious, or maybe she just doesn't like talking about her past unless it's on her own terms. "What for?"

"School project," I say with a shrug. "About our origins."

I'm good at thinking on my feet. Have I mentioned that?

Mom laughs and swirls her bracelets around to the high-pitched cooing of "You Make Loving Fun." "Your origin was in the back of a VW van after this one particularly magical night on the Oregon coast. . . ."

I put my hands firmly over my ears, jump to my feet, and remove myself from this blatantly unacceptable situation.

In my room, I throw on my metallic headphones and click the Walkman back on. French tape 2, side 1, "Greetings and Goodbyes" comes on, but the soothing monotone of the woman's voice saying "Bonjour! Salut! Coucou! Allô? Au revoir! Je suis désolée, mais je dois y aller" just isn't doing it right now.

I turn to my limited selection of actual music and put on Stevie Nicks's solo album *Bella Donna* to compete with Mom's eternal Fleetwood Mac. It's a small act of rebellion, but it scratches the itch. I skip straight to the über-dramatic opening to "Edge of Seventeen." The music spills over me as I fling myself down on the carpet.

I stare at the ceiling.

The ceiling stares back.

I'm stuck here, definitively stuck, and I don't know what to do. Stevie Nicks—in her gravelly way—is reminding me that I'm not anywhere *near* seventeen. There's some kind of hope in seventeen, some promise of adventure that I can only dream about. Past that, eighteen is waiting. And freedom. And the rest of my life.

I'm only fifteen and a half.

Nobody sings about that.

HAWKINS
HIGH SCHOOL

CHAPTER FOUR

SEPTEMBER 10, 1983

In Hawkins, even a trip to the grocery store can be fraught.

I'm only here to pick up the requisite junk food for my Saturday hangout with Kate, but I get stuck in the checkout line behind a mom I recognize from school. Mrs. Wheeler. Her daughter, Nancy, doesn't seem to be with her, but there are four small people in tow—at least one of them is her offspring. They're all swarming around instead of helping her, bombing down the cereal aisle, shouting cryptic things at each other through walkie-talkies.

"All right, Mike," Mrs. Wheeler calls in her most indulgent tone. "Not *too* wild, okay?"

Mike, her extremely pale child, snarls at her and runs away.

"They're complete hellions," Mrs. Wheeler admits to the grandmotherly woman working the checkout, and they both chuckle.

What a great joke.

Mrs. Wheeler's wearing a white dress and pink high heels, and her hair is teased into a blond tempest. There's an enormous amount of food in her cart, but she seems to nutritionally crave small talk. She literally won't stop chatting up the checkout lady. She talks about the new stop sign they put in. (Traffic patterns are apparently a big deal when you have nothing else to look forward to.)

When everything is scanned, she turns. Her facade slips for a second, her voice coming out more like a drill sergeant than a saccharine TV mom. "Mike! Bring your friends over here and help with the bags!"

Her ghostly child with a frightful dark bowl cut shrieks, "Mom. We're busy!"

The streaks of rouge on her cheeks pull tight as she grimaces. "Fine, Mike, just . . . meet me outside?"

Mike grumbles and pushes a button on his walkie-talkie. "We're meeting the Blond Medusa outside."

Mrs. Wheeler sighs. She looks miserable, but she's got her teeth locked in a tight smile as she turns to the bag boy.

"Can we hurry it up here, please?" she asks.

"Sorry, Mrs. Wheeler."

She frowns and continues to berate him—with a smile

on the whole time—because he's not packing the bags "correctly." Mrs. Wheeler seems perfectly comfortable treating this guy like a servant, like he's in some way beneath her. It feels like I'm watching the social order of high school out in the wilds. None of it stops when we graduate, not as long as we stay here in Hawkins—it just evolves, takes new forms.

When Mrs. Wheeler (finally) budges, I drop my M&M's and slightly melted Milky Way bar on the counter and wait for the checkout lady to ring me up as I dig through the pockets of my jean jacket for change.

Mrs. Wheeler looks straight at me and says, "Oh, sweetie, just candy? You are *so* lucky that you don't have to worry about your figure yet." She smooths down the front of her dress—showing off a seriously toned Jazzercise stomach. "I remember being like that in high school. I was just like you."

I laugh. I can't help it.

There's no way Mrs. Wheeler was like *me* in high school. She was probably top-shelf popular.

"Oh, you think I'm being a silly old lady," she says, even though she's not remotely old. "But I grew up in Hawkins, and I can tell you that those high school days are golden. You should enjoy them. You have to enjoy things . . ." She looks out the glass front wall of the grocery store, where the four feral small people are pretending to be spies. "While you still can."

What happens to the people who already aren't enjoying any of this? I want to ask. *How much worse is it going to get for* us*? What* *horrible fate does this town have in store for anyone who isn't starting at the top of the social order?*

I don't ask her any of that, of course.

I dump a bunch of change on the counter, take my candy, and run.

CHAPTER FIVE

SEPTEMBER 10, 1983

By the time I get to Kate's, the Milky Way is mostly melted.

"Come on in," she says. "Parental coast is clear."

Kate's got the kind of parents who go to church twice on the weekends and stay there basically all day. Once we started high school, she was allowed to decide if she wanted to skip Saturday services, as long as she went to youth group on Tuesday nights. It didn't take her long to realize that the brownie points she'd score for a double church weekend could never outweigh having one-seventh of the week to herself.

She's already changed into her secret wardrobe. (She keeps a weekend outfit in her backpack.) We're both wearing stirrup pants and oversize T-shirts in bright, semi-clashing colors. (Teal and highlighter-yellow for me, fuchsia and orange for Kate.) My everyday style is a little more jeans and secondhand T-shirts, but Kate loves it when we match.

We make popcorn on the stove—her parents don't believe in microwaves—and pour it into a big bowl. I pour the entire box of M&M's in. I had to pick up them up on the way over because none of our parental units believe in processed sugar.

"Ahhh," Kate says, digging in with both hands. "Food of the gods."

"Isn't that ambrosia?" I ask.

"If there are gods in Hawkins, they would definitely eat this," she says, crunching down on a bite.

"I heard that *if,*" I said, teasing her with my flat-as-a-Midwestern-farm voice. "And gods? Plural?"

"Blasphemy squared! It's a good thing I don't have any younger siblings to snitch on me."

Neither of us has siblings. My parents had me by accident (nobody gets pregnant in a VW van on purpose), whereas Kate was adopted. In some ways, we have a lot in common, and in other ways, our families could not be more different.

We made a list once, comparing and contrasting the two. In one column, we had things like "doesn't trust the government" and "too many steamed vegetables." In the other, we had things like "Kate's house is always spotless" vs. "Robin's house smells like dogs even though we don't have any."

"Let's take this to the den," Kate says, grabbing the bowl and a cold ginger ale for each of us. Her parents have a weird loophole for ginger ale—apparently since it's made from a root, that's okay.

We settle into the brown plaid couch and I turn on the TV, flipping around until I find the news. The anchor is in the midst of a segment about Radio Shack and some new color computer they're releasing, the CoCo2.

"CoCo2?" I ask, test-driving the name. "That sounds more like an experimental chimpanzee than a computer."

"Scientists are great at discovering things, not naming them," Kate points out. "Why do you think they defer to Greek and Latin? It makes everything sound fancy and respectable, when really they're just hiding the fact that, left to their own devices, they'd name planets things like Neville, after some random scientist who happened to have his telescope pointed in the right direction."

"Hey," I say, fake affronted. "Robin would be a superlative planet. Free one-way tickets for anyone who needs to start over."

Wow, joking about leaving Earth should not make me so wistful.

"Can we change the channel, please?" Kate asks, grabbing for the remote. "It's my one day off from a fully educational diet. I want my MTV."

"You know my dad thinks the government puts subliminal messages in the news. I have to get my fill of the outside world while I can."

"Fine," Kate sighs. "I guess it keeps me up-to-date on things I might need to know for debate."

"Right. Like whether or not CoCo2 will develop sentience and Radio Shack will lead the fight for human survival in the robot uprising."

"I'm taking the negative stance."

"So . . . the robots win?"

"You really don't know anything about debate," Kate sighs. "I wish I could guilt you into at least one after-school activity."

"Not likely."

Kate, Dash, and Milton are all joiners. In addition to marching band in the fall and concert band in the spring, they're all officers in student council and various other clubs that I can't even imagine signing up for. No matter how much I need to blend in to avoid a fate like Sheena Rollins's—just another nerd, nothing to see here—the one thing I can't seem to stomach are semi-academic clubs where people spend all their time trying to intellectually one-up each other. They make me roll my eyes to the point of actual strain.

The newscaster moves on to sports. Something about Martina Navratilova doing something with a tennis ball.

Kate sits down crisscross in front of me, which means I can't really see the TV, but that's fine because we still have five minutes of sports before they switch back to meatier topics. It's a perfect amount of time to French braid Kate's hair. We did our home perm kits together back in August (so the smell would fade a little by the time we started school), but she swears by sleeping in braids anyway. To "double her volume," as she puts it.

“Thank you.” She pats the braids like well-behaved pets when I’m done. “Do you want me to do yours?”

“That’s okay.” My curls don’t need any more encouragement. “I really should just cut my hair off.” I hate this perm, but it *does* help with the whole blending-in business. It’s band-nerd standard. “At the very least, I should hack off the parts that touched old gum. It’s been days, and I swear I can still feel it. . . .”

“Do you want me to shave your head with my dad’s beard trimmers?” Kate asks.

I know she’s kidding, but I seriously consider it for a second.

“My dad would *never* get over it,” I admit. “Which is funny, because he talks a good game about sticking it to his own parents by growing *his* hair out. Mom would pretend she’s proud of me to make Dad feel like he’s given into the Man, but I’m pretty sure she’d secretly hate it, too. Just going to feel ghost gum in my hair forever, thanks.”

“I can’t believe that happened in front of Steve Harrington and he didn’t even crack a single horrible joke,” Kate says. “Maybe he’s evolving.”

Kate is always holding out hope for boys and their evolution, like they’re a species that hasn’t *quite* caught up. That’s not really it, though. They’re just held to completely different standards, like when we do the limbo in gym class and suddenly, after the bar has moved lower and lower to the floor for everyone in turn, it flies back up to the starting height when a super-popular boy gets to the front of the line.

Okay, now I'm wondering *why* we do the limbo in gym. In what way does standing in line for most of the period and then nearly breaking our backs make us more athletic?

"Steve Harrington is always going to be the same," I say. "He's going to suck exactly this much forever."

Kate swivels to me, scooping the last of the popcorn out of the bowl. A few M&M's rattle against each other. She lets me eat the pieces of candy that get covered in salt, along with the burnt kernels—I'm the weirdo who likes them best when they're half-exploded. "I heard that Steve likes Nancy Wheeler. That seems like new territory for him."

Kate is extremely plugged into junior gossip because she's so advanced in a few of her classes that they had to skip her ahead.

"Really?" I ask with an unwelcome spike of interest. "Nancy Wheeler doesn't seem like his type."

"Who does?" Kate asks. Not defensively—she really wants to know. She likes having all the data points.

I think about Steve Harrington smiling at Tam in history class. It's happened every morning, like clockwork.

Every time, she turns bright red.

Maybe she's having an allergic reaction?

"I don't know. Steve just seems to like girls who are a little more . . ." I think about Tam, singing every morning. Does he notice what she looks like when she's really into it, down to the way her eyes crinkle shut at the edges? Does he see how she tips her head back on the low notes?

"You seem to have a pretty vested personal interest in this

topic, Robin," Kate says. "If I didn't know better, I'd think *you* liked Steve Harrington."

I'm about to protest with all of my heart.

But then the newscaster switches tones, and it feels like thunderclouds gathering in the big open sky. My skin prickles. I know that tone. It's the way they always sound when they're talking about the epidemic.

"As of yesterday's report, the CDC has ruled out all forms of casual contact," the anchor announces. "The AIDS virus cannot be transmitted by food, water, air, or environmental surfaces. While this eliminates a number of vectors for the disease, the transmission rate among homosexuals is still high enough to cause . . ."

Kate heaves a sigh and clicks the TV off, conclusively. "Maybe that will get my parents to stop talking about this whole thing like it's going to invade their perfect lives."

I don't know if she means gay people or AIDS.

A lot of people in Hawkins seem to be talking about them as basically the same thing—a contagious disease, either way.

Whenever I hear something like this, my throat freezes up and a deep chill starts to spread through my body. As soon as the words hit my brain, my vital functions start shutting down. I can't quite breathe, or talk, or eat.

Nobody else seems to react as strongly—not even my parents, who have zero tolerance for dehumanizing talk. They don't seem to freeze up like I do, though. I don't know why I'm the only one with an icy brick where my stomach used to be when someone brings up *the homosexuals.*

"All right, back to the matter at hand," Kate says, tapping the remote against her palm. "You're not getting out of this."

"Out of what?" I grab the popcorn bowl and leave the den. As if putting distance between me and the TV will change what the news was about.

"Who do you like?" Kate asks, dogging my steps.

"Oh. Ummm. Who do *you* like?" I ask numbly.

"No, no, no," she says. "You're not going to deflect this time. And besides, you know I like Dash. I've been talking about it nonstop all summer. You haven't talked to me about any crushes since eighth grade."

"I haven't *had* any crushes since eighth grade."

And that one was made up. At a Halloween sleepover party at Wendy DeWan's, everyone pushed so hard that I blurted out a boy's name even though I didn't really like anybody. In middle school, saying you liked a boy felt important bordering on compulsory.

"You're sure you're over Matthew Manes?" Kate asks.

Matthew Manes is a boy who spends most of his time at the roller rink working on solo routines like he's an ice dancer training for the Olympics. I like ice dancing as much as the next person, but Matthew Manes was just a name I pulled out of nowhere. He was never someone I wanted to kiss. Or even pair-skate with.

I grab another ginger ale. Isn't this stuff supposed to cure stomachaches? But my whole stomach is still a single huge ache, and this conversation isn't helping. "I just think that I'm going to wait until after high school to cultivate a love life."

"Why?" Kate looks genuinely perplexed. She's one of those students who are so good at homework that when people are more complicated than algebra problems, she gets a little frustrated.

"High school relationships are fleeting," I say. "Whereas band squads are forever."

Kate laughs at my deflection, but I haven't quite shaken her off. "That doesn't negate my point. You should get a boyfriend. Any boyfriend."

"You wouldn't tell me to settle for just any study partner, but you think I should just grab the first guy I see in the cafeteria and . . . what? Start making out with him? And then inform him that we're going to spend every Friday night together to fulfill the social contract?" My stomach is seriously a Gordian knot right now.

She sighs. "You're making it sound so onerous. Dating in high school is fun. It's good for you. It's *practice.* You wouldn't go to the state tournament in debate if you hadn't practiced, right?"

"I'm going to take the negative stance."

"You don't even know what that means!"

"I know that I can't imagine *practicing* on any of the boys in our high school. And what exactly are we rehearsing for?"

"Life," Kate says dreamily. "We're going to grow up at some point, Robin. Soon. Think about it mathematically. We're closer to marriage and babies than we are to being little kids. . . ."

And just like that, I throw up in my mouth a tiny bit.

No offense to Kate, but . . . ew.

All I can think about is Mrs. Wheeler blocking the end of the grocery store checkout in her desperately nice outfit, her fake smile locked in place.

There isn't enough ginger ale in the world to wash this weird taste out of my mouth, but I chug the rest of the can anyway. "I don't want that," I state, with the last of the bubbles still tickling my nose. "I want anything *other* than that."

"That's going to be a problem," she points out firmly. Her tone isn't nasty or condescending. It's more like she wants me to hear and understand every word of what she's saying. "Our lives are pretty much graphed out already, and anyone who wants to change that has to draw a bold line in a new direction, which might be harder than you think. Because you're not a rebel, Robin. You're a nerd."

"Kate," I say, putting down the ginger ale and flinging myself at her in a whirlwind hug. "You're a genius."

"Right!" she says, smooshed against my shoulder. "Because I, too, am a nerd."

And then I'm out of the back door, grabbing my bike, Kate calling after me.

"Wait, where are you going? You promised me we'd finally listen to Madonna together!"

CHAPTER SIX

SEPTEMBER 10, 1983

An hour later, I'm standing on my bed, staring down at the floor, which is covered in old, glossy photographs.

Evidence of rebellion.

Ninety-five percent of the floor is devoted to my parents' rebellions. They didn't just sit in their high school classrooms and wait to get devoured by banality. They didn't stay still and give in.

They skipped school for days at a time, took off for entire summers, kept moving instead of committing to college right away, traveled up and down the West Coast and all over the country when they were only a few years older than I am. Their photos look sun-bleached, unposed. They stare at the camera or off into the distance through round sunglasses. My mom is topless in some of them. (Yikes.) My dad has a beard that birds could nest in. They stand with their arms casually and yet somehow defiantly wrapped around friends and people they were dating. Except they didn't use that word.

I can't quite get myself to say *lovers,* even in my head.

My mom loves to talk about free love. But do they really believe in that, still? Now that they're married and have things like meat loaf Tuesday? How long do you have to stay in Hawkins before you become immutably normal?

I get down on the floor, making room for myself in the middle of all the photos. I plucked them out of the photo albums as soon as I came home from Kate's. She told me I wasn't a rebel—and she was right.

My parents went to protests and parties, slept on beaches and the floors of the friends they'd made earlier that day. They put flowers everywhere they could imagine putting them. There are hundreds of photos of them on my floor. So many that I can't see the beige carpet underneath.

A sad, small portion of the floor is dedicated to my rebellions.

The time when I put gum in my hair on purpose and Mom cut out a big chunk of it with kitchen scissors. (Which, in light of Miss Click's class earlier this week, feels ironic. Or maybe just portentous.) The time I refused to go to Grandma Minerva's for Christmas because she always made me wear a scratchy pink velvet dress, and it got too small when I was in middle school, so I stayed home with the eggnog and spiked a cup with something that smelled like nail polish from Dad's liquor cabinet—which I promptly threw up. The time when I was just starting high school and realized they didn't offer foreign languages, so I decided I would only respond to people in French for weeks.

I can't find a single rebellion in the last year.

That's not really a coincidence. I thought that camouflaging myself as a band nerd and keeping my head down for the rest of high school would get me through four harrowing years, but I'm not even halfway.

And then there's life *after* high school. What kind of monsters are waiting in Hawkins when I'm done? What if Mrs. Wheeler is right and it really only gets worse from here? If I don't learn how to escape now, maybe I never will.

Of course, it's not like I can just run into the waiting arms of the hippies. This is the eighties. Teenagers don't leave their lives behind for boundless freedom and bell bottoms anymore.

But that doesn't mean I have to stay in Hawkins every minute until I graduate. There must be other possibilities, ones that play to my strengths. I look at the stack of books on my desk, the novels that I can now read in three other languages, the well-loved language dictionaries that I bought to teach myself new words and expanded ways of thinking.

Dad knocks on my door. (I know it's Dad; he always gives a single, solitary knock. Mom would just keep pounding.)

"You in there, Robin?" he asks.

"I am," I say, eyeing the lock to make sure it's turned.

"Stew tonight," Dad reminds me. "Your mom put in the carrots this time, the way you like it."

Wow. So much to look forward to.

I can hear Dad move away from the door, and I push my back against the bed and stretch my legs all the way out as I sigh.

I'll tell them my plan when it's all lined up and everything's in place. They'll understand—they'll have to. They're the ones who doomed me to life in Hawkins. They're also the ones who made it clear that you didn't have to wait until you're a full-blown adult in the eyes of the world to make your own choices. I'm going to be sixteen by the end of sophomore year, old enough to travel on my own.

I need to go somewhere with a completely different culture, a place where *marching band* and *sophomore year* and *Steve Harrington* are foreign concepts. A place where I can use all the words I know and send postcards back to Hawkins in languages that nobody else understands. A place that's so different that it won't matter if I'm different, too.

I grab my chunky gray Polaroid, turn it to face me, and click. After a few minutes of flapping the plastic rectangle until my face emerges from the murk, I throw it on the floor, adding it to the tapestry of bold decisions, to make this one official.

I'm going to Europe.

CHAPTER SEVEN

SEPTEMBER 12, 1983

"I call it Operation Croissant," I whisper to Dash.

We're in third period English on Monday morning. I had to wait twenty whole minutes to whisper this, because we're sitting too close to the front of the classroom, and therefore, the teacher.

But right now Mr. Hauser is walking up and down the aisles as my classmates stub their brains against the question he's put on the board: *If no man is an island, what kind of landmass are we? Discuss.* Which gives me a chance to tell one of the Odd Squad the plan that's been fizzing inside of me since Saturday night like a lit sparkler.

"Wait, so you're moving to Europe?" Dash asks, doing

the patented high school boy move where he twists his entire body around to face me and his little chair-table combo (aka chable) is forced to come with him.

"No, I'm *going* to Europe," I clarify.

"Like, for vacation? With your parents?"

I give him a half-strength glare. He's trying to understand, but only Dash would think escaping Hawkins is a luxury travel opportunity. He's probably only ever flown first class. If I actually pull this off, I'll be lucky to be sitting in the back row of the plane, where it smells like very small bathrooms and the people who smoke cigarettes in them. (I can't believe they let people smoke on planes. I've only been on a plane once in my life, but the fact remains that they are tiny metal canisters that run on flammable liquid.)

(Oh my God, I'm going to have to get on a plane to get to Europe. By myself. I've only been thinking about the part where I have to *afford* the flight.)

(One thing at a time, Robin.)

"All right, everybody, let's go on and get those books out," Mr. Hauser says.

Dash and I prop our copies of *Lord of the Flies* on our desks, pretending to be dutifully reviewing the chapters that were assigned over the weekend. I feel bad doing this to Mr. Hauser—the one person at Hawkins High who seems to have missed the memo that he no longer has to care about his job. He seems to truly, unironically love teaching English. And that makes me respect him in a way that I've basically stopped respecting the rest of my teachers.

But life-changing plans wait for no one.

"I'm going to *travel* next summer." It feels good to say that. It feels grown-up and exciting and like it's the exact opposite of agreeing to stay in Hawkins. It's anti-Hawkins. It will negate a little bit of this place's hold on me.

"How does that work?" Dash whispers.

I shrug. "I'll be sixteen by then, and I'm tall, which means people always think I'm older."

"No, I mean, how are you going to do it?"

I wish that Dash's first reaction wasn't pure, uncut doubt. At least I'm ready to answer his annoyingly dubious question. "I'll take the train to Chicago first, obviously, and then a flight across the Atlantic. In Europe, you can get around most cities just by walking." Though I'd love to rent a bike in Italy or France . . . "And trains connect most of the cities."

"Yeah, I know that," Dash announces a little peevishly. "I guess I just don't see the point."

"Of *travel*?" I ask. "That thing where you leave quotidian existence behind, and what you see and do and experience changes your entire life?"

Dash just keeps staring at me like I'm some weird question on an essay test.

Mr. Hauser passes between us, and we both put our books up like our lives (or at least our participation grades) depend on it.

Mr. Hauser lingers near us, and Dash improvises a sentence about the signal fire that the boys light with Piggy's glasses and how nerds always save the day. He genuinely believes that nerds will inherit the earth; I've heard him give impassioned soapbox speeches on the subject whenever a jock is celebrated in this school for doing something rote and unimpressive—like throwing a ball through a hoop or winning another blond trophy girlfriend.

"Intellect will always win out over popular opinion, in the end," Dash says. "Being smart is the long con. It's often a matter of losing a few plays strategically in order to come out on top of the game."

"But what if man's intellectual response is to make a play for safety?" Mr. Hauser says. "Wouldn't he then want to be in with the in-crowd?"

"No, because he realizes that any crowd will cannibalize him as soon as they're given half a reason," I say, completely off the cuff.

Mr. Hauser raises his sandy eyebrows. I can't tell if he's impressed with my answer or a little worried at how quickly it came out of my mouth.

As soon as Mr. Hauser moves along, Dash turns back to me in a hurry, seeming to remember that talking to me about my plan to escape our particular civilization is more exciting than talking about boys rebuilding civilization from nothing, while also battling the darkness of their own souls. (I've read this one already. It doesn't turn out well.)

"Where are you going?" Dash asks.

"I'm delighted you asked," I say. The truth is, I've spent a lot of time thinking about this. All of Sunday, I kept the door closed and told my dad I had my period. He probably told my mom I had a stomachache. (Is what we have really civilization if boys still can't say the word *period* out loud? Discuss.)

"I'm going to start in Italy. Rome, then Tuscany, the Amalfi Coast. I thought about Sicily, but they speak Sicilian there, which is pretty much its own language, and I only want to go to places where I feel confident talking to people." I don't want to be just another American bumbling around, assuming everyone is going to change the way they speak for me. The rule I came up with is that I won't go anywhere I can't order breakfast without reverting to English. Hence the name Operation Croissant. "And then I'll go north to Spain. I'm thinking about spending at least a week in Barcelona for the Gaudi architecture alone, and France will be last, but I don't want to park myself in Paris like a tourist. I'm going to see Dijon and Lyon and Orléans first. . . ."

Dash taps the paperback cover of his copy of *Lord of the Flies.* They all have the same cover with the judgy staring face of the boy whose hair is twined in the greenery, like the island is eating him alive. "That sounds . . . extensive." Dash squints. "Are you going full expat on us? Will we be losing a member of Odd Squad? I just need to know, because next year is big for college admissions, and our marching band reputation needs to be sterling." Really? *This* is what he's worried about? "How long do you think this jaunt is going to last?"

Something in me sparks and I snap, "Until I bottom out and don't have any more money or junior year begins.

Whichever comes first." I'm more convinced than ever that I need to get away—not just from Hawkins, but from opinions like the one Dash just came out with.

Maybe I won't keep doing band next year.

I might be too continental for it. High schoolers in Europe don't march around fields before sports matches, blaring out stupid brassy marches and mangling pop horrors in the hopes that it will give them some proximity to the coolness of sports or another point for their college applications.

Dash is tugging at his lower lip now. It's one of his "thinking" gestures. Kate insists that it's cute, but I'm not so sure.

"What?" I ask him.

Dash uses his pencil to point at my entire outfit, shoes to hair. "You're going to need new clothes if you want to go anywhere cosmopolitan."

"What's wrong with my clothes?" I'm wearing perfectly normal—if a little bell-bottomed—jeans and an unobtrusive baseball T-shirt with orange sleeves. My perm puffed out more intensely than usual this morning, which I tried to balance by putting on extra eyeliner, but it's possible that makes me look like a raccoon who knows how to play baseball.

Dash, on the other hand, is wearing one of his infamous gray sweaters over a white V-neck. He seems to think that if he layers enough V-necks it will unlock some kind of superpower. And besides, just because he looks ready for lunch at the country club doesn't mean he's cosmopolitan.

"Come on, Dash. If you're going to make fun of the way I look, you should at least have the data to back it up," I say.

"There's nothing wrong with the way you look, Robin. In *this* context."

"Let's talk about context," Mr. Hauser picks up in a voice that's meant for the entire class. Then he shoots me and Dash a special glance to let us know that he's heard every word we're saying.

Oh, good.

"And, Robin, come see me after class."

Even better.

HIGH SCHOOL

CHAPTER EIGHT

SEPTEMBER 12, 1983

The class flees at the first shriek of the bell. Even Dash leaves me alone to face the music. I just don't know what kind of music it's going to be. Classic rock (aka Mr. Hauser pretends to be hardcore but actually acts like any standard teacher who's been interrupted during class)? Sappy pop (aka Mr. Hauser tries to bond with me)? New Wave (aka Mr. Hauser says things that don't technically make sense but sound kind of deep)?

After everyone else is gone, I stand there, balancing my notebooks on my hip, waiting for Mr. Hauser to actually speak.

"Am I in some kind of trouble?" I finally ask.

"Probably," he says as he erases the chalkboard, leaving the names of the characters from *Lord of the Flies* there in white, ghostly imprints. "But not with me."

How much did he hear me say to Dash?

Is he going to tell my parents?

I'm not ready for them to know about Europe until the plan is in better shape. Right now, it's just a bunch of desperate decisions I made in the last thirty-six hours, fueled by sleeplessness and my clandestine stash of Cheetos.

I need (more) time. And (any) money.

Mr. Hauser doesn't seem to care that passing period is only two minutes long. I'm going to be late for my next class. Not that I really want to *go* to my next class. I just don't want anyone to notice me not being there.

I don't want anyone to notice me at all, until I'm gone.

Mr. Hauser sits down slowly and frowns at me. He's probably about thirty, but he frowns like an eighty-year-old. It's a masterpiece of concerned wrinkles. His eyes pinch up behind dark, nearly square glasses. He looks old and wise and not happy about either of those things. It doesn't help that he's wearing a brown tweed jacket and shiny brown shoes, both of which add at least ten years. Maybe he does it on purpose, since he has a little bit of a baby face.

Wow, the second bell just rang, and he's *still* frowning.

It's starting to feel like time is stuck. Or Mr. Hauser and I have fallen into some kind of weird temporary paralysis. I wave my hand in the air, just to make sure that we're not actually frozen.

"What are you doing?" he asks.

"Checking for a glitch in the space-time continuum."

Mr. Hauser shakes his head. "You're very strange, Robin."

I don't know if teachers are allowed to say this to us, but the way Mr. Hauser does, it doesn't sound like a bad thing, like he's ridiculing me because he knows he can get away with it. (Some people never grow out of that behavior, and I'm starting to wonder how many of those people become high school teachers. It must become some kind of horrible comfort zone.) When Mr. Hauser tells me I'm strange, though, it sounds almost like a compliment. "In fact, you might be the Weirdest Girl in Hawkins, Indiana."

The way he says it, I can tell it's capitalized.

But I can't tell if it's a good thing. Mr. Hauser clearly thinks it is, but he also must know that it's not easy to be *that* weird. A tiny pinch of weird is like spice on the top of someone's personality. When you're seriously weird, monumentally weird, Sheena Rollins weird, you only have two choices: tone it down for everybody else every single day or live with the consequences.

Mr. Hauser pulls out a sheet from his desk. It's mostly blank, with a few names written on lines. And the words *Our Town* at the top. "Robin, have you thought about signing up for the play?"

"You wanted me to stay after class because I was talking too much to say that I should talk onstage?"

"Maybe it's a better outlet," he says.

"I'm already in band," I say. "I play the French horn, well

actually it's a mellophone for marching band, which is basically the same thing, but I'm the only one, which means I really can't skip out. Plus my squad would . . . well, I don't know if they would miss me, but there would only be three of them and they would definitely have to fix all the formations and I'd never hear the end of that, so whatever glorious future I had as a thespian looks like it's over before it started. Sorry."

What I don't add is this: I don't have time to add another activity if I'm going to get a job and make enough money for a round-trip plane ticket and European hostels and train rides and a bike rental. Oh, and croissants.

Every single day, I'm going to eat one for breakfast. That adds up to a lot of croissant money.

I'm going to need time to build up to that kind of small fortune. Some kids in Hawkins (like Dash) get allowance just for existing and maybe picking up a piece of trash or two around the house. Kate gets money every birthday and Easter and Christmas, as a payout for good behavior. Her parents never call it that, but last year she skipped a youth group meeting to get her ears pierced, and even though she got little crosses for her studs, there were no fat envelopes in her Christmas stocking. Some teenagers in this town would be halfway to buying their plane tickets without even lifting a finger. But my parents told me that they're not going to *commodify my childhood*.

Even if they did, I probably would have spent it all on records and books by now.

Mr. Hauser pushes the audition sign-up sheet across the desk. "I can make sure none of your rehearsals conflict with band. I just think that you should give it a chance before you rush off to Europe."

"You heard that part?" I ask with a cringe.

Mr. Hauser's face goes stony. It doesn't look parental, though. The old-man act falls away, and suddenly he seems like he's only a few years older than me. Like thirty is a stretch. Like he's barely on the other side of his own shitty adolescence. "Robin, if you ever feel like you are about to run away, I need you to find me."

And do what?

How could Mr. Hauser help me *not* run away?

Besides.

"I'm not running." Why doesn't anyone seem to understand this? "I'm *traveling.*"

"Right," he says, the old curmudgeon shtick falling back into place. He takes off his glasses. Wipes them on his shirtfront. "Well, if you're ever going to spontaneously travel because you can't stand being here anymore, let me know. Okay?"

"Okay, okay," I promise.

"And, Robin? You should bring someone with you."

"Who?" I ask, reflexively.

Kate would theoretically be an amazing person to travel with, in terms of her interest in art, history, architecture, and food. But would she really be able to focus on those things with all of the international hotness surrounding her? What if she spent the whole trip pushing me to grab the nearest French guy and *practice*?

No. Just. No.

Dash has already proven that he's not the right choice for this particular venture.

Milton and I aren't very close—and besides, his anxiety level would be a little bit difficult to navigate while also trying to find my way around the (infamously confusing) streets of Venice.

Outside of Odd Squad, nobody else comes to mind.

"Seriously, I'm drawing a big old blank here," I say.

"I can't tell you who to bring on your trip of a lifetime," Mr. Hauser says. "That falls into the category of trying to control your life, instead of just annoyingly nudging you in the right direction."

I laugh, right out loud. Which is weird, indeed. Teachers aren't supposed to be *funny.*

"I just know that if you have someone to share your history with, it stays alive."

I lean in and pretend-whisper, "I hate to tell you this, but you're not a history teacher."

"No, I'm an English teacher. Which means I know that plenty of better books than *Lord of the Flies* have died in obscurity because nobody remembered them. While *this,*" he says, slapping a paperback onto his desk, "seems to live forever because the school board just won't let it go."

"Hmm," I say. "Maybe you have a point."

My parents definitely keep each other's memories alive. Sometimes their entire dinner conversations are just long, two-person reminiscence-fests. And if that wasn't enough, they get together with their old friends every December (they call it Hippie Christmas) to relive their best stories and let their hair down. (Though they can only do that part metaphorically at this point. I feel bad for the balding hippies who spend their time talking about the lost glory of their long, glowing manes. Is that how Steve Harrington is going to feel when he's forty?)

My mind goes back to those pictures on the floor. How my parents never seemed to be alone, no matter where they went. Being on an adventure with other people—the *right* people—might have made them feel a little braver, push a little further, show the world even more of themselves. (And I'm *not* talking about the photos of my mom at a nude beach.) Besides, when I think about going to Europe, it's not as much fun to imagine sitting at coffee shops and riding bikes and being moody on trains without someone else right there. To share it all with.

(Not the croissants—those are mine.)

So, I don't just need money to get to Europe. I need money and someone to go with me.

My workload just doubled, which means I need to get busy.

I push the audition sign-up back toward Mr. Hauser.

"Sorry," I say. "I just don't have the time."

Mr. Hauser sighs. "Well, this will be up in the main hallway of the school next week if you change your mind. Auditions are next Friday."

"Got it," I say.

"Here," he says. "Let me give you a late pass."

He fills it in with a quick scribble and then I finally leave. The hallways are shiny and silent and empty except for the hall monitor, Barb Holland. She's wearing jeans that are nearly as out of fashion as mine, though hers are a faded country-western blue, while mine are indigo. Her shirt is both plaid and ruffled. Her hair is both short and feathered. She exists on the edge of the nerd kingdom; she's definitely as nervous as Milton and as into school as Kate, but she's also best friends with Nancy Wheeler. Who *must* be edging toward popular if Steve Harrington really wants to go out with her.

Barb looks bored, standing with her back against a locker. She's got a glazed look on her face. But maybe she's in the middle of some great daydream, because she's got a hint of a secret smile.

It reminds me of when we were friends, a million years ago. We weren't inseparable, like she and Nancy are now, but we were definitely drawn to each other. Always on the same playground equipment. Laughing at the same jokes. Splitting our grape juice boxes because we agreed it's the superior flavor. We drifted apart as we got older, which is normal, I guess. Plus, at some point she and Nancy became an official duo. But I remember that look, like she was smirking at all of reality, creating an alternate version of life in her head, and if you were lucky, she'd tell you about it.

She's managed to get out of an entire class period by volunteering as hall monitor. It's really a very sneaky way to ditch, if you think about it.

Way to go, Barb.

"Hey, can I see your pass?" she asks, about two seconds after I walk by her in the hall.

"Sure," I say.

She looks at it and snorts.

"All right, you can go."

I wonder what that snort meant. I look down at the hall pass Mr. Hauser wrote for me. He filled it out dutifully with his name, my name, the date, and the class period. Under *Reason for Tardiness,* he wrote, *Fixing a glitch in the space-time continuum.*

Wow. Well done, Mr. Hauser.

HIGH SCHOOL

CHAPTER NINE

SEPTEMBER 13, 1983

It's one thing to decide that Mr. Hauser is right, and my plan will fare much better if I have someone to skip town with next summer. It's another thing completely to look around and try to figure out who that person should *be.*

So far, I've ruled out half of the marching band.

Practice is in full swing, by which I mean that everyone is standing around either lofting or hugging their instruments, depending on how heavy they are, waiting for Miss Genovese to tell us what formation to make next. The fact that we don't actually play our instruments while we practice drills for our ill-fated sports interludes makes the whole thing much more awkward.

Band practice: this time, without the pesky music!

The only person who does play is one of the drumline, who has to keep us all on beat. Today the honor has fallen on junior Craig Whitestone, who is exactly as white and stoned as his last name implies. Despite the haze in his eyes and the leafy smell about his person, he hits the snare with stunning regularity, and now we're all supposed to move around in arbitrary shapes that make people looking at us from a distance happy for some reason I will never fully understand.

"Let's run the Juggling Balls again!" Miss Genovese yells from the bleachers, her feet clanging on metal as she runs up and down to check how we look from every possible place in the imaginary crowd. She's switched out her kitten heels for sneakers, but other than that, she wears her usual outfit—pencil skirt, high-necked blouse, blazer with shoulder pads that would make a linebacker proud. Some poor gym teacher has been harassed into letting her borrow a whistle.

Milton, Kate, Dash, and I are grouped together on one side of the field in an O shape. Except Kate and Dash are so intent on flirting with each other that they kept making our O lopsided because they can't stay four steps apart.

"You two! Stop canoodling!" Miss Genovese shouts. And then adds a blast from the whistle, just for good measure.

Kate and Dash drift apart, but they're laughing so hard I know it's only a matter of time before our O collapses all over again. Making the shape is only the beginning of our collective torment. Now we're supposed to be exchanging spots with various other Os all over the field.

The clarinets—a polished, perfect squad led by Wendy DeWan—are poised to switch with us. Only as we make it partway across the field, Craig drops a beat, and nobody can figure out when they're supposed to be stepping. The whole thing dissolves, and Kate and Dash take this opportunity to pretend-run-into each other.

I roll my eyes. Milton rolls his eyes.

We catch each other mid-eye-roll. And laugh.

"Mr. Whitestone! Get it together!" Miss Genovese shouts with a double whistle blast.

"Ugh," Nicole Morrison, one of Wendy's sub-clarinets, says as she brushes imaginary grass stains off her skirt. "What is the team going to think of this disaster?"

"The team?" Wendy asks suspiciously.

"You know she just means Steve Harrington," Jen Vaughn says, waving her clarinet around wildly. "She's been trying to get his attention since the school year started. She wants him to see how good she is at the Juggling Balls so he'll ask her to juggle *his*—"

"Earth, Woodwind, and Fire Squad!" Wendy shouts, to get them back in line. The clarinets have the longest squad name, by far, but it's also one of the best. "That's enough, okay?" Wendy purses her lips and tightens her ponytail in a simultaneous power move. She's wearing a sparkly white miniskirt that makes her dark brown legs look about ten miles long. She's got braces, and she makes stellar grades, but otherwise you could easily mistake her for a popular kid. "You should have become a cheerleader instead of a clarinet player if all you wanted to do was impress some second-rate jock with a styling gel addiction."

Wendy's thorough dismissal of Steve Harrington is a wonder to see. Maybe someday I could say something that honest right to his face, instead of just thinking about how ridiculous he is all the time.

"Let's get our O in order," Wendy says.

Part of me wonders if I could befriend Wendy and ask her to come to Europe with me, but the practical part of me knows that (a) she already has plenty of friends, and (b) she's a senior. She's not going to be wanting to traipse around with some sophomore next summer. She's going to be planning for college in the fall or finding a genuine adult job. Moving on with her life. Instead of stuck here, on this horrible, horrible island we call high school.

Maybe it's all that *Lord of the Flies,* but I can't help thinking about what would happen if our entire marching band was stranded together. How long would it take before we turned on each other? Who would start the signal fire to get us back to civilization? (Wendy and Kate, definitely.) Who would devolve and start attacking each other? (All of the trombones, aka Bone Squad, a name they just barely get away with every year.) Who would go rogue and disappear into the forest, never to be heard from again? (Sheena Rollins.)

I give her a quick look. She has to wear her marching band uniform like the rest of us for field practice and games, the only exception I've ever seen to her all-white wardrobe. Somehow it makes her look even *more* pale. Sheena is definitely enough of an outsider that I can imagine her wanting to escape Hawkins for a summer, but I also can't imagine spending that much time with someone who doesn't want to talk to me.

And I don't mean the kind of small talk that all of the adults in this town inevitably seem to give in to. I want to make actual, life-size *conversation* with someone. I want to talk about all the big things, the ones that matter. The truth is that I've always loved to talk. It's one of the reasons that I hoard words in so many languages.

Now I just need someone worth talking to.

"All right, keep marching," Miss Genovese says, and everyone converges into straight lines. Now we're supposed to march down the field in perfect lockstep. One of the other drummers elbows Craig sharply. Nobody wants to practice this more than once.

Craig more or less gets it together.

Everyone's instruments shift into position. We're ready to pretend to play. We're eager to march. There's only ten minutes left in practice. I need to figure out if anyone here is a good candidate for Operation Croissant, and I can't keep crossing people off the list one at a time.

Miss Genovese blows her whistle and we all start moving to the strict rhythm of the quads. Except, this time, when we get about halfway, I sit right down in the middle of the field. The grass is slightly wet, and the ground is strangely cold for September. I can feel dampness seeping into the butt of my jeans.

"What are you doing?" someone shouts.

Everyone just keeps flowing around me. Dash has to step over my head. Milton swerves, but he hits someone in the line next to him, and I can hear the cussing that happens as a result. Then Kate, who's not tall enough to step over me and is far too stubborn to go around, trips right on top of me.

"What the hell?" Kate shrieks.

The entire marching band devolves into chaos. Nobody seems to get what I'm doing. Well, crap. I was really hoping that one of them would be willing to break the pattern with me.

I'm ruining the practice all on my own.

Miss Genovese's whistle is blowing over and over. She can't seem to stop. I think I broke her.

"Get up, Buckley," Dash says.

"Seriously, Robin, what are you doing?" Kate hisses.

"Anyone else suddenly feel like this is a ridiculous way to spend their free time?" I ask. "No? Just me?"

I catch Milton laughing behind his trumpet. But he wasn't willing to stop marching.

Fine, then.

I'll just have to find someone else. Someone who's not afraid to step out of line.

CHAPTER TEN

SEPTEMBER 16, 1983

I've spent the rest of the week scouring my classes for someone who might fit the description. But the closer I look, the more everybody seems locked into their high school lives. It's all so banal that I actually fall asleep in history class, halfway through the fall of the Roman Empire.

Miss Click snaps her fingers right in front of my face.

"Nice French tips," I say with a yawn.

"That's detention," Miss Click says.

Wow. Detention. I've never gotten one of those before. Often, simply being known as a nerd is enough to fend off serious disciplinary action from most teachers. But not Miss Click. She means business, apparently. (At least when it comes to falling asleep in class. Last week, when a bunch of guys started donkey-laughing about how gay the Greeks were, she pretended not to notice.)

I steal a glance over at Tam. Did she see that I got in trouble, or is she really, really into her notes about the Goth invasions? Does *she* ever get detention?

We've been in school together since we were kids, but I don't know all that much about Tam. I know that she's not an outsider, a nerd, a loner, or a burnout. She might not be immensely popular, but she exists in the same realm as the popular kids. That's easy enough to explain: Tam is pretty. Not paint-by-numbers pretty, either. Her nose is a little sharp and her eyes are this mild, sweet brown. She doesn't have the kind of curves that seem to shatter boys' brains on impact; she's small and trim, with smooth lines everywhere. She's the kind of pretty you have to think about, the kind that you can't take in all at once so you have to keep coming back to consider her from a new angle. Which means that she's the kind of pretty you can't *stop* noticing once you start.

Tam might be mildly popular, but I can say with confidence that she's not an ass about it. In fact, there's something soft and sweet and silly about her personality that doesn't usually translate well into the harsh lexicon of popularity. In fourth grade she used to spend every rainy-day recess "rescuing earthworms" from the blacktop, tossing them back into the dirt. She gently calls out her friends when they get catty and gives them better things to talk about. I've even seen her give Sheena Rollins a pep talk after she was bullied for taking too long to choose a dessert in the lunch line. Tam gave Sheena her little bowl of rice pudding—and gave the jerk who was messing with her a solid punch on the shoulder. Which I thought was improbably cool.

Under that chopped red hair, there's a good heart.

But is there a hint of rebellion?

She sings before class starts almost every day, and maybe that's not textbook rebellious, but it does feel like something that most people would be too cowardly to do. (And maybe not being textbook rebellious but finding your own way to go against all known grains is, in fact, *extra* rebellious.)

I still have to rule her out as my escape partner for Operation Croissant, though. To be able to ask her to go to Europe with me someday, I'd have to spend lots of quality time with her, and to do *that* I'd have to actually talk to her first. And I can't seem to do it. I get shy around her in a way that . . . well, it's not like me. Maybe it's because I don't have a good place to start—when you've technically known someone for ten years but you've barely spoken to each other, it's hard to launch into things. Or maybe it's because her friends are always around her, and while I can imagine talking to Tam, I can't seem to get past their social-climber glares.

Or maybe it's just Steve Harrington's fault.

At least five times since the school year started, Tam and I have been on the verge of talking. Once or twice we've even gotten past the part where we exchange pleasantries.

Tam: Do you have an extra pencil?

Me: Yes.

Or . . .

Me: Do you have the notes about the Ottoman Empire? I left mine at home.

Tam: Sure thing.

But then Steve strides into the room and it's all over. Tam's eyes slide to him and never slide back. (Unless Miss Click is commanding the room's attention with her historical anecdotes, which are drier than my mom's Thanksgiving turkey. She was a vegetarian for ten years and she still hasn't really figured out meat. I keep telling her: if it tastes like wood pulp, you've taken a wrong turn somewhere.)

And then, because Tam is staring at Steve, all of a sudden, *I'm* staring at Steve. Which is not what my eyes would do under any natural circumstances, but nothing about being fifteen-and-a-half is natural.

He must be so used to having people stare at him that he doesn't even notice anymore. He's the kind of popular that has its own gravity and draws everyone in, inexorably. (Kate calls it the black-hole effect.)

Even right now he doesn't seem to feel the death ray of my eyes. So I keep on staring, even though I must look creepily obsessed, because I need to figure this out. I need to understand why Tam can't stop looking at him. He's like a riddle hidden inside of a jock and buried under an ocean of perfect waves.

What is it about him that girls can't get enough of?

It can't *just* be the hair. I refuse to believe that one part of someone's physiognomy can be all-powerful. It exerts an otherworldly force on what sometimes feels like half the girls in school. I'm immune, but so many people aren't.

Okay, now I'm not just looking at Steve Harrington, I'm specifically hate-watching his hair.

It's a low point for me, I know, but here we are.

I watch for long enough that I can't help feeling like the hair is sending Tam subliminal messages.

Steve's hair: *I'm everything you've ever wanted.*

Tam: (blushes)

Steve's hair: *Lustrous. Rule-defying. Gravity says no, and I say* whatever. *I'm the hair that most guys—and let's face it, also some girls—wish they had. Which means that whoever I belong to must be important. And whoever is seen with me? Goes out in public standing next to* this? *You get the picture. You should probably also be thinking about how silky and full I am to run your hands through during make-out sessions— Oh God, is he making a face? Is it supposed to be flirty? Please someone tell him to stop doing that. While you're at it, can you remind him that I've been doing the heavy lifting for* years.

Tam: (giggles)

Steve's hair: *I'm so glad we agree on these things.*

Tam writes a note, folds it, and passes it off to one of her girl friends. (Sorry, but I am never smashing those two words together. It's so weird to me when people say "girlfriends" when they clearly mean girls who are friends. Compound words have their own singular meanings; we all know this, yes?) Anyway, her friend unfolds the complicated origami of the note and looks back at Tam, scandalized and delighted.

What does it say?

What is she thinking about him?

Why does he merit thinking about *at all*?

This is a mystery that I'll probably never solve, so even though Tam is undoubtedly special, I have to keep up the search for a travel partner. Because every time I look at her, I seem to get stuck in this impossible loop.

And I can't find my way out.

CHAPTER ELEVEN

SEPTEMBER 22, 1983

I kept hoping it wouldn't come down to this, but a week later I'm standing in front of the sign-up sheet for the school play.

It's not that I'm anti-theater. I did costumes for the spring play last year—*Anything Goes.* The songs were cheesier than the entire state of Wisconsin and nobody really knew how to tap-dance, which made the whole two hours sound like a metallic stampede. But I had a surprisingly good time putting together all of those sailor outfits.

It's just that when you're deciding what kind of nerd to be in high school, there are only a few tracks you can pick. Kate, Dash, and Milton have all committed (in some cases, overcommitted) to band and academics. Doing crew for the play can fit into any kind of nerd profile, but actually getting *onstage* is reserved for a very special kind of nerd, which in some cases also has crossover potential with the lower ranks of popular kids, but which always involves singing in public and flirting a lot and laughing so loud that your back teeth show.

Not really my thing.

I take a step closer, and I can see that the sheet is much more filled in than when Mr. Hauser had it. Those first few names must have been the people who knew to find him and get their spots before the list went up in such a public forum.

I look around once, twice, making sure that nobody's watching. It seems like the monster that is Hawkins High is slumbering—or maybe it's just busy devouring someone else, in some far-off classroom that I can't see.

I step closer and the names on the list come into focus. Picking up the pencil dangling next to the list by a piece of string, I hunt through the time slots tomorrow afternoon for one that's still open. And then I see it.

Right there, in loops and swirls.

Tammy Thompson.

She's going to be at auditions.

I go back into the loop from class—me staring at her, her staring at Steve, me staring at Steve.

I think about how she sighs and looks at him with that sort of dreamy unfocused longing that makes the whole world seem to soften at the edges. That sort of thing doesn't come naturally to me, but when I see her do it, I feel sort of dreamy-by-association. Tam is a romantic. It infuses her singing. It probably makes her a good actress, too.

I put my name down, squeezed at the bottom of the sheet because there aren't any spots left. Who knows. This might be my chance to talk to Tam without Steve Harrington around.

This is my way out of the loop. This is my chance.

"Hey, Robin, are you signing up for this?" someone behind me asks. I whip around so fast that the pencil—which is still in my hand—comes detached from the wall, and the string whips Milton directly in the eyes.

"Ah. Okay. Ouch."

"Why were you skulking like that?" I ask.

"Skulking? I'm not sure you know the definition of that word. I'm right in the middle of the hallway." He laughs at himself nervously. Then he blinks a few times. "Can you, um, look at my corneas and make sure they're not scratched?"

I put my face weirdly close to his face and inspect his eyes, which are dark brown, and have a bit of his black bangs falling into them. I have to hold his bangs to one side and push my face toward his again and then rotate so I can see his corneas in all kinds of different light. My face just keeps switching angles, and his face becomes blurry and then sharp and then blurry again.

I wonder if this is what kissing feels like. Minus the lips.

It's . . . not that thrilling.

"Um, so why did you freak out so bad when I walked up to you?" Milton asks quietly. He's probably worried that I don't want him around. Milton is always a little afraid that people don't like him.

I don't want him to worry about that. But I definitely don't want to mention why I whipped around so quickly and nearly impaled his left eyeball. (Which is *not* scratched, thank goodness. I don't have money for his optometry bills if I want to go to Europe.)

The truth is, I was touching Tam's name. My fingers were just resting on it, lightly. I turned around so fast because I didn't want anyone to see that and think that it meant anything, because it didn't.

"I just . . . You'd look good with an eyepatch," I deadpan. When in doubt, sarcasm. "Like Kurt Russell in *Escape from New York*."

"You think I look like Kurt Russell?" Milton asks, perking with some kind of delight that I really didn't expect. "A half-Japanese Kurt Russell, of course." Milton's mom is Japanese. He doesn't talk about it that much, and honestly there aren't that many kids at Hawkins High who are something other than white or Black. It must be weird for him, in ways that I can't really begin to fathom.

"Of course," I say.

It's more than we've talked one-on-one since the beginning of the year. Last year, Milton and I talked way more. We'd write notes back and forth in the margins of our sheet music—mostly about music we liked more than whatever stuffy old march Miss Genovese had us playing. But for some reason Milton's been weirdly quiet around me since we got back from summer break. Maybe it's because Kate and Dash take up all the air with their flirting.

Or maybe it's because he can sense that there's something off about me—something different. My band nerd camouflage might be fading. The ways that I'm different from my friends feel like they're multiplying. My heartbeat plays triple time as I reattach the stupid dangling pencil to the wall.

"Are you trying out for the play?" Milton tries again, pointing at my cramped signature on the sheet. It's already there, so I can't really say no.

"I think so. I might not actually make it, I might have to stay home and shampoo the dog or—"

"You don't have a dog, Robin."

"Which is why I am going to get really good at dog shampooing to help convince my parents I should have one." Why am I lying? Why am I lying *about dogs*? Am I really afraid that Milton will tell everyone that I'm trying out for the play and acting generally bizarre? Will he report back to the rest of the Odd Squad? Has Dash already told everyone else about Operation Croissant?

I'm suddenly feeling very protective of my whole plan. My whole existence.

Is it because a small part of me already wants to jump ship on band and spend the rest of the season in play rehearsals with Tam? Because even though we haven't talked quite yet, I can see us becoming inseparable?

"I'm just doing this to make Mr. Hauser happy," I lie, because the truth is a little too intense to admit. "He really, really wants me to try out."

CHAPTER TWELVE

SEPTEMBER 23, 1983

Mr. Hauser doesn't exactly beam when he sees me walk into the auditorium, but his lack of a frown feels like the same thing.

I can tell that he's happy that I made it. And for a single moment, I feel weirdly guilty that I'm mostly here to see if I can find someone to (currently) befriend and (eventually) go to Europe with. Yes, my first hope is Tam. But it feels like, if there are people in this school who are going to care about culture, they're going to be in this auditorium . . . right?

Looking around, I get the sense that maybe my initial estimation was wrong.

Sprawled over the folding auditorium chairs, freshman

girls are working on their makeup en masse, trying to get the perfect electric-blue eyeliner and pouty, puffy magenta lips. A mixed-gender group of upperclassmen down in the orchestra pit are gleefully giving each other back rubs. I can't for the life of me figure out how random back rubs are supposed to make someone a better actor. Are these people all here to show off and hit on each other? If so, why bother putting on a play?

"Robin," Mr. Hauser says, brandishing a handful of paper in my direction. "I want you to read for Emily."

"Great," I say, taking the pages and heading for the door. I have an excellent exit strategy. I'm going to pretend I want to practice my lines privately in the hallway. Then I'm going to run.

But in the row right before the double exit door, I see Tam sitting by herself, quietly mouthing lines as she scans the script pages. (Which I guess are called sides, because Mr. Hauser keeps saying that as he hands them out.) Mine still have that burnt, fresh-from-the-Xerox smell to them.

It combines with the smell of Tam's raspberry-scented product (soap?), and deep down I know that those two smells will remind me of her from now on. Fresh new pages and tart red sweetness. That sounds right to me, for some inexplicable reason.

Maybe it's just more evidence that I'm the Weirdest Girl in Hawkins, Indiana, as Mr. Hauser dubbed me.

I'm still not sure I want that crown.

Tam looks like she's pretty focused, head down. I don't

want to interrupt her while she's getting ready. But this might be my only chance to talk to her without the threat of Steve Harrington looming nearby.

I think about her singing in class. I think about how she wasn't afraid to be seen, to be heard, to be different.

What if Tam really is the person I'm looking for?

I go and sit down in her general vicinity. Just to see if she's interested in talking to someone. Of course, now that I'm sitting, I need something to do, so I look through the sides. But my eyes aren't really absorbing the words. They seem to bounce right off and go back to Tam.

The third time, she notices me looking.

"You have Emily too?" she asks, craning over to see my pages.

She's looked so bold and carefree to me since the start of the year, but right now she seems a little nervous. Like she's afraid that I might poach her part. (As if I could honestly hold someone's attention as well as she could.) "Yeah, but I didn't ask Mr. Hauser to give me these. It was a random page assignment."

"Really? You're not trying out for the lead?" she asks, her upper body hovering over the seat that separates us.

"No," I rush to assure her. "I'm cool with anything."

Those are not words that have ever left my mouth before. In any permutation.

Still, I can see that whatever I said made Tam feel better. She settles back into her chair and smiles. Not a big, fake showy theater smile. Not a vague I-know-you-from-history-class smile. She's looking at me like I'm any other girl at Hawkins High.

For some reason, that terrifies me.

Because I'm *not* any girl at Hawkins High. I'm the one slinking around, trying not to be noticed, because I'm weird enough that even teachers can see it from a mile away. I might want to be friends with Tam, but what if she doesn't like me? The *actual* strange, scrappy, me? That seems like the kind of rejection I don't need to put myself through. And it might catch other people's attention. What if people think I'm trying to climb the social ladder by spending time with her? What if this is what awakens the monster, its mouth waiting for me like a dark pit when I inevitably fall? Will I be ridiculed so hard that I don't even speak for the next three years, like Sheena?

"Are you okay?" Tam asks as I get up, wobbly.

All I can think is: this is why I have to leave, this is why I have to leave, this is why I have to—

"Robin!" Mr. Hauser calls. "Why don't you come up and get us started?"

I can hear my voice, but I can't feel it leaving my throat. "I haven't had any time to go over—"

"I'll go first, Mr. Hauser!" Tam says, popping out of her chair so fast that it folds back up behind her.

It's nice of her, I think, to volunteer like that. To save me from whatever humiliation was waiting. But the bang of her chair was a little too loud and her hair looks so red and I'm really, really overwhelmed right now.

“Thanks, Tammy,” Mr. Hauser says in a voice so flatly chipper that I can tell he’s full of shit.

He didn’t want Tam to read. He wanted *me* to read. I can’t begin to understand why he cares so much. It can’t be because he thinks I’m the next great high school leading lady. I’m clearly not cut out for acting. Even just getting to the part where I actually audition is proving difficult.

I shove myself back into my seat and stay put, because now I know that if I *do* leave, Mr. Hauser will see it happen and he’ll want to talk about it next week. And besides. Tam is standing onstage, taking a deep breath. Diving into that monologue headfirst. It wouldn’t be fair to interrupt her by slamming the doors.

And I want to see what she does.

Tam nearly shouts the first few lines, which are all about being dead. People in the audience snicker, probably because they don’t know how this play ends. Most of it takes place in a pitifully normal small town named Grover’s Corners, but toward the end, the main character, Emily, dies and becomes a ghost and—well, she stays in Grover’s Corners.

Forever.

(I only know this much about *Our Town* because I read it during my existentialist phase. I made Kate binge Jean-Paul Sartre and Simone de Beauvoir and Richard Wright with me. Most people think that Thornton Wilder is a product of pure apple-pie Americana, but he was part of a desperate global search for meaning, and his work can be as searing as Camus’s if you’re really paying attention. Most people aren’t.)

"Can you start again, Miss Thompson?" Mr. Hauser asks. "A little less volume this time. Really let us know what Emily is feeling. What she wants to say to her mother. What it feels like in that moment when she realizes no one who's alive will ever hear her again."

Tam nods and nods, like she's really taking in what Mr. Hauser is saying.

Then she starts over. And does the same thing.

Toward the end, after Emily asks to go back to her grave, Tam opens her mouth wide and starts to sing. I don't recognize the song—something churchy. It takes everyone a second to figure out what's going on, because none of us are expecting it.

Mr. Hauser paces in front of the stage, two fingers pinched on the bride of his nose. "Miss Thompson, if you could just pause there—"

She must know that he's about to tell her that he's seen enough, because she launches into a breathlessly fast explanation. "I just think Emily could be a singer. You know, maybe she sings with her church choir? That would fit into the script, the way it's already written."

"There's no singing in *Our Town,*" Mr. Hauser says. "It's not a musical."

"It doesn't have to be a musical to have music in it." Tam looks proud of this statement. Like maybe she thought it out beforehand. She stands with her hands clenched tight on her script pages, waiting to be asked to continue.

"That's an interesting theory." Mr. Hauser claps, which is

a signal to the rest of us to applaud her audition. "All right, thank you. Please stick around in case I need you to read with scene partners later."

Tam leaves the stage, looking distinctly upset. Part of me wants to follow her, to tell her that I think she was brave.

"Robin," Mr. Hauser says. "Are you ready?"

No. Not close. Not even remotely.

"Sure," I say.

As I make it to the front of the auditorium, I catch a bit of a quiet argument that Jimmy Blythe is making to Mr. Hauser. I know Jimmy from *Anything Goes* last year. He was the set designer, nominally, but he spent most of his time backstage hitting on the chorus girls who were waiting for their cues.

"Seriously? Two ladders and a dining room table set? That's the entire set? This is my senior year and you want me to do . . . nothing?"

"It's not *nothing,*" I say. I know that I'm trying to fly under the radar, but sometimes I can't help myself. Mr. Hauser is watching me now, waiting for what I'll say next. "Thornton Wilder was adapting Asian theater practices where there's minimalist set design, and one physical item could stand in symbolically for all kinds of things. He's trying to stretch your limited little imagination."

Mr. Hauser gives a single chortle. As soon as his back is turned, Jimmy mutters, "I'll punch your limited face."

Yep. This is definitely the haven for the most cultured kids in school.

There are no stairs to the stage, so I have to slide up on

my butt and then get to my feet. "Go ahead, Robin," Mr. Hauser says.

I look out at the audience.

Nobody really seems to be watching me. Most people are doing homework, or buffing their nails, or passing notes.

It should be a comfort, knowing that nobody cares. But for some reason it just makes Emily's words ring true. She says that none of us really notice every minute and detail as they pass us by.

She says that we're all missing our own lives.

And we have no one to blame but ourselves.

"Oh, earth, you're too wonderful for anybody to realize you," I say, quoting from the script, but also meaning it.

This is why I want to travel. To see this world. To fill my life with things that *matter.* (Art, music, food so good it makes you cry, conversation so interesting it keeps you up all night.) And I want to do all of it with someone who understands, someone who appreciates it as much as I do. I honestly think that I'm a misanthrope by accident of geography, not by nature. If I weren't surrounded by dinguses, I'd probably have plenty of friends.

Standing here and saying Emily's words—about growing up in a small town and never leaving and then dying and *never leaving*—is making me so claustrophobic that I'm walking around just to escape the sound of my own voice.

And then there's the infamous staging that Jimmy was complaining about. Emily's grave? It's a metal folding chair in a row of metal folding chairs, where she has to sit with other people in her town who've died. She has to stay there, *with them.* She can't even switch spots and try out a new cemetery view. She's stuck. Literally. Eternally. When I think about it, I can't breathe right, and my voice comes out raw and winded.

"Nice, Robin. Keep going." Mr. Hauser thinks I'm making acting choices, when I'm just plain old freaking out.

Part of me wants to power through this moment. To spend the next three months in rehearsals, telling off a-holes like Jimmy, making Mr. Hauser not-frown, seeing Tam every afternoon. Spending enough time together going on a trip as best friends is just the natural next step. Tam wants to be a singer, right? You can't be a singer if you stay in Hawkins your whole life. We can break out of here together. Stage a two-person rebellion against everything that makes our lives small and bleak.

Only a few lines left. Almost there.

But I run out of breath, and then I can't get it back.

And everything goes blacker than black.

HIGH SCHOOL

CHAPTER THIRTEEN

SEPTEMBER 23, 1983

When I open my eyes again, things feel weird.

At first, I'm sort of hoping that sophomore year has slipped away into nothingness and we're far, far into the future. The day before graduation would be nice. (It would also explain why I'm in the auditorium.) But as my brain settles, I realize that only a few moments have passed. And I'm staring up at the auditorium from the floor. But the weirdest part is Milton hovering over me, waving his fingers slowly in front of my eyes.

"Milton?" I ask. My voice sounds creaky.

I didn't even realize he was at the auditions. And now he's *right here,* in my face.

I hear Mr. Hauser's voice somewhere in the distance. "Are you all right, Robin?"

"Blink twice if you're all right," Milton nearly shouts. "No, wait. Blink once if you're all right, twice if you're *not* all—"

I swat his fingers away. "I'm fine." I shove myself up to sitting.

Now that it's clear I'm not dead or gravely injured, everyone in the audience feels free to laugh at me—which is exactly what they do. "Exit, pursued by assholes," I mutter, getting up and rushing off behind the curtains so I won't have to backtrack through the auditorium.

The truth is that nobody actually pursues me, except for Milton. He stays on my heels as I shoulder through the back exit. I'll have to circle all the way around the squat, sprawled-out, one-story brick school to get my bike out of the rack. I'm not even sure I can ride it right now. My breath is still a little scratchy and shallow, and I don't know how hard I hit my head when I went down.

But I'm absolutely not sticking around for the rest of this audition.

"Robin, are you sure you're okay?" he asks. "You could have a concussion. When you fell, your head made this sound—"

"Thanks for filling me in, Milton, but I really don't need you to describe what happened in excruciating detail."

Milton keeps up with me, even in his squeaky leather shoes. This side of the school is lined with bushes and a fence that separates it from the playing fields. I edge along, practically walking through the bushes. What if Milton rumples his khakis? What if his button-down doesn't make it out of this unscathed?

"Did you eat enough today?" he asks. "Did you drink any water before you went onstage? Have you been sick?"

"What are you, a doctor?" I ask as we round the corner of the building together. I speed up. Milton's worries are getting so big that I don't think I can spend any more time with them.

My parents don't believe in worrying. When I was a little kid and they caught me worrying, they'd make me chant affirmations. Mom would put a crystal on my forehead. Sometimes those things made me feel better. But mostly? They made me worry a lot less, not because there was less to worry about, but because I got the message that it wasn't really a welcome emotion.

"I just know about fainting spells," Milton says. "I used to have them when I was a kid. If you answer those questions, I'll get a better sense of—"

"Yes, yes, no." We reach the bike rack, and I grab mine, standing it up. The cool metal frame grounds me.

I'm going to be fine.

Even if I did just panic-fall in front of the entire drama crowd. Even if I did just ruin another potential way to find the travel partner I need for Operation Croissant.

"I'm worried about you," Milton said.

"Why didn't you tell me you were going to audition?" I ask. "We were both standing there in front of the sign-up sheet, chatting about Kurt Russell. You could have brought it up at any point."

Or he could have found me while everyone was hanging out in the auditorium. But he didn't bother. This only confirms what I already knew—the Odd Squad and I might be friends because of band, but that doesn't mean we're close. We're friends of convenience. And marching band formations. Milton and I aren't bosom buddies: he's more like my assigned dance partner.

"It was a last-minute decision," he says, shrugging. "And I thought your audition was really good. You know. Up until the part when you . . ."

I touch my head. It really does feel awful.

"Robin, I think I need to check your pupils," Milton says. His voice is so grave that it takes me a minute to understand what he wants to do.

"I guess it's only fair," I say begrudgingly. "I did inspect your corneas yesterday."

It's hard to stand still and not blink while he gets close, then closer. He examines my eyes, and I examine his pores.

They're nice. He has perfectly nice pores.

I try not to think about how this is the second (third?) time our faces have been this close to each other in the last two days. At least he doesn't get any kind of gooey or dreamy or otherwise romantically fogged look in his eyes while he's there.

"I don't think you have a concussion," he says, stepping back. "But I do think you need pie."

"Is that a medical diagnosis?"

"Kind of," he says. "When I was little, my parents always took me out for pie after I passed out. It turns out I dehydrate really easily. I think doing the whole thing over and over made a groove in my brain. Passing out equals pie? Besides, this is a good way to keep you from riding your bike when you really shouldn't. I don't want you throwing up over the handlebars."

"Is that . . . ?"

"A thing that can happen when you hit your head really hard," he confirms.

He nods me toward the other side of the school where the student parking lot is waiting. Milton has a car. It's only his mom's old station wagon with the wood paneling down the side, nothing that the popular kids would get excited about, but it's trustworthy. I've been in it a few times after marching band games when Kate and Dash wanted to go out and celebrate with fries and shakes instead of going straight home.

And I don't want to go home. Not yet. I don't want to sit alone in my room all night and face the fact that my plan is falling apart almost as quickly as it came together.

"They have cherry, right?" I ask.

"With a lattice top," Milton assures me.

He pulls the keys out of his khaki pocket and opens the back of the car. Because it's a station wagon, there's no trunk, just a wayback seat. He folds it down so we can fit the bike inside. I marvel slightly; it's perfectly clean in there. It even looks like the rug has been vacuumed. How did he get the vacuum all the way out to his car? And what teenager keeps the wayback of their station wagon perfectly clean?

Milton Bledsoe, that's who.

I lift my bike and toss it into the trunk. I don't mind being the messy one.

"All right," I say. "Falling down pie it is."

CHAPTER FOURTEEN

SEPTEMBER 23, 1983

By the time Milton and I leave the diner, it's dark outside and I've devoured three slices of pie (two cherry, one apple).

He's not wrong. I feel much better.

At least, physically speaking.

"Should I drop you off at home?" he asks. "Do you have a curfew?"

I sigh upward at the moon. "I . . . have the opposite of a curfew." My parents are always disappointed that I'm not wilder. Whenever I go to my room at eight p.m. to read, they start up a long, long description of all the things they used to do at night when they were teenagers. (For example: sneak out, go skinny-dipping, beg cheap beer off friends' older siblings, howl at the moon. You think I'm exaggerating on that last one, but I'm not. My mom actually still howls at the moon sometimes, but now she's wearing pink fuzzy slippers and taking the garbage out. It makes for an interesting contrast.)

I wonder what they'll think about me running off to Europe.

Will they be proud? With a sprinkle of jealousy on top? Will they remember why they loved the big, wide world, and want to pack up and move our family out of Hawkins forever? Will we, as Dash so poetically put it, "go full expat"?

Sure, that last one is highly unlikely, but a girl can dream.

"Do you want to go back to my house?" Milton asks. At first I'm worried that he thinks something date-like is happening. But then he adds, "My mom and dad always have game night on Fridays, and they rope me in if I don't have any other plans."

"Are they going to rope *me* in?" I ask

"That depends. How good are you at Scrabble?"

I shrug. "One time I won with the word *xenophobe,* and the *X* was on a triple-word score."

"Yeah, they won't want you to play. They get really competitive."

"Milton, how do you feel about Hawkins?" I find myself spontaneously asking.

"This town?" He looks around contemplatively. "I hate it."

"How do you feel about croissants?"

"I just brought you all the way across town for pie," he

says, nodding at the diner's big neon sign. "I'm a fan of flaky butter pastry." When he smiles, there are deep dents around it, like full brackets around a parenthetical thought.

I wonder what he'd look like in anything other than khakis. (Not that it would change how I feel about him. Not that I'm suddenly susceptible to the kind of fluttery loss of function that happens to other girls when they're around guys in acid-wash jeans. I just feel like Milton deserves to wear pants that don't have a crease down the front so sharp it could probably cut glass.)

"Do you speak any languages?" I ask. "Other than English?"

"I know a little Japanese. Mostly from my grandparents. I want my mom to teach me more, but she's always busy with work and my brother and sister and . . ." He pauses, like he's not sure if he should add the next part. "I do speak Elvish."

"A few words of Elvish or . . . all of Elvish?"

"It's actually a language family, so technically I speak Sindarin and Quenya and—"

"And you don't seem shy about it! Good for you?"

"It's not like I go around telling everyone that. Only my good friends. So Dash knows. And now . . . you."

Wow. Milton's list of friends is almost as short as mine.

And he thinks that due to our recent bonding experience with the unexpected passing out and the ritual dessert consumption, we just became *good* friends. Maybe I was wrong about the Odd Squad only liking me for my semidecent playing.

Or maybe I was just wrong about Milton.

"Did you go to the auditions because I signed up?" I ask.

He shrugs. "I've always wanted to try out acting. I guess knowing you'd be there made it easier."

Hmmm. Maybe Milton just needs company to help him feel adventurous. Maybe I could provide him with an opportunity. . . .

"I guess we can go back to your house," I say. "*If* the snack options are adequate."

"You just ate three pieces of pie."

I shrug.

Milton laughs. He doesn't have the sickly bray that most teenage boys do. His laugh is soft, low-pitched. It's an objectively nice laugh. But it would probably sound a lot nicer to a girl who's not me.

I tell myself that this is a good thing.

It would be the Worst, categorically speaking, to get a crush on someone I was planning transatlantic travel with. Milton is starting to seem like a possibility in a way that I never would have considered yesterday. And we have the rest of the year to become better friends, while I build up the funds for Operation Croissant.

We're lingering in the parking lot, in that awkward moment before you fully commit to getting in the car, when a family comes out of the diner. It's Jonathan Byers, who I know from school (pale, quiet, takes a lot of photographs), and his mom, who I recognize from the general store (anxious, pretty, offers me a discount on replacement tape heads because I wear mine out so often listening to my language tapes). There's a younger kid with them, too, Jonathan's little brother. I saw him at the grocery store with Mrs. Wheeler . . . so, one of her son's friends? He's trailing behind his mom and brother, looking around sort of aimlessly, clutching a fantasy novel to his chest like body armor. I don't remember his name, but he's got a bowl cut that looks like his mom did it by snipping around an actual cereal bowl. (I had the same haircut in second grade.)

Anyway, this kid seems like a serious nerd-in-training.

Milton and Jonathan nod at each other in that self-conscious way that teenage boys do sometimes.

I catch the kid's eye. For just a second. I want to tell him that life here is going to get better, but I don't have any comforting words.

I wish I could just tell him to run.

But you can't say that to a random middle schooler you barely know. So Milton and I wait as they load into their car and Mrs. Byers lights a cigarette on her way out of the parking lot, the smoke trailing behind her in a long, smooth line.

Milton and I climb into his car, and he drives us down the street through the dark, dark town. I put my feet up on the dash, roll down the window, and stick my head into one of the first real autumn breezes.

Here's the thing.

Hawkins is *nice* during the day.

But when you can't see the painfully identical white houses and the Main Street that somebody stole off a postcard, this place is different. In the dark, the town stretches out and grows. It feels alive in a way that it doesn't when everyone is watering their lawns and showing off their new vinyl siding. These are the parts of town that people don't bother to notice, because their heads are always down or up their butts, respectively.

But I look around and see it all: the trees and meadows, the quarry with mist hovering on dark water. And the open stretch of sky, with its big moon draped in smoky-gray clouds the way Stevie Nicks drapes herself in shawls. There's a weird sense that if none of us were here, this place would go back to being . . . kind of perfect.

A place where I could be myself. Not just the barely socially acceptable, mostly quiet nerd but every sharp, strange Robinesque bit. I could dig up the feelings that I'm so good at keeping six feet underground. I could let out the edges that I'm always trying to hide.

But I don't live in that place.

Milton speeds up, and I whisper goodbye to Hawkins in Spanish, French, and Italian, practicing for the day when I can leave all this behind.

PART TWO

HIGH SCHOOL

CHAPTER FIFTEEN

NOVEMBER 6, 1983

Milton and I are watching MTV.

Let me rephrase that.

I'm reading a dual-language edition of Dante's *Divine Comedy* while Milton plays keyboard over the Duran Duran video unfolding on the TV. He doesn't just mimic the song, either, trying to keep up with chord progressions. He's actually adding another layer of music on top of everything he listens to. Sometimes it meshes with the original song. Sometimes it's an odd, quirky counterpoint. Sometimes it feels like he's scribbling over the original, making something better. He's got the volume on the TV turned all the way up, which the rest of his family hates, which is how we keep getting the den all to ourselves.

"Milton!" I shout. "Which one do you like better? Duran or Duran?"

He reaches over and grabs a pillow from the couch and throws it at me with one hand without missing a single, literal beat.

We've been doing this every day for weeks.

I first came back to Milton's house after auditions—which got neither of us cast in the play, surprise! Tam did get a small role, *not* Emily, which she tried to be cheerful about when the cast list went up, but I could tell she was more than a little disappointed. I've apparently stared at her in history class enough to know that when she's upset, she tugs in a half-hearted way at the red wisps of her bangs. Anyway, when I first got to Milton's I was shocked to find this setup, as well as a bedroom that Milton has wallpapered with the posters and liner notes of his favorite punk and New Wave bands. I knew that he was both musical and a nerd, but Milton is an enthusiast on a whole other level. He's obsessed with the details of aural history, and he plays about nine instruments *besides* the trumpet and keyboard.

One of them I hadn't even heard of before. It's called a theremin, and it's absolutely bizarre. It's electronic, but Milton doesn't even have to touch it—he just moves his hands, and these two metal antennas can sense where they are and release sound accordingly. It looks like a keyboard, minus the keys, plus a lot of old-timey magician waving.

Right now he's playing his pride and joy, his Yamaha.

The first time Milton asked if we could watch MTV together, I thought it was the beginning of the end of our very short friendship. MTV is what everyone in our school watches. But Milton doesn't watch it like everyone else.

When we sat down together—or I sat down and Milton hovered over his keys—I found myself watching with a dropped jaw as he fiddled out a brand-new harmony over the strains of David Bowie and Queen's power team-up, "Under Pressure."

"You don't even own a single band T-shirt," I said, incredulous.

"I wear the clothes my brother wore before he left for college," Milton said, looking down at himself like he'd never really thought about it before. "They're clean, they fit okay, they're dorky but I guess I am, too."

"You can't have an entire hand-me-down personality!" I insisted. "There are parts of you that nobody can see. Important parts. Doesn't that bother you?" (Of course, as soon as I spouted all of that, I realized that I was wearing my mom's old jeans and a T-shirt from a secondhand shop.)

Milton cocked his head, really thinking about it. "My brother is the oldest son, which means that he gets new everything, the best of everything, but he has to pay it all back by being perfect. And he doesn't seem to mind living up to the expectation. Personally, I don't mind having less pressure on my life, if the only real trade-off is wearing old khakis." Milton shook his head without turning away from the keys. "Besides, *I* know that I'm into music. Why do I have to prove it with a shirt?"

"That's far too healthy an attitude. Please say something angsty to balance it out."

"Oh, believe me, I have plenty of angst under all of these hand-me-downs," Milton said evenly.

Right now, he's got some of that feeling on display, frowning with distaste at the visuals of "Hungry Like the Wolf" even while his hands pound out an alternate melody.

"I thought you loved Duran Duran," I say.

"I appreciate them as early users of complex electronic audio layering. Their night versions are some of the first ripples of the New Wave. But the visuals?" So far, the vague concept seems to center on the band running around, pretending to be multiple Indiana Joneses. "They're using an Asian country because they think it's exotic. I bet they don't know a single thing about Sri Lanka. And the sexy cat-woman thing is . . . "

I cringe as the phrase *sexy cat-woman* becomes a much bigger part of the story line. "Yikes. I was wrong before," I admit. "Healthy and angsty aren't opposites. This is very healthy angst."

"Yeah, they can't seem to make a single video that doesn't treat people other than white British men like props and scenery," Milton says. "Hey, I got angsty enough to use a double negative."

"I'm so proud of you. And so not proud of this band," I say, clicking the channel, and then turning the TV off.

Milton slides into a new song, which seems to be a symphonic version of Prince's "Little Red Corvette."

Even though I completely threw off his rhythm, Milton doesn't seem nervous or upset. I've realized that whenever he's in his element (playing music, at home, or even better, playing music at home) his nerves melt away to basically nothing.

"How do you do it?" I ask, setting my chin on the arm of the couch, my legs kicked up behind me.

"We've talked about this, Robin. How do you read poetry in a revolving door of four different languages?"

"Three of them are in the same language family," I say with a smirk.

Milton throws another pillow, but this time I'm ready with a counterattack, throwing one that knocks his down in midair, with a second pillow lined up to hit him right in the chest. "It just makes sense in my head," I say, sitting back victoriously. "It's like, as soon as I can see enough of the words, the second I unlock some kind of understanding, the rest starts to fill itself in."

"That's how it is with music, too," he says. "You know, for a band nerd, you don't think in music. You think in words and puzzles and problems to be solved. What *do* you like?"

He's goading me, and I know it. Milton has a lot of talent, but he thinks of himself as a fan, first and foremost. He *loves* (not necessarily in this order) sci-fi novels, cult films, comic books, and every form of countercultural music. (He has a soft spot for New Wave, because the electronic instruments they use come from Japan, and as he told me the second time we watched MTV together: "That makes it half Japanese. Like me.") I don't happen to share his love of fluffy-haired singers and pulpy paperbacks with solemn-looking aliens on the cover, but I must be a fan of *something,* according to Milton.

There's a lot to dislike out there, though. It's a veritable buffet of bad choices. There's so much that I'm dead set *against* that sometimes it can be hard to remember what I'm *for.*

"Echo and the Bunnymen. Brian Eno. Cyndi Lauper."

"Cyndi Lauper is a pop singer," Milton says.

"And you're a pedant," I shoot back. "Have you listened to her album? Or do you just sneer at the singles?"

"Ouch." Milton clutches his chest. Then he turns back to his Yamaha. " 'All Through the Night' is a great song," he mutters, and immediately takes up the weird electronic bagpipe solo, note for note.

"You do know what I like," I say. "How else did we end up dressed as Annie Lennox and Boy George for Halloween?"

Milton hasn't dressed up since we were in elementary school, so he let me pick the costumes. I've always favored music videos that involve some kind of cross-dressing or general gender smashing. I found a suit at the thrift store that actually fit me, and an orange wig at the party store that I cut perilously short, ringing my eyes in the blackest of black eyeliner. Milton subjected himself to a long, ratty wig that I added a few thin braids to, and spent all night with his floppy, lacy cuffs falling into the candy bowl at Dash's nerds-only Halloween party.

"I still can't believe that you sang 'Sweet Dreams' in front of the entire marching band and half the student council," he says.

"Dash dared me," I remind him. "Because Dash was very, very drunk."

He clearly thought I wouldn't do it. He thought he had me all figured out.

I wanted to prove him wrong.

"Robin Buckley?" Milton's dad asks, sticking his head into the den. (He always says my full name, for whatever dad reason.) "Are you staying for Sunday night dinner?"

"That sounds really great, Mr. Bledsoe," I say. "Is that . . . ?"

"Okay with me," Milton says. "As long as you don't keep teaming up with my little sister and stealing all the rolls."

Sunday dinner at Milton's house is great, as usual. I hope my parents managed to feed themselves without me around. I've been cooking about half of our dinners since I started high school. My parents both hate domestic chores. Milton's parents cook *together,* even on weeknights, leaning their heads over the pots in tandem and feeding each other spoonfuls to test things. Milton's mom cooks as much Japanese food as she can with the nearby grocery stores. I remember, in middle school, that Milton would come in every day with a bento box lunch—and have to endure pretty much everyone gawking at it. (In high school, he gets hot lunch like pretty much everybody else. Bagged lunches are enough to get you beaten up all on their own, courtesy of the monster.)

Tonight, we have ramen with a miso egg floating right at the top among the broth, meat, and green onion. Milton and I contribute to the feast by making the one dessert I'm good at: buckeyes. We all stuff ourselves with balls of chocolate-dipped peanut butter. Milton's sister, Ellie, puts one in each of her cheeks and pretends to be a squirrel. I do it, too, pretending I'm twelve again.

Amazingly full and strangely happy, I bike back home, my front wheel making a lazy S back and forth on the sidewalk. It's ten thirty, maybe edging closer to eleven. The streets are quiet and the air is cold. It won't snow for another month probably, but I can feel the first sharp threat of it in the air. I pull my flapping open jacket across my body with one hand as I steer with the other.

As soon as I run out of sidewalk, I have to bike a single mile through almost-country from Milton's neighborhood to mine, which is set farther out toward the edge of town. I keep to the thin margin of asphalt between the road and the white line. There's a rustle in the undergrowth at the side of the road.

I try to ignore it.

I do whatever I can to keep the strange skittering sound from sending nervous flicks of fear across my skin. I ride faster, my wheels now blazing a straight arrow down the road. I hum a little bit of the first song I can find in my head, "Hungry Like the Wolf," but the rustle seems to get louder in response.

I shout the lyrics at the top of my lungs.

Songs about being hunted aren't really helping right now.

So I try to think about Operation Croissant.

I'm going to tell Milton about it. Soon. I'm going to ask him to come with me. I know that he's ready for life beyond Hawkins, too. He's already been to Japan with his family, and he's got amazing travel tips, things that I never would have thought about. How to roll your clothes when you pack, instead of folding them. How to find the nearest public restroom without looking like a complete loser. How to decide which books are worth your very limited backpack space.

I'm already starting to think that if Operation Croissant works out, we could branch out and visit more countries together. And what about Milton's bands? We might need to plan a road trip to see live music in Chicago and California and New York. . . .

There are so many places that aren't here.

So many places where that rustle in the bushes isn't something I have to think about, ever again.

Headlights pierce the night behind me, and the rustling goes quiet as a car passes. Right when I let myself believe it's gone, it comes back. Louder. Closer. There's another sound beneath it, soft and pulsing. Something like blood rushing through a heart or breath dragged up a windpipe. I pull onto my street and by the time I drop my bike in the driveway, I'm running scared and I don't care who knows it.

I sprint to the door—thank God it's unlocked—slam it shut, twist the lock behind me, and push my back against the solid wood.

I wait. For what? I honestly don't know.

It's dead quiet in the house. My parents must be asleep.

The phone rings *so loud* that I jump and let out a little shriek—the way you sometimes let out a little pee when you laugh too hard—and I pick it up, hoping for a voice.

Any voice. I hear a second of hard breathing and I think that whatever just happened to me is happening to someone else in Hawkins.

"Robin!"

I sink down to the floor, bringing the receiver with me. The familiarity of the voice on the other end erases a good 50 percent of my fear.

"Kate?"

"You didn't answer the first five times I called! What's going on? Are your parents being weird about phones now?"

"No, I just . . ." I can't imagine telling her what just happened. What would I even say? A raccoon was skittering around in the underbrush and I had a full breakdown? "I guess I stayed at Milton's later than usual," I offer, faintly.

"Well, I'm glad you're finally home, because I have an update." I can hear the glow in her voice.

"What is it?" I ask, knowing that she'll talk about Dash, and for once I'll want to hear it. They've been having sloppily secret make-out sessions ever since Halloween, but it isn't official yet, which I know is killing her.

"We went out tonight," she breathes. *"Out."* She starts in on the details of their latest almost-sort-of-date. Her voice wraps me up in a blanket of normalcy. I twist the phone cord around me. Once, twice.

I've almost stopped thinking about whatever was out there in the dark.

And then, with a crackle, the phone goes dead.

CHAPTER SIXTEEN

NOVEMBER 7, 1983

It turns out there were outages all over town last night. My house kept power, but Kate's didn't. When I see her on Monday morning, that's the first thing she tells me. The second: "Look at *this.*"

She sits us both down in front of her locker on the linoleum floor. "He just gave it to me in the parking lot." Kate shows me her foot, adorned with a brand-new anklet. The chain is thin, the nameplate chunky. Kate's and Dash's names are smashed together, written in a looping font that I think is supposed to look romantic but just makes my eyes hurt. There's even a diamond chip right next to Kate's name.

"Diamonds are for when it's really serious." She's vibrating with excitement. Her voice sounds like she just chugged an entire pot of coffee. "This is not just boyfriend-girlfriend. This is a *first love* anklet."

I know she wants me to admire it. The best I can do is a thinly spread smile, barely covering the fact that this is only going to make things weirder for the four of us. At least I have Milton.

"Are you going to get a necklace chain?" I ask.

"I don't know," she says, stretching her leg out into the hallway, turning her ankle this way and that. She's taken her foot out of her shoe. (Probably because she's wearing a pair of Reeboks, nothing special. Judging by her outfit, she really didn't know this was going to happen today, or she would have dressed for the occasion.) Her foot is bare, except for the loop of stretchy fabric around her ankle from the stir-rup pants. Her dainty little toes make mine look like they belong to a yeti, but when she sticks them directly into the sophomore hallway traffic it still causes a minor commotion. A few people roll their eyes or flip us middle fingers, but then they see that Kate's anklet is the cause of the new traffic pat-tern. A few of the girls even stop to get a better look. Which is exactly what she wants. "It looks cute the way it is, but I can't really put my foot in everyone's face when I want them to see it."

"You're really making me feel special," I say.

"You *are* special," Kate affirms. "And now it's your turn to find someone."

That statement brings down a frigid wave of dread, like I just stepped into the ocean in mid-January. At least, that's what I'm guessing it feels like. The biggest body of water I've been in at any time of the year is Lake Michigan.

I carry my dread around with me as I watch Tam watch Steve Harrington in history class.

I hold it close as I pass Dash in the hallway and he smirks like he's done something truly impressive—all he's really done is wait months and months to make Kate happy because he knew very well how much she likes him.

I try to smother it in ranch dressing and French fries during lunch.

I take it home and sleep with it under my pillow.

I don't think anything can wash this feeling away. But then, the next day, something does.

Band period is just about to start. Over by the practice rooms, Wendy DeWan is whispering with the rest of Earth, Woodwind, and Fire Squad. I find myself drifting toward their conversation, even though I'm not part of their group. There's something serious about the way they're talking to each other. Their eyebrows are tight, but their postures are loose, like they're not sure what to do with themselves. Even from twenty paces, this doesn't have the air of regular high school gossip. At ten paces, I can hear their voices—not quite the same as when the newscasters on TV are talking about the epidemic. But close.

"What's going on?" I ask.

Wendy turns to me. The rest of the group stays huddled, like they need to feel close to each other. Protected. "You know Jonathan Byers?"

"Pale, nervous, takes a lot of—?"

"Photos, right. His kid brother is missing."

"My dad was one of the volunteers in the search party last night," Jennifer adds.

"Missing?" The word trembles through me, shakes things to the ground. "What does that mean?"

"Nobody knows," Nicole jumps in. "It could mean anything. Maybe he just took off. Maybe his dad showed up and took him away from his mom. You know he came from a—"

"If you say broken home, I'm going to break something, and there are decent odds it'll be your nose." Kate has appeared right at my side, glaring at Nicole with laser precision. Nicole leans back in her chair, as if Kate's stare burns a little.

Kate knows what it's like when people start gossiping about which families are acceptable and which ones aren't. Her adoptive parents might be the most upstanding, Hawkins-y couple to ever bring a hot dish to a church social, but for some reason people feel entitled to gossip about the endless possibilities of her birth parents. She's overheard classmates (and nosy office secretaries and overbearing PTA members) speculating that her biological parents must have been split up, or they were never really together, or they must have been drug users and that's why she came out so short. . . .

The list goes on.

So Kate has made herself the defender of kids who don't

have the picture-perfect married-mom-and-dad scenario that people in Hawkins seem to think is the one true option. She swoops in whenever someone is about to say something dumb and unnecessary just in time to slap them down. It's one of her superpowers.

Kate grabs me, hooking my elbow, and pulls me away from Earth, Woodwind, and Fire Squad.

"That poor kid," she says.

"Will," I strain out, finally remembering it. "I think his name is Will."

"I don't know what happened, but he'll be okay," Kate says conclusively. "Hawkins is a safe place."

Kate is good at statements like that. I'm usually good at believing them. Her certainty can be so contagious—but this time something isn't ringing true. There are monsters here in Hawkins. Ones that nobody is paying attention to, because people have decided that this town is safe, and if you start questioning whether that's true or not, you have to deal with all the shadowy truths you find on the other side.

We go back to our section, the spot at the side of the room where the brass players hang out. Kate slides straight onto Dash's lap, her arms falling around his neck. I can tell that she's comforted by his presence, but it turns my discomfort all the way up to eleven.

"Hey," Milton says, riffling through his sheet music. "You want to hang out tonight? Ellie is asking again. I think she thinks you're *her* friend. . . ."

Knowing that Milton's house is there, waiting for me,

definitely helps. But. “I should probably go home after field practice today. I didn’t really see my parents last night and they both left early this morning.”

“Everything okay?”

I can tell he hasn’t gotten wind of this. Milton is watching me now, raising his dark eyebrows, waiting for me to fill the blank space with what’s no longer okay. “Do you know about what happened to Will Byers?”

CHAPTER SEVENTEEN

NOVEMBER 9, 1983

It's my third day in a row going straight home after school. Yesterday, my parents shut themselves in their room as soon as they were both home from work. Within a few minutes the sounds of an argument leaked under their door. Usually when they get mad, they just go to their separate corners. Dad sulks, Mom meditates. But last night they really hashed something out. I couldn't help feeling like, whatever it was, Will Byers's sudden disappearance acted as the catalyst.

Tonight is even weirder.

I'm in my room listening to Spanish tape 6, side 2, "Questions and Answers": "A dónde vas? De dónde eres? Dónde estás?" My parents don't even knock, they just crack my door open and tell me they need me in the kitchen. I click the Walkman off but bring it with me, the headphones still resting around my neck, the foam earpads scratching at my skin.

"Robin, will you sit down, please?" Mom asks.

She's standing to the side of the round wooden dining room table, where we never eat. Dad is hunkered down in a chair, where he never sits. He's usually installed in one of the big reclining corduroy armchairs in the living room. They're like thrones where my parents relax after work, reading or listening to music or talking to each other about how much they hate their respective jobs. I spend most of my time in my room, alone.

"We're having family dinner," Dad grumbles.

"No, we're not," I say.

I click the Walkman back on. Spanish words and phrases trickle out of my headphones.

But before I can get them back on, Dad says, "Leave those off, please."

I lower the headphones, but I don't stop the Walkman. Endless, tinny questions fill the air as I look around.

The table is fully set—something I haven't seen in years. There's salad in a bowl I didn't even know we owned, yellow with flowers around the rim. There's bread and margarine on a little plate, steamed carrots in a colander, a plate full of chicken that looks even paler than I probably do.

"Thanks, but I'm not hungry."

"You're going to sit down and eat something, though," Mom says. "Your father spent a lot of time on those carrots."

"*You're* the ones who told me that family dinner is patriarchal BS and the four food groups are a corporate scheme by Big Dairy."

"Don't tell us what we said, Robin," Dad growls. "We don't need you to be our Dictaphone. You're our daughter." They look at each other—sharing some kind of parental moment of strength.

I grab a chair and sit down, defiantly occupying only the smallest corner. "Yeah. I am. That's why I know this is stupid and we can just skip to the part where you start a conversation you don't really want to have."

"Fine," Mom says. She looks at Dad again. "The Byers boy . . ."

Then she grabs for a napkin and dabs at her eyes.

Okay, I didn't see that coming.

"We know that you probably know Will Byers is missing," Dad says. He's not looking at me. He's staunchly looking anywhere else. "And your classmate, Barbara Holland, didn't come to school today."

I shrug. "So she's not feeling well."

"They found her car. . . ."

Well, that sounds ominous.

Mom picks up where Dad left off. "She never made it home from a party last night. One young person missing in this town was bad enough. But now *two* are gone, so quickly, with no explanations?"

"It reeks of secrets," Dad says. "Something they're not telling us."

"They?" I ask. "Who is they?"

But I already know what they're talking about, in a vague shadowy sense. The government, the police, whatever people in power don't want us to know the truth and therefore are using their authority to quash it.

"Okay, but what about Occam's razor?" I ask, reverting to nerd mode—not that it always works with my parents the way it does with Odd Squad. "Barb probably didn't disappear at all. She's not a little kid. The most likely explanation is that she saw how horrible this place is and ran away."

I could totally see Barb doing that. She's a weirdo, an outcast, a loner at heart. Like me. She must have gotten to that party, reached a breaking point in dealing with prisses and popular kids, and cut out for good. She's too smart to hitchhike, so she probably just walked to the train station. Barb pulled off the escape I've been planning since the beginning of the year. Which makes her my new personal hero. No wonder we were friends in elementary school. Now I'm just sad that we didn't stay close. We could have escaped together.

"Robin," Dad says, bringing me back to reality.

A reality where kids are going missing from Hawkins, and that's just the beginning of the weirdness. Because something even stranger is happening in our kitchen, right now. This fear is turning Mom and Dad into the suburban parents they hate.

"Things are going to have to change," Mom says, picking at a piece of bread. She's not eating it, though. She's slowly tearing it to shreds.

"What kind of things?" I ask, crossing my arms. Maybe it's ultra-petty, but I'm not going to make this easy for them.

"Well, for one . . ." She looks at Dad.

"We're taking away your bike," he finishes for her.

"What?" I jump up. "That's how I get everywhere! That's how I get to school!"

Dad raises a hand, like it's a stop sign and I'm supposed to obey the law without question. (This is the same person who taught me to *always* question authority.) "You'll have to ride the bus."

"That's not the problem," I say. Even though the bus sounds like a perfect nightmare. "My bike is more than just a mode of transportation." It's the only way I ever feel like part of my surroundings. It's the only time I have completely, entirely to myself. It's also how I get home from Milton's. After school or practice, he loads my bike in the wayback of the station wagon. Whenever we're done hanging out, I ride home.

For a second, my nervous system goes back to the other night, when I was riding in the dark. That was the same night Will Byers disappeared. I heard someone say that they found his bike in the woods.

Abandoned.

The only thing that I hate more than thinking my parents are being wholly unreasonable is thinking that maybe—just maybe—they're right.

No. That was just a raccoon in the underbrush. Or some other small mammal. Logic is on my side here. Like Milton said, I'm good at solving puzzles and applying my intelligence to problems. Forcefully, if necessary. Especially when other people give up and decide to throw in the towel.

There's no reason to think that whatever happened to Will or Barb had anything to do with my raccoon or fox or whatever was skittering around. If there was an animal out there attacking kids, they would have found something by now. And no animal would track down three people in two nights, when there's no history of animal attacks in Hawkins. It couldn't have been a person, either. I was riding my bike as fast it would go—nobody could have kept up with me at that pace on foot.

The only option would be a nonhuman, non-animal creature that could move quickly all over town, that was specifically hunting people. And that makes exactly *zero sense.* Will must have gotten confused in the woods or lost. Maybe he hit his head.

Barb left. I'm sure of it.

"We'll make sure you get where you need to go without being . . . snatched," Dad says.

"Sit down, Robin," Mom says. "Please."

"I can't," I say. "I feel like staying here right now would be indulging this behavior." I'm suddenly, extremely tired of them treating me like a child when I've been talking to them on an adult level since I was eleven years old. It makes me want to throw the margarine dish and watch it streak, greasily, down the wallpaper. To remind them what an actual childhood tantrum looks like. "I'm fifteen and you won't teach me to drive, but you'll take my bike away?"

"It's your mother's bike," Dad says.

"She hasn't ridden it since 1975!"

"We just don't want you to do anything that could put you in danger right now," Mom says.

"You mean like every night you spent sleeping on a beach or in a stranger's van?"

"That was a different time," Mom mutters to her carrots, as if they're the ones that need convincing.

Dad barrels forward. "You can't be out at Milton's house as late as you like anymore. Until we know what happened, until we're sure the danger has passed, you'll need to be right here in your bed by ten p.m."

"You're giving me a *bedtime*? I've been a latchkey kid since I was in fifth grade! Can you two hear a single thing you're saying? You're pod people! I have pod parents! It's like . . ." It's like my entire family has turned upside down, overnight.

Dad sighs. "We're not grounding you, Robin. We're not putting you under house arrest. We just need to know that you're safe." He puts his hand on my shoulder. Confusion, frustration, and disappointment battle inside of me, but disappointment wins the day. My parents are starting to behave like everyone else in this town. Maybe they've been living here too long.

Or maybe it's just not as safe as they thought it was.

HIGH SCHOOL

CHAPTER EIGHTEEN

NOVEMBER 10, 1983

They found Will Byers. In the quarry.

The Odd Squad is huddled together under one of the Missing posters that Jonathan hung all over the school.

No one's taken them down yet.

Kate gently lifts it off the wall. "Should we go to the funeral? I heard they're having one tomorrow."

"We didn't really know him." It feels disrespectful, somehow, to go to a funeral for a kid you didn't know. "I have no interest in being a tragedy leech."

"And it's not like we're close personal friends with Jonathan," Dash adds.

I was trying to be considerate. Dash just sounds like a dick.

But I can't say that, because Kate's got her arms wrapped around his neck. They're like one symbiotic creature now. She can't even walk down the hallway without one of his arms slithering around her waist.

"I guess all of that's true," Kate says. "It just feels weird to be this close to what's happening and do . . . nothing."

"That's exactly what my parents expect me to do," I say. "Possibly forever."

Finding out that Will drowned in the quarry didn't exactly set my parents' minds at ease. It's like a genetic switch flipped or something. Their parental instincts, long dormant, have gone into overdrive. It's like they've suddenly become aware the world is actually full of dangers.

"Just come over tonight," Milton says, kicking at my shoe with his. "I'll give you a ride home." He's been weirdly calm through this entire purgatorial week. Apparently, he's the kind of person who expends all their anxiety on everyday events and when a big crisis comes along, he doesn't have any left.

I could really sponge some of his serenity right now. Dealing with my parents has been difficult, verging on impossible. I actually stomped away from them after finishing "family dinner" last night. I've felt the teenage drama spiking higher and higher with each passing day. I'm not that kind of person, usually.

But they're ruining Operation Croissant.

If they won't even let me ride my bike around town, they're not going to give their blessing when I announce I want to ride one around Europe. Even if Milton is with me. They don't even want me to stay out at his house past nine thirty anymore.

"You two have been spending a lot of time together," Kate says, eyeing me and Milton with an impenetrable look on her face. I can't tell if she thinks this is good, bad, or indifferent. "Why don't we all hang out? Moonbeam Roller Disco on Saturday night? I could really use some time together, the four of us."

"You mean besides every band period *and* field practice?" Dash snarks.

"Hey, the season is almost over," Kate says, sounding fake-wounded. "I want to make sure we all stay friends."

It's true that we've been spending more time as pairs than as a group lately—me and Milton, Kate and Dash.

"Robin, are you in?" Kate asks, looking at me with such hope that I don't have the heart to say no.

"All right," I say. "But you have to rent the skates. And find me ones that don't smell like the last person used them to age cheese."

"I will valiantly smell skates for you," Kate agrees.

"I won't," Dash says.

"Dash!" Kate slaps his chest.

And then they're gone, disappearing down the hallway toward their shared first-period chem lab.

Milton lingers with me, hands shoved deep in his pockets.

"How is your family doing?" I ask. I've hardly seen them all week, and maybe it's weird, but I miss them.

"My parents won't let my little sister out of their sight," he says. "And my brother is always calling home from college for updates. He calls five times a day at this point. Part of the whole perfect-son thing." He shrugs. "I'm flying under the radar. Middle-kid birthright."

"I'm feeling pretty jealous of that right now. Can you please scare me up some siblings?"

"Robin, anyone would be scared to be your sibling."

I push his shoulder. "Ha."

This feels like our normal. And that feels good. Milton and I are friends, and it doesn't matter that my parents have gone into complete filial lockdown. Their parents tried to keep them from doing what they knew was important, too. I remind myself that it's not a real rebellion if it's parent-sponsored. I promise myself I'm going to tell Milton about Operation Croissant at the roller rink on Saturday.

Right now, I have to face history class.

"Sorry, gotta go," I say, leaving Milton behind and ducking into the girls' bathroom. I won't be able to focus on the Protestant Reformation if I have to pee this badly. I close myself in a stall right as a group of girls come in. I can see their fashionable shoes through that missing bottom strip of the door. (Why do they leave it like that? Do they think we all need to see each other's feet while we're peeing?)

Wait. Those are Tam's dusty pink sneakers paired with turquoise leg warmers.

"He had a party that he didn't even *invite* me to."

And that's Tam's voice. She doesn't seem upset—more angry.

"It's not like we got invited, either . . . ," one of her friends says, trailing off.

"It's just a party, Tam," says another.

I can almost hear her shaking her head. I can picture her red hair flying. "You can stop pretending you didn't hear about it. Everybody heard about it."

"Heard what, Tam?" the first friend asks, pretty clearly faking innocence.

"He had sex with Nancy Wheeler."

Carefully, I ease open the stall door. It squeaks like a dying rat, which is excellent. Everybody looks up at once. Tam's a wreck, both blotchy and pale, and the second she sees me she starts blotting at her cheeks with a scratchy brown paper towel. I slide my eyes away as she pulls herself together. I don't want her to think I was listening on purpose, but it's also not like this is a particularly big or soundproof bathroom.

"You're going to get past it, Tam," promises the first friend. She's a blond Jennifer.

"You're going to get Steve away from her," swears the other friend, a brunette Jessica.

I install myself in front of the sinks, back turned to all three of them, and run the water.

"Linger much?" Jessica asks.

"Jess," Tam says. "It's the bathroom. Robin has every right to be here. It's not like Steve Harrington should ruin another girl's day."

I knew, on some theoretical level, that Tam knew my name—but knowing that and hearing her say it are apparently different things. Her voice brushes over words, and having it brush over *Robin* makes it feel almost like she reached out her hand to touch my arm. We've barely talked since the auditions for the play, but I'm shocked back into that feeling, like we're right on the precipice of knowing each other better.

"Oh, sweetie," Jennifer says. Jessica gives her a big hug. Her friends are all fawning over her. Like this is a tragedy on par with what happened to Will Byers. Nothing that we're doing right now feels quite so huge or terrifying or all-important with that perspective.

And somehow that knowledge is what gets me to finally take a few steps toward Tam. Her friends eye me like I'm some kind of invasive species. "Are you okay, Tam?" I ask. I like saying her name as much as I liked hearing her say mine. It makes whatever tiny connection we have feel solid and real. "I couldn't help hearing. . . ."

The bell rings. We're all supposed to be in class right now.

"Oh, it's just dumb *boy stuff.*" She says those words with a bite, the way I've heard myself say them before. Tam swipes at the pools of mascara beneath her eyes. "Ugh, I hate that I'm this messy about it. This is ridiculous."

"Don't be so hard on yourself, Tam," Jessica says.

"No. I'm over it. I'm over *him*."

"Good," I say.

The word just leapt out of my mouth.

Everyone is staring at me now, three sets of unblinking eyes, one of them ringed in watery black.

"I just mean . . . Steve's an asshole."

"He really is, isn't he?" Tam looks genuinely delighted by the notion. "I mean, I heard he broke Jonathan Byers's camera. . . ."

"Right?" I say. "Who does that to a guy who just went through a complete tragedy? Who's, like, I know what I'll do, I'll find Will Byers's brother and break the one thing he cares about, because he definitely hasn't been through enough? Steve Harrington, that's who."

"He's a complete and utter *asshole*!" Tam says, really getting into it now.

I keep going. I can't seem to help myself. "He's an asshole raised to the power of asshole. An *exponential* asshole."

Tam laughs so hard that her neck and the shoulder she's got peeking out of her off-the-shoulder sweater turn bright red.

Her friends are full-on glaring at me now.

But I don't care, because making Tam laugh is the best feeling I've had since . . . umm . . . It's possible I've never felt this good.

"Come on, we're late," Jessica says, grabbing for Jennifer's hand. They leave in a combined huff. They clearly don't have the same tolerance level that Tam does for social underlings.

She doesn't seem to care that they're gone, either.

Maybe she needs new friends.

Maybe I could be that person. . . .

"Thanks, Robin," Tam says, breathless from laughter. She turns on the water, ducks her head, and wipes off what remains of her mascara. When she comes back up, her face is naked. I don't think I've ever seen her without makeup on before. Her cheeks have a faint natural blush under the rouge, and her brown eyes look lighter without all the eyeliner and mascara amplifying them. She's pretty both ways. She's pretty all the time. "Being that honest made me feel so much better."

"No problem," I say. "I'll take down douchey guys any day of the week."

She giggles one more time. Then she looks at me. Really looks. And smiles, like she did that day at the auditions. Except this time, I don't feel scared.

This time, I'm ready for it.

"Hey, are you coming to see the play next week?" Tam asks. "I know you didn't end up getting cast, but—"

"Oh, yeah, I'll definitely be there," I say, even though I had zero plans to go until this moment.

Tam lights up. "Great," she says, pushing down the leg warmer on one calf with her other foot, a sort of nervous tic. "I think it's going to be really, really good. I'm *so embarrassed* I sang at auditions, though." Her face goes raspberry red, and she puts one hand over it, then peeks out at me from between two fingers. "I should have just read the part and given it my all. Like you did."

"Umm. I guess I did? And then I gave the floor all of my face."

She laughs again, softer this time. "Well, you would have been a great Emily. It'll still be good, though. Mr. Hauser did a great job."

I've never heard a non-nerd student in this school compliment a teacher. And it was Mr. Hauser, the only teacher really worth complimenting.

"See you in class, Robin?" she asks.

"Yeah," I say, breathless, but not from laughing. Breathless for absolutely no reason. "See you."

I let her leave the bathroom first, because I'm not quite ready to face Miss Click (and Steve Harrington's existence) yet. When the door flaps closed, I look at myself in the mirror. Under my wilting perm and half-hearted makeup, there's someone Tam keeps smiling at.

"Wow," I whisper to myself in the mirror. "Okay."

I didn't think anything could possibly feel good today, and then I got to make fun of Steve *and* make Tam feel better all at once. At least I'll have one thing to remember fondly when I'm halfway across the Atlantic.

HAWKINS
HIGH SCHOOL

CHAPTER NINETEEN

NOVEMBER 12, 1983

I show up at the roller rink a few minutes late—my parents insisted on dropping me off. The rest of the Odd Squad is already assembled at the counter when I walk in.

Kate and Dash are both dressed up for Date Night.

Milton is dressed like . . . Milton. (Or his older brother, really.) I'm wearing the same high-waisted jeans that I usually do, along with a fuzzy black sweater with white polka dots, since it's starting to get cold. I threw on some electric-blue eyeliner right before I left the house. Kate swears that it looks good. (My eyes are already a color that's close to electric blue, so the effect is creepily monochrome, if you ask me.)

Kate shoves a pair of size 9 roller skates into my hands.

"Pre-sniffed," she says, beaming.

"Excellent."

We sit down on one of the benches and swap out our shoes for skates, watching a half dozen people straggle onto the floor to attempt the YMCA while rolling in a circle. How did I agree to this?

I look over at Milton, who's cringing at both the music choices (endless disco) and the sound quality (fuzzy as an earmuff). I shake my head and grab his hand, rolling him right to his feet. At least I have a partner in disgruntlement. We're the perfect pair to travel together. We can marvel at everything worth marveling at, and when things are subpar, we can cringe in stereo.

Kate is by far the best skater in our group, so Dash, Milton, and I follow her out onto the scratched-up wooden floor like fledgling ducks. It's a quiet night at the rink. Probably because of what an intense week it's been in Hawkins. Apparently, Steve Harrington and Jonathan Byers got into a knock-down, drag-out fight earlier today, and nobody could tell which side Nancy Wheeler was on. Steve's face got messed up, his hair no doubt got mussed for the first time, and Jonathan even got arrested. Nothing to keep the popular crowd away like drama that can be endlessly dissected.

The only two people I recognize here are Matthew Manes of the fake eighth-grade crush, working on his routines like he always does, and Sheena Rollins, who's out there in an ankle-length white skirt and a cropped white sweater, rolling endless circles by herself.

"All right," Kate says, clapping her hands like she's the official Night Out on the Town Coach. "Let's at least try to have some fun."

Dash grabs her around the waist and she shrieks as he pushes her backward on her skates.

"No shenanigans," says a disembodied voice over the speaker, interrupting the music for a few seconds before it picks back up.

"YMCNoShenanigans?" Milton asks.

"It's an obscure B side," I say.

Kate and Dash subside into skating side by side. She has to keep slowing down because he can't keep up with her, and every time she circles around to herd him, he gets a little more pissed off.

"Wow, super fun," I say. "Is that what dating looks like?"

Milton gives a little shrug. We have the exact same level of experience with these things. Or inexperience, as the case may be. We sail around the rink a few times, and I stretch my arms out for balance.

"We should really make a run at the next Olympics," Milton says as we both slam into the wall, palms first, because we're not very good at braking.

The voice over the speakers crackles from on high again. "All right, this one is for the lovers. Couples only, please. This is your couples' skate."

Matthew Manes sighs, like couples' skate is the bane of his existence. Sheena Rollins vacates the rink quickly, with a backward glance and a sigh that makes me wonder if she's lonely—if all of the bullying she endures at school hasn't *completely* quenched her interest in other humans. I tried to talk to her at school all through ninth grade, but all she did was nod and run away, so at some point I stopped trying.

A plinky piano intro starts up, and then Bonnie Tyler comes on, singing "Total Eclipse of the Heart."

"At least it's not disco, right?" Milton tries.

As I trudge-skate back toward the benches, Kate laps us and grabs my hand, whipping me away from Milton. She leans in close and whispers, "You should ask him to skate."

"Milton?" I ask. "Are you kidding?"

"You two clearly like each other. Dash and I are together. Wouldn't it be so perfect if we were two couples? Think about the symmetry of it."

"Math isn't how you choose a boyfriend," I mumble. "Are you going to use an algorithm to find me a prom date next?"

Kate has already told me at length about how she's going to get herself into prom this year, even though she and Dash are both sophomores, and obviously getting a junior or senior to ask her is out of the question. She's got an elaborate scheme involving lots of volunteering on the prom committee. (I guess it's worked for a few overachievers in the past.)

Kate nudges me gently toward Milton, until my skates roll me toward him without my express permission. I rock my heel up and hit the brake. Hard.

"Look, I'm not skating with Milton!" I say. I don't say that I don't like Milton. Because I *do.* I like Milton a lot. Just not in the way Kate wants me to. He's basically my best friend, and it's been so long since I've had one of those that the last time, there were juice boxes involved. I hate that in high school caring about someone doesn't count for as much if it's not romantic. If it doesn't come with a gold anklet and a diamond chip.

Across the rink, Dash has cornered Milton. They're barely moving—you're not allowed to stop in the rink—and Dash has his arm around Milton's shoulder.

"Was this whole thing a *setup*?" I ask, suddenly furious.

Kate tries to be cute about it, shrugging and waggling her dark eyebrows. Can she really not see how pissed I am? Or does she just not care?

"I thought we were hanging out as friends tonight," I say, my voice coming out all scratched up.

"This is better. Think of it as enhanced friendship. Friendship *plus.*"

Milton skates over. He holds out his hand.

Ugh. I guess we're doing this.

I take his palm. Why is it so sweaty? Is *mine* that sweaty?

We clunk along together. It's probably the worst collective skating ever done in the history of the Moonbeam Roller Disco Rink.

"This is Tam's favorite song," I blurt as the song swells into the wildly melodramatic chorus.

I don't know where that came from. I just needed something to say.

"Who?" Milton asks.

"Tammy Thompson? She's in my history class."

Even though Milton and I have been hanging out all the time, I've never talked to him about Tam. I've never really talked to anyone about her. And for the first time I wonder why. Am I really that worried that people will think I'm a social climber? Am I afraid that they'll remind me of Tam's obnoxiously huge crush on Steve Harrington, which I already know plenty about from firsthand observation? What, exactly, is so secret about my not-quite-friendship with Tammy Thompson?

"Robin, you're scowling."

"Sorry. I'm concentrating."

"On skating? It's not making us any better, so you can just relax."

I'm not fixated on my footwork, though. Milton told me once that my brain works in puzzles, logic, problems to be solved. Why can't I figure this out? Why is Tam a mystery that makes no particular sense to my brain? Why does thinking about her sometimes make me intensely happy, and other times make me feel like the high school monster is right behind me, breathing down my neck? Why is the idea of talking about her to somebody else inherently terrifying?

I speed up a little bit.

There are four or five other couples breezing around us in circles. They look so smugly proud of themselves, like dating in high school is some kind of accomplishment instead of a way to deal with the increasingly tight boa-constrictor-squeeze of obligation.

Then I catch sight of two girls bombing around the rink, going twice as fast as everybody else, laughing so hard they can barely stand up. They're probably just doing it as a joke, but nobody's stopping them. And unlike most of the boy-girl couples making their way around the rink, they look so *happy.* Their hips bump together on the beat. One of the girls brushes the other one's lower back with her hand, then dips her right in the center of the rink, her long hair brushing the floor.

I pull my fingers away from Milton's sweat-slicked palm and leave the floor, fast.

"Where are you going?" he asks, skating after me.

"Snack bar," I shout back.

I need to ground myself with some grease. I don't know what's going on right now. Holding hands with Milton? Wishing I could skate with some pretty, popular girls instead when they would sooner laugh me off the face of the planet?

This night is getting totally out of control.

I settle my arms on the snack counter and order two baskets of curly fries. I'll leave one for Kate and Dash—an apology for cutting out. The other is all mine. I'm going to scarf it and then walk all the way home.

That's what my parents get for taking my bike.

I look down the counter and find Sheena Rollins perched on a stool, drinking a vanilla milkshake. I wonder if she likes vanilla best, or if this is just unshakable commitment to her all-white aesthetic. When I plop down next to her, the red vinyl stool squeaks horribly. She looks up from the book she's reading—something by Anne Rice—and cocks her head at me.

Sheena studies me unabashedly.

I study her right back.

I've felt bad for Sheena every time I've seen her dealing with bullies and bullshit within the confines of school. But now that I see her in a different context, I can't help thinking she looks like she's doing her own thing, instead of following the crowd.

I'm officially a tiny bit jealous.

"You're lucky," I say. Sheena scrunches up her button nose with a questioning look. "I wish I were reading a good book right now instead of dealing with social fallout." I think for a moment, then emphatically add, "The couples' skate sucks."

A dent, the faintest dimple, appears on one of her pale cheeks. She shrugs one shoulder and goes back to her milkshake.

Milton reaches the snack counter right as my fries are dropped in front of me. I grab the baskets, but they're viciously hot, and I overturn one of them, scattering hot-fry-projectiles all over both of us.

"Could you just . . . give me some space, please?" I shout, much harsher than I meant to.

Oh, great. Now I'm being shitty to Milton because I don't want Kate and Dash pushing me to date him.

Milton gives me a weird look. Like he's hurt, and not just by the fries.

I don't want to hurt Milton's feelings. I hate that he's upset right now. I hate that any of this is happening.

"I'm sorry, I didn't . . . ," I start, but he's already turned and is skating away.

I'm stuck there with my oil-soaked fries, scarfing them all alone, which is exactly what I thought I wanted. Sheena Rollins sits a few stools down, reading silently, probably judging me. Intellectually speaking, I know that the fries are delicious, but I can barely taste them.

"This whole night sucks," I mutter.

I push the basket away and stand up. Rolling over to the skate rental counter and asking for my sneakers means that Kate and Dash will realize I'm leaving and stage some kind of intervention that will make this whole thing *worse*—so without breaking stride, I roll straight out the doors onto the dark pavement. For a second, I think about Will Byers and wonder if I'm safer waiting inside and calling my parents to pick me up.

But I can't live like that, afraid of every shadow. I rattle across the parking lot, picking up speed as I hit the sidewalk. I hate to leave my sneakers behind, but they're a necessary sacrifice. I'll get home much faster this way, and if they never let me back in the Moonbeam Roller Disco Rink because I fled into the night with a pair of size 9 skates, so be it.

HIGH SCHOOL

CHAPTER TWENTY

NOVEMBER 18, 1983

The Friday of the play, I'm sitting squeezed between Milton and Wendy DeWan. I've apologized twice for what happened at the snack counter, and Milton's accepted my apology both times—and laughed about my new status as Hawkins's most wanted roller skate thief—but it still feels like something between us is strange and strained. And I don't like that, at all.

I want my best friend back.

And I want him back before the end of marching band season, when the bonds that tie Odd Squad will naturally loosen a bit. The other three members will return to their regularly scheduled high school excellence while I mildly slack around and make plans for Europe.

So I keep stubbornly putting myself right next to Milton, waiting for this weird feeling to dissolve and for everything to go back to our normal MTV-fueled, banter-laden, couch-pillow-throwing routine.

"This play had better not suck," Dash says, leaning over from the row behind us.

"It's a school play, Dash," Kate says. "I know that you're the only one here who's seen a show on Broadway, but you might have to lower your standards a little bit."

"That's what I'm best at," he says with a smirk at Kate.

And she doesn't destroy him.

She doesn't exactly look happy about it, either, but she just rolls her eyes like it's no big deal, like this is just the kind of crap thing boys get away with saying once you're dating them. Oh, Kate. I'm bristling enough for both of us.

"Buckley, are your eyes okay?" Wendy asks as Dash and Kate settle back into their seats. "You're squinting *really* hard."

"I'm fine," I say. "And the play is going to be really, really good."

Those aren't my words—they're Tam's. I hear them come out of my mouth, like I couldn't help echoing her.

"Either way," Wendy says with a shrug that sends her black ponytail bouncing. "I'm just here for those sweet, sweet bonus points."

"What about you, Milton?"

"Oh, you know," he says.

But I don't. Is he here because he wants to see how the

play turned out, even though we didn't get cast? Did he just tag along because more than half of the marching band is here, so we've got critical mass for another almost-obligatory social outing? Does he *want* to be sitting next to me?

His gaze shifts from me to Wendy, then back again. "The play came so fast, right? I can't believe the season is almost over."

Tomorrow we have a game, one of the last of the season. Everyone in marching band who wants to see *Our Town,* or get the extra credit in English for seeing *Our Town,* is packed into the auditorium tonight.

After Tam asked me to come—specifically *made sure* I was coming—I couldn't imagine skipping it.

Mr. Hauser catches sight of us in the audience and waves. I can tell, somehow, that the wave is meant more for me than anyone else. And then, to make it officially awkward, he shouts, "Robin! So glad you could make it!"

"Are you two friends?" Wendy DeWan asks, pointing between us with her lavender nails. "It's always so funny when teachers try to act like they know us outside of class, like because we're nerds, maybe we're on the same level of cool as actual adult teachers."

Milton laughs. Chortles, really. I've never seen him do that before.

"Mr. Hauser really likes Robin," Dash says, leaning over from the row behind us again to haunt my conversations.

"Are you kidding? Mr. Hauser *loves* Robin," Kate adds.

"He waxes poetic about her papers in my class, and she's not even in my English period."

"Wow," Dash says. "That's an even creepier amount of love than I thought."

"He's just being nice," I say confidently.

I don't understand why he singles me out, but there's no question in my mind that he's trying to be helpful. His increased attention probably has something to do with the fact that he can tell I'm underperforming in English class. On purpose. I sail by with good-enough grades, but I'm always holding back.

"I don't know," Dash says, watching Mr. Hauser with a tight focus as he paces up and down the auditorium in his best brown suit with a bright-red tie. He's double-checking everything in preparation for opening night (which is also the night before closing night). "There's something about that guy that I just don't like. He's creepy to the max."

"Mr. Hauser is not a creep," I snap. "Maybe you're just smelling your own cologne and getting confused."

"Robin!" Kate says with a stupidly theatrical gasp.

"Why are you defending him?" I ask. "He's being a dickwad about a teacher you like."

Kate's eyes get all big and wounded.

"That cologne really is wafting all over us," Wendy confirms, waving the thickly perfumed air in front of her face.

Dash is about to launch a rebuttal, but at that moment the lights go down, so we don't have to talk anymore.

Thank God.

I can't really handle much more of this. I'm feeling

hemmed in on all sides by the marching band. I can't wait for the end of the season, when I can focus on getting a job and raising money for Operation Croissant.

Milton and I will still hang out, of course. Once he knows the whole plan—which I had to bail out of telling him at the roller rink, but I'm going to tell him soon, maybe even tonight—we'll have so much to talk about that we won't need anyone else for the rest of the school year. I'm sincerely looking forward to the whole "I don't need a social scene because I've got a best friend" scenario.

As the play starts in the best, overeager tones that the Hawkins High School actors can muster, I shoot a look over at Milton. He's sunk into his seat, looking dismal. Maybe that's just the forced exposure to bad theater.

But maybe it's something more.

Is he upset with me? Is he upset because our friends are pushing us together?

I catch a glimpse of red hair and my eyes snap to the stage.

It's Tam. In the end, Mr. Hauser cast her in the role of Rebecca, the younger sister of one of the main characters. She's wearing a long black skirt and a high-necked lacy blouse, and her hair is pulled back in two short French braids. She's making the most of her time onstage. But she's not overacting.

I've noticed that in the morning, when she's singing and she gets the sense that people are watching her, she's got a tendency to really *perform*. But sometimes I catch her in moments when nobody else is watching, and her voice travels over the words of a song like she's going somewhere new.

I can only look at her out of the corner of my eye, because it would be so weird to stare. Besides, it might change how she sings.

Right now, I can look at her full on, because everyone is staring in the same direction. (Except Milton. I think Milton's looking at me.)

When the play is over, all of the actors are mingling in the hallway, most of them still in costume. Tam is standing by the spot where the audition sign-up was posted. Her stage makeup, which didn't look like much under the heavy lights, is caked on so thick that it looks like she's wearing a whole extra skin. So many of the other actors are surrounded by parents and grandparents and siblings and friends. The girl who played Emily (the one Mr. Hauser cast after my little audition debacle) is holding a bouquet of white flowers.

Tam's arms are empty.

I have the weirdest thought: I wish I'd brought her flowers. Stargazer lilies, those are my favorites.

"I should go over and say something to Tam," I say to the Odd Squad as we work our way through the choked hall.

There, I did it. I talked about Tam out loud—and I didn't die.

But I *am* subjected to immediate scrutiny.

"Why?" Dash asks.

"She invited me." Didn't she? That day in the bathroom?

"It's the school play, Robin," Milton points out. "Nobody has to invite you."

Fine. But that's not really the point. "I think she did a great job. And somebody should tell her."

"It doesn't have to be you, Buckley." Dash is already herding band nerds toward the door and Friday night freedom. "I want Hawkins Diner. Only their cherry soda can wash out the taste of amateur theatrics. Let's goooo."

I know that if I push right now, everyone will push back—Kate with curiosity, Dash with impatience, Milton with confusion. They'll want to know *why* it matters for me to say something to Tam.

And I honestly don't know why.

I don't want that stumbling block of a conversation tonight—another bit of distance between me and the only friends I've got.

I send one last look back at Tam. She's got people with her now. Friends. Assorted Jessicas and Jennifers. (No Steve Harrington in sight. Of course not. He's still getting over his bruises from that fight with Jonathan, and I don't think he likes to be seen at anything less than his prettiest. Not that he would be caught dead at a school play, anyway. Maybe I shouldn't be quite so glad that I'm here to see Tam's performance tonight and he's not, but I dislike him so much and he's so deeply unaware of me that sometimes private gloating is the only victory I can get.)

Anyway, Tam's not alone. Someone will tell her she did a great job. Obviously, it doesn't have to be me.

Why would it?

When we get to the car, it's Milton's station wagon, but Dash is dangling the keys. "I'm driving."

"Did you take my keys?" Milton asks, checking his pockets as if there isn't already visual evidence they've been stolen.

"Shotgun," Kate cries.

Everyone else piles into the car as quickly as possible.

Milton and I are left standing in the dark, cold parking lot. There's only one seating option left.

"The wayback it is," Milton says.

CHAPTER TWENTY-ONE

NOVEMBER 18, 1983

"Do you feel like they planned that?" I mutter as Milton and I shove our way into the small, cramped space. This bench seat, a godsend for suburban moms who can't seem to stop having kids, is usually occupied by small children, not two high schoolers who could both vie for the Gangliest Teenager trophy.

We settle in and fumble at seat belts and buckles in the dark, our hands bumping more than once.

"Yeah, this feels about as scripted as *Our Town,*" Milton says.

I can see the barest outline of his face in the dark. He's

turned all the way toward me. I can hear his breathing, heavy and fast.

Is he frustrated by this whole setup? As frustrated as I am?

I thought Kate and Dash were going to back off after what happened at the roller rink. But that was far too hopeful. If Kate thinks we should be together, she'll make this her new extracurricular activity. She'll be de facto president, vice president, treasurer, and secretary of the Milton and Robin Must Date Club. I genuinely can't tell if Dash is participating in this charade to make Kate happy or because messing with us gives him something to do.

At the diner, I get a brief break from Kate's scheming. (I also get my nearly broke go-to order, a plate of chocolate chip pancakes, which are shockingly cheap and unfairly delicious. I ogle Dash's club sandwich with extra curly fries, but anything expensive I eat in Hawkins is one more meal I won't be eating in Europe.) As soon as we leave the diner, everyone lightning-bolts for their original seats in the car—leaving me and Milton stranded together yet again.

"Our friends suck," I say, loud enough for everyone in the station wagon to hear.

They laugh, like I just told the best joke of the night.

"I don't know," Milton says. "It's not so bad back here, right?"

"At least you keep it clean."

"Until *you* put your bike grease all over it."

Me: Wait. This feels strangely flirty.

Me: This is just how Milton and I banter.

Also me: Then why is Milton breathing so heavily and leaning his thigh against yours? Is it really that tight back here? Or is this something *he* wants?

The idea hits my brain all at once. Maybe Milton told Dash that he was interested in dating me, and that's where this whole aggressive plan to push us together came from. Kate and Dash might have decided that Milton needed help telling me. That drastic measures must be taken.

Milton hasn't been acting like he has a big must-tell-Robin-or-I'll-die-type crush.

Has he?

We've been hanging out for two solid months and he's barely ever seemed nervous. He's never gotten mysteriously sweaty or looked at me with pre-kiss intensity. (My only kiss was with Joe Flaherty at a seventh-grade dance, but I'll never forget That Look right before he dove in and mashed his braces against my closed lips.) Milton hasn't been weird with me, ever.

Why would that change now? Did a crush descend on him out of nowhere?

"So," I say. "What do you think happened with Will Byers?"

Yikes. I'm so uncomfortable with my almost-best friend possibly having a crush on me that I dropped *the* question. The one everyone's been asking all week, until we ran out of things to speculate about and the conversation shriveled up.

There's only one thing we know for sure: Will Byers is back.

Not the body in the quarry—the *actual* Will Byers.

"I guess the coroner made a mistake," Milton says. "I'm just glad my parents can finally relax about Ellie."

"Yeah," I say. "I wish my parents got that particular memo."

They still haven't restored my life to normal status, even though Will is back, and Barb (as I have maintained throughout this entire catastrophic autumn) probably just ran away and found herself a better life somewhere else.

"Your parents just want you to be safe. And I know your bike being gone sucks, but it's almost winter. You walked it in the snow most of the time anyway. And I mean . . . you can always take the bus."

"A public school bus? The yellow kind that looks and smells like pee on wheels? Milton, I would gag, but that would ruin your pristine wayback seat." He laughs. I can hear the sound perfectly, even though it's low-pitched and barely audible. I suddenly realize that everybody in the front is quiet—and band nerds are never quiet in large numbers. It's like when you take our instruments away, we have to overcompensate by making a cacophony all on our own.

They're listening in. Waiting to see what Milton and I will do when we're stuffed together in close proximity.

I drop my voice to the lowest of whispers, lean in until my face is nearly touching Milton's, and say, "What about this beautiful luxury vehicle that you've been so kind to chauffeur me around in?"

"I'm only a chauffeur if you're riding in the back seat and I'm alone in the front," Milton says, his voice as quiet as mine.

The sound in the rest of the car resumes. My plan to keep us from being overheard is working. But what if it's only playing into Milton's crush? Our faces are basically touching right now.

Oh, God. What happens to Operation Croissant if Milton has big, unrequited romantic feelings? If I ask him to come, knowing that he likes me, am I just leading him on? Is that as cruel as Kate and Dash treating us like zoo animals they're trying to get to mate?

"Umm . . . Robin?" Milton asks gently.

And then he *takes my hand.*

How did I get to fifteen completely unprepared for the moment when a fully decent boy tells me that he likes me? Should I give him a chance to tell me how he feels? Or should I cut him off now right now—before he says something he can't take back?

I can't seem to open my mouth.

"I feel really bad only telling you this now. . . . I mean, I should have brought it up a long time ago . . . but we were having so much fun and I . . ."

"It's okay," I blurt. "It's not like we ever talked about crushes, in general."

Milton pauses, like I threw off his rhythm. (Finally. I tried to do it with so many pillows and weird, random comments while he was playing his instruments. Apparently all I had to do was say the word *crush,* and the world would more or less stop turning.)

"That's true," he admits. "We didn't broach the subject. Either of us."

Of course we didn't.

That wasn't the *point* of our friendship, but it was certainly a bonus. Being around a boy who wasn't constantly bringing it up felt sort of like finding an escape hatch. Girls like Kate expect me to talk about boys with them. Milton seemed happy to talk about music and movies and their strange bastard children, music videos, forever. He didn't need me to dissect my feelings. He didn't push me to tell him my deepest secrets.

Not that I have any.

My biggest secret is Operation Croissant. And I'm supposed to tell him tonight. I can't let a little crush get in my way. High school crushes fade. They aren't forever. Milton and I will get back to being friends by holiday break. We'll laugh about that one awkward time in the car, when Milton declared his feelings to me. All of this will be okay. But first, we have to push through this.

"Milton, I need to tell you . . ."

But his voice is already crossing paths with mine in the dark. His words are already hitting my brain. "I like Wendy."

"Oh!" I say.

That's . . . not what I was expecting.

"That's excellent news!" I'm glad for him. I'm glad for Wendy. They're both amazing. And now the level of nervous close-talking makes sense, because Wendy is in the car with us. Milton isn't ready to tell her yet, but he's ready to tell me. And for someone as socially nervous as Milton, that feels like a big step.

I squeeze his hand. "You two are going to make a genuinely not-awful couple."

"Thanks, Robin." He clenches my hand tight. "You're the best. Which makes this the worst." He winces in the here-then-gone light of a streetlamp. "There's something you said at the roller rink. . . . You asked if I could give you space, and I think you're right. We need to spend less time together. Everyone thinks . . . They think . . ."

"That we want to date and we're *so* shy and nerdy that we just can't get our shit together?" I ask. There's a slight edge to my voice. (Okay, there's a whole razor blade in it.)

"Exactly!" Milton whisper-shouts.

"But *we* know that's not what's happening," I say. "Isn't that what matters?"

Even as I say it, I can feel the monster tracking us down. Breathing in the dark. Waiting for its prey. The truth about who we are has never been what matters most at Hawkins High. What matters is what everybody else thinks about you.

"I'm sorry, Robin," he says. "But I don't know how I can ask Wendy out if everyone thinks I'm secretly in love with you."

"Kate and Dash can take a flying—"

"Ten other people have asked me if we're going out since Halloween." Well, crap. We shouldn't have gotten our costumes together. Even if they *were* fantastic. "Even my sister assumes I have a huge crush on you."

"But you don't," I say, really letting the relief of that part sink in. "We don't need to hang out all the time!" I offer, ready to help now that I know what we're dealing with here.

"There are other things we can do." Like plan a big, friends-only, no-kissing-under-the-Eiffel-Tower trip.

"I don't want to stop being your friend." He lets go of my hand. "I just need some time."

"How much?"

Two minutes ago, I thought I'd be letting him down gently, and here I am sounding needy.

"Give me until prom tickets go on sale?" he asks, like he knows it's a lot. Like he's aware of just how bad a friend he's being, in the name of love and not letting other people around us have a new excuse to be awful. "I really want to ask her, but I know it's a big deal. Especially since it's her senior year. I won't be the only guy who wants to be her date. And . . . you know me. I have to work up to it."

"I mean. Yeah. You needed two months to work up to telling me, and I'm not even Wendy."

We're riding backward. My neighborhood unfolds in reverse as Dash turns onto my street.

"Robin, now that we're talking about it . . ." Milton sounds antsy, like he knows we have a limited amount of time left before I get out of the car. "Is there anything you want to tell me? About liking anyone?"

When Kate asked me this question, I was angry. It felt like she needed me to have an answer. Like it was required. A question on the test that you can't just *skip.*

"I don't get crushes," I say absently. It's my standard response.

"Are you sure?" Milton asks. "Back at the auditorium tonight, I wondered if maybe—"

"I liked you?" I ask. "I thought, for a second back there, that you liked me, too. What a sitcom, right?"

Milton gives me a strange look—like maybe he had a completely different idea back at the auditorium. But before I can ask him what that look was about, Dash brings the station wagon to an abrupt, coughing halt.

"All right, Buckley. This is your stop."

I wait for someone to come release me from the prison of the wayback. (It's impossible to open the door from the inside, which seems like a serious safety issue.) Kate takes her time getting out of the car and walking around, probably because she's hoping that we're mid-make-out back here.

Little does she know.

When Kate finally opens the door, I leap out.

It's gotten stuffy in the station wagon, but the air that comes in is bracing, nearly winter.

"Robin—"

"Bye, Milton," I say as I close the door and Kate returns to her seat. As the car ping-pongs off down my street, I add, "I'll see you soon."

I might understand everything Milton just said, and I obviously want him to find happiness with the girl of his dreams, but I'm not giving in to this enforced friendship break. I don't know if it's fixable, but I know I have to try.

And I'm going to use my entire puzzle-solving, problem-fixing brain to do it.

HAWKINS
HIGH SCHOOL

CHAPTER TWENTY-TWO

NOVEMBER 20, 1983

This time, I'm the one who suggests a scary movie night at Dash's house. But it's only three of us: me, Kate, and Dash.

We settle into Dash's room quickly. It's filled with a king-size bed *and* a couch, and the furniture is a combination of black wood and smoked glass that looks extremely out of place in a seventeen-year-old's bedroom but matches the decor of the rest of the house. Dash turns on the TV and pops *The Evil Dead* into his very own VCR. As the tape starts to play, Dash and Kate settle onto the couch with a bag of Ruffles between them, their fingers doing a weird little dance as they both reach for the same perfect chip.

Yeah, not watching that all night.

I sit right below Kate and let her French braid my hair. She looks far too delighted to have some girl time as well as her boyfriend right at her side. I think this is the scene she's been dreaming of since the beginning of the school year. Even though I know she's still terrified of this movie, she's grinning down at me as she grabs big, tawny chunks of my hair and gets to work.

We've had a long, late-season weekend of marching band. My entire body is exhausted because carrying a mellophone around for hours on end is bizarrely strenuous, and I melt into the rhythm of Kate's fingers, the combination of smoothing and tugging that helps me forget all my worries, then brings them back into sharp focus.

I remember my mission.

"Hey, guys," I say, looking at them both upside down, because I can't imagine saying this straight on. "I'm sorry things have been so tense lately."

I don't mention that their pushing is one of the prime reasons for that tension, and that I'm still pretty mad at both of them for pulling on strings that they should have left alone. I'm giving them both one big chance to make it up to me before this whole situation gets out of hand and I'm not allowed to speak to Milton until after the spring thaw. (It hasn't even started snowing.)

"I just think that everyone should know that Milton and I are friends. Just friends. *Really great* friends."

"Then why isn't he here tonight?" Dash asks with a smirk.

Anger flares up my throat, but I douse it with a bit of

preparedness. "Milton is the one who asked not to see me right now, and, honestly, it's pretty upsetting. He's afraid that people are going to keep seeing us as a couple, and he doesn't want that. Neither of us do. I would really appreciate if both of you would help me spread the word through the marching band."

The marching band nerds will tell the choir nerds. The choir nerds will tell the theater nerds. The theater nerds will even tell the popular kids—if any of them care. And so the information will snake its way around Hawkins High, and Milton will be free to go after Wendy DeWan without any false gossip hanging over his head. Then Milton and I can go right back to where we were as friends, and Operation Croissant will be back on track.

"Hmmm," Kate says, narrowing her eyes. "You want us to spread . . . the antidote to a rumor?"

"Exactly," I say with a sigh of relief. I should have known that Kate's megabrain would be able to keep up.

Her hands tug the roots of my French braid so tight that I can feel it in my sinuses. "I still don't get it. Milton is great, and you clearly like him. Are you sure you don't want to at least kiss him once, to see how you feel?"

"Kate, you know how scary this movie is to you? You know how your skin crawls every time you look at those zombies?"

"They're demons, Robin," Dash says.

"Shut up, Dash," Kate and I both say at the same time.

"That's how I feel when I think about dating a boy at Hawkins High." I feel like this makes sense, like it's conclusive.

"Are they really that bad?" Kate asks, patting Dash's knee. "*My* first boyfriend is from Hawkins High. Are the boys here really not good enough for you? Milton is amazing! I hate to say this but . . . I feel like maybe you're just holding out for someone who doesn't exist, Robin."

My mind flashes on Tam smiling at me in the school bathroom.

And everything wobbles.

Kate finishes off my braid and I stand up suddenly, my head still off-balance. I tell myself it's from the too-tight braids. I touch them and find that they're so firmly set in place that a tornado couldn't take a single wisp out.

"Where are you going?" Kate asks.

I look down at her absently. "More chips," I say, picking up the empty bowl and clutching it to my chest.

My feet make almost no sound on the dark stone circular staircase at the center of Dash's house. Not that I have to worry about bothering anyone. His two older siblings are out of the house already, and his parents aren't home—they're hardly ever home. We originally bonded over being latchkey kids, but it's different when one person's parents are working late to keep the bill collectors from swarming, and the other person's parents are driving out of town to much fancier places with much fancier parties.

I breathe in the stillness of the kitchen, which is all glass and chrome with the most cutting-edge everything. It takes me six tries to find the chips, as I rip open cupboards and find that half of them are empty.

When I finally locate the food, I stand up to find that Dash is watching me with his arms crossed and his eyes brightly amused.

He grabs the chips from me and pours them into the bowl—like I can't do it myself. "When Kate won't let go of something, she can be so annoying, right?"

"Don't you mean cute?" I ask.

He looks at me, not blinking. We're in some kind of standoff that I don't fully understand.

"I think I know why you won't date Milton. . . ."

"Finally!" I say. "Thank you!"

And then he ducks in and tries to kiss me.

"Are you kidding?" I ask, pushing him away so fast that he nearly lands butt-first on the cold, dark stone. The heel of his hand catches on the glass kitchen island and he staggers back to an upright position.

"Yikes, Buckley. Those are some strong reflexes." He steps closer. "Want to try that again?"

I shake my head so fast that my French braids whip my face. "No!"

"Look, is this just because Kate is upstairs? We can do it another time. . . ."

"Dash, you are supposedly smart," I say. "So you should definitely understand one of the simplest words in the English language. *No.* I'm not interested in kissing you. Now, later, ever. No."

"You're being weird again," he says, still acting amused—which for some reason makes this all worse. "You told me all about your little plans to go to Europe! You didn't tell Kate. You think I don't know what that means? You and I have *secrets,* Buckley." He smiles at me, and I feel twice as sick as that time I drank that spiked eggnog. "Maybe we should take that trip together. Wasn't that what you were hoping? I have enough money that I could pay for the whole thing. *And* I speak three languages. I have a very talented tongue."

My upchuck reflex kicks in, and I release a retching sound. "You're . . . ugh, you're the worst, Dash."

He shrugs, grabbing a cherry soda to bring upstairs, like none of this just happened. Like we're all going back up there to watch the movie together. "Whatever, Buckley. Your loss is Kate's gain."

"Were you seriously going to break up with her if I said yes?"

He shrugs. "High school relationships don't last forever. Smart people know this. They don't get bogged down in sentiment and attachments that can't possibly stay static. Evolve or die, right? Besides, you're the one who said that sophomore year is the dead zone of our education. We're all just killing time."

Maybe that's true for some people, but no matter how much she acts like she's just *practicing,* I know that dating means a lot to Kate. Way too much, if you ask me, but still. What Dash just said is so cold and self-centered that I actually stagger backward into the pristine steel refrigerator.

"I can't believe you just used your intelligence as an excuse to cheat on our friend," I say.

"How can nerds rule the world if we're supposed to be *more* moral than everybody else?" he asks with an aggressively bored shrug. "It's a double standard, and I'm not interested in living up to that." Dash has taken the concept of *nerd* and twisted it, until it's something dark and self-serving, just another way to be awful.

I storm up the stairs, Dash quick on my heels.

"I'm leaving," I say to Kate as soon as I reach the bedroom. Demons fill the screen and Kate clutches a throw pillow. "Come with me."

"What?" Kate squeaks. "Why?"

"Because your gross boyfriend is being gross," I snap. I know I need to tell her the rest, but it'll have to wait until we get out of here. Dash is glaring at me now, and I don't exactly want to relive the scene in the kitchen right in front of him.

Kate looks like she's the one being tortured as the demons on the screen behind her start wreaking havoc. "Robin . . . please don't make me choose between the two of you. My boyfriend and my best girlfriend?"

"Don't use that word," I mutter.

"You *know* that's not fair," she whines playfully. She clearly still thinks we're playing some kind of game.

"I have to get out of here," I say. "I never should have come here with just the two of you."

Kate sighs like I'm a lost cause and her voice goes hard. "Robin, if you're feeling lonely, you have nobody to blame but yourself, okay? I *keep* trying to help you. There are *plenty* of boys who would go out with you."

I feel the shriek bubble up in my throat right before I release it. "I don't like any of the boys at school!"

"Okay, okay," she says, placating me and petting my braids, then looking over at Dash with a quick eye roll, like I'm obviously overreacting. "We'll find you a way better boy. From a way better school. Somebody you really like, all right?"

"You're not listening to me," I say to Kate, nearly in tears.

She just stares at me like I'm a word she can't possibly translate.

Dash pauses the movie and stares at me. "Are you done stomping around my house?" he asks. "I want to watch the part where Cheryl goes rabid demon on the rest of them."

"Just go, okay?" Kate says. "I'll talk to you later."

"No," I say. "You won't." Because that's when I know that I'm done with all of the people I've previously thought of as my friends. Milton needs time away from me. Kate can't understand me. And Dash . . . well, Dash was always a wolf in a really nice wool sweater.

I leave his house early and start the long, lonely walk home.

We might have a week left in the marching band season, but as far as I'm concerned, Odd Squad is over.

CHAPTER TWENTY-THREE

NOVEMBER 21, 1983

Living in an unexpected state of suburban parental lockdown, losing the friend they wanted to go to Europe with (along with their other ones into the bargain), and having exactly zero dollars in the bank because they were focusing on said friendships and getting through the remainder of marching band season, some people would let go of their plans.

I'm doubling down.

Marching band is over in one week. By then, I'm going to have a job where I can make enough money for not one but *two* people to get to Europe next summer. Something about the way Dash (creepily) offered to pay for the whole trip made me extra determined to raise the funds all on my own.

By the time my friendship with Milton is officially reinstated, he won't have time to fund his own plane ticket, though my hope is that he'll be able to contribute to the "trains and hostels and moules frites" fund. I've called and priced out every airline while my parents were asleep. If we leave from Chicago, round-trip tickets for Charles de Gaulle Airport near Paris will cost eight hundred dollars each.

If I work for the rest of the school year and combine that money with the saved-up funds I get from my rogue relatives who send birthday and Christmas cards stuffed with twenty-dollar bills, I might just have enough.

In the meantime, I'll wait for Milton to fight his battle with the high school monster. Maybe I should be mad at him for bailing on me, but I understand his choice better than I want to. There are things the people around us just don't understand or accept. Girls like Sheena Rollins, who won't talk to anyone, refusing all forms of social connection, even though they're the constant target of bullies. Girls like me, who won't cave to the pressure to date a boy—any boy—even though it means losing longtime friends. And boys like Milton, who can manage to be friends with girls like me.

I trust Milton, though. He'll ask out Wendy, go to prom with her (okay, I judge him a *little* for caring so much about prom), and then we'll be back on for Europe. It would be weird to tell him about it now, when we're in friendship purgatory, so I'll just keep planning in his absence.

And in the meantime, I'll look for a backup candidate—just in case.

My brain is clicking away with all of this as Mr. Hauser starts into the topic of Shirley Jackson. We finished *Lord of the Flies* back in September, slogged through *The Catcher in the Rye* in October, and for November are on to short stories by a bevy of assorted writers. Last week was Hemingway's "Hills Like White Elephants." (Even Mr. Hauser looks bored when we talk about Hemingway. When I wondered aloud why he keeps it on the syllabus, he revealed that he isn't allowed to set the readings. They're based on school board approvals and whatever copies remain after the previous year's students descend on the beat-up old paperbacks like a plague of locusts.)

This week we're reading our first woman author of the year. (Yes, I've already pointed out that it's late November and asked how it took us so long.) We're focusing on her story "The Lottery," which was originally published in 1948 and feels like it could have been written about Hawkins yesterday.

"What are you getting from the opening lines?" Mr. Hauser asks. "What secret messages are folded up in that first paragraph?"

I love when he talks about stories this way. Like they're filled with meaning that could leap out and surprise us at any moment. And depending on who is reading them—and when and where and why—different meanings are waiting for us to discover. He doesn't treat stories like dead things on display.

Dash holds up his hand and starts talking at the same time. "This town doesn't really like the lottery, but they've figured out how to live with it. It's a commentary on how people minimize evil in their own minds." Which is pretty rich, coming from a person who tried to cheat on his girlfriend last night and then acted like it was no big deal. "Most people just want to get the nasty bit over with so they can get back to their regularly scheduled programming."

"But the nasty bit *is* regular to them," I add quickly, stomping over the satisfaction he clearly feels about his answer. "It's right there in the opening paragraph. They do this every year. They sacrifice someone *every year.* Like clockwork. And their town isn't the only one who does it." It makes me think about how the United States was the first country in the world to try to standardize time, because they wanted the trains to run from place to place without any confusion. So everybody had to match. "It's a story about how this country is . . . standardizing evil."

Dash looks pissed, like I hijacked his point.

Good.

I raise my eyebrows in a challenge. Boys like Dash, the ones who've turned the idea of "nerd" to the dark side, hate it when you show them up in class, but I no longer have the capacity to care about his poor hurt feelings. He and Kate are not exactly on my list of favorite people right now.

I do feel bad for Kate—still stuck dating a slithering excuse for a boyfriend—so I decide to leave her a note in her locker later today, telling her everything that happened in Dash's kitchen last night. But I'm not talking to her directly. I don't have it in me to face another round of her "why aren't you just like me?" interrogation.

Mr. Hauser gives me a dry smile. "Robin, can you stay after class?"

There are some laughs, poorly hidden behind hands.

My cheeks startle with red. If I'm being pulled aside or punished for something, I have the right to know what.

"Did I say something wrong?" I ask.

"Not at all. But you've been writing notes in Italian since the class period started, and if you'd check your schedule, I believe you'll note that this is English class."

I glance down at my black-and-white marbled composition notebook, where I have indeed been scribbling an update on Operation Croissant. Now that I'm getting worried about secrecy, and the importance of hiding these plans from my parents (and anybody else who would block my much-needed escape route), I've started writing in a mix of Italian, French, and Spanish. Anybody who speaks even one of those languages can't translate the notebook in its entirety. They'd need to know all three.

And if they did, I'd probably ask them to come with me.

Today my notes read things like: *L'ostello costa cinque lire a notte.*

I put a protective arm over my notes. "What if I like to write about Shirley Jackson in other languages?" I ask. "That can't possibly be against the rules. In fact, I'd think you would encourage such flexibility of thought."

"I would, indeed. And in that case, I would love if you could translate your notes for me. After class."

The laughing notches up a little higher.

As soon as class is over, I find myself in front of Mr. Hauser's desk, awaiting my sentence.

"Robin, do you need somewhere safe to spend your time?"

"Wait. What?"

"Before school. At lunch. During free periods. If you ever need somewhere to be, you can come here. I won't bother you. In fact, I'll barely speak to you, since I have two hundred mediocre essays to grade every week."

My body releases a metric ton of tension, and I realize how relieved I am by this offer. I hadn't really been aware of how much I was freaking out about facing down the wilds of the hallways or the endless indignities of the cafeteria without the Odd Squad at my back. If I'm mad at Kate and Dash and not spending time with Milton, who else do I have?

Exactly no one.

"Thanks, Mr. Hauser."

An uncomfortable memory barges into my mind. Dash told me not to spend time with him alone—that he's creepy in some indefinable way.

But Dash is the worst.

And I trust Mr. Hauser. That much I know. Maybe there are things about him beyond what I'll ever learn in school, but that's the deal with teachers. They exist at school with us, and they exist in their own personal lives, but there's no real overlap. It's like a Venn diagram where the circles don't touch.

And yet they see so much of our petty little personal lives unfolding in the hallways like a bad play. . . .

I wonder what Mr. Hauser saw that made him think I need somewhere to be, away from all of my classmates.

"How did you know that I—?"

"In case you haven't noticed," Mr. Hauser says, seeming to have anticipated this question, "you're one of the only students who actually engage with the material. And young people who do that tend to be under constant onslaught from the slings and arrows of outrageous teenagers."

"I'm pretty sure Shakespeare never said that."

"The unit on *Hamlet* isn't until senior year," he says, setting his sandy eyebrows in a firm line. "Are you sure?"

Mr. Hauser goes back to his papers, marking a C- on one before flipping it over and turning to the next.

"What did you think about the play?" he asks, multitasking.

"*Hamlet*?" I ask.

"Our Town," he says.

Honestly, I haven't really thought much about it since the curtain dropped. I haven't thought about anything but Tam standing on that ladder, giving her one big speech of the show, her face shining in the lights and her voice eager. "Some of the actors gave . . . really strong performances."

"There were a few surprises, that's for sure," he says. "I'll miss it. Not because it was the world's greatest production. But it kept me busy."

"I'm getting a job," I blurt out.

"Good for you," he says. "Still dreaming about Europe?"

"More than dreaming." I clutch my composition notebook.

He nods briskly. "We might never have an easy road to what we want, Robin. But that doesn't mean we stop wanting."

I don't know who *we* is. The general *we*? The people who think too much, dream too hard, refuse to standardize themselves—even when it means we might lose the next lottery and have to face a horde of entitled townspeople who are just going through the motions of anger and fear?

The bell rings. I'm already late for next period, but I don't care anymore. Besides, Barb was the hall monitor, and they never replaced her.

I hope she's far away by now.

I hope she's somewhere incredible, living a life that nobody in this town could ever dream, far away from the people she was forced into close proximity with for so long—the people she called "friends," even though in the end they were just as much a part of the high school monster as anyone else.

Heading for the door, one more question stops me cold. "Mr. Hauser, why are you doing this? Letting me come to your class whenever I want and invade your free time?"

"I wish a teacher had done it for me." He doesn't look up from the stack of papers, just grades the one on the top with a swift hand and keeps going.

CHAPTER TWENTY-FOUR

NOVEMBER 21, 1983

I have to make it through one more nightmare before this day is through.

Without Mom's old bike or Milton's trusty station wagon in my life, there's only one option left for getting to and from school. Dad dropped me off this morning on his way to work, but he made it clear that would only be happening sporadically, when he had the extra ten minutes to spare (he's notoriously late leaving the house in the morning) or when there's a blizzard in the forecast.

For the most part, I've been condemned to a new fate. Or really, an old one.

I step onto the bus.

I haven't been on a school bus since fifth grade. I started riding my bike in sixth, with a flock of other kids at first, and then alone. All of my memories of this process are dated. They're circa the elementary school bus, which always smelled like milk.

I'm not an idiot. I know that the high school bus bears no resemblance to that one. They're the same genus, but completely different species. Even as I reach the top step of the bus, things already seem dire. For one thing, the bus smells like it's on fire.

The black rubber on the stairs matches the burning rubber in the air, which is probably from the tires. The driver gives me a cursory glance, then looks through the windshield with a thousand-yard stare.

She doesn't even know where I live. How is this going to work?

"Um, Robin Buckley," I say. "Forty-Two Magnolia Drive?"

The driver gives no indication that she's heard me. She's a woman probably in her early forties, wearing a T-shirt stained with something that looks like fruit punch, but her eyes seem unfathomably old. Ancient, even. Like she's been driving this bus since the dawn of time.

The bus pitches forward as I start walking back, and I stumble down the aisle. There's no assigned seating, not even a suggested plan based on what grade you're in. In other words, it's a complete free-for-all.

I don't see any of my people.

What's the point in letting everyone think I'm a generic

nerd if it doesn't offer safety in numbers? Even without Dash and Kate and Milton in my life, I should at least have other bandmates and related types to stick close to. I touch my perm, like a talisman. I hate this hairstyle more and more with each passing week. But when people see it, when they watch me lug my instrument case around the hallways, when they notice the way that I dress, they know what I am.

Even if they don't know *who* I am.

That's enough to get most people not to look any closer.

But on this bus, I might as well be naked with a target painted on my back.

"Buckley! Buckle up!" shouts a horrible junior named Roy from the back row.

"There are no seat belts on this bus," I remind everyone. Loudly.

"That's not the kind of ride I was talking about," Roy says, giving a hip thrust that makes me gag. Also loudly.

Roy plays a little bit of victorious air guitar and returns to the backseat kingdom of upperclassmen metalhead burn-outs who don't bother learning to drive because they'd rather congregate here, where they can headbang in peace and stash their drugs in the hollow seat backs that have been ripped and then covered back up with brown sticky tape. The front half of the bus is packed tight with freshmen. They're only a year younger than I am, but somehow they look like newly hatched chicks. Fluffy hair, unsuspecting manner. But they can be vicious in groups. A nonstop spitball factory and gossip machine.

I wedge myself into the no-girl's-land in the middle of the

bus, a swath of seats where I can push myself between two seat backs like a piece of toast in a toaster. I slide down and I stay down.

Pulling out a pen, I open my composition notebook to work on some Spanish phrases for traveling.

Sí, yo soy Americana.

Sí, mi país es el peor.

I mutter the words out loud. My parents have their soothing mantras. I have mine.

But it's not enough to counteract this bus ride. By the time we make it to the third or fourth stop, there are so many spitballs in my hair (how? The angles don't even make sense) and about four dozens variations of the "Buckley, buckle up" joke have been shouted in my direction.

"Hello?" I call out to the bus driver. "What are you doing to curb this madness?"

The driver doesn't even glance in the rearview mirror. I can only see the strip of her face from eyebrows to upper lip. She remains impassive. Unmoved. This is how she survives, I guess. By pretending the bus is empty. By acting like whatever's unfolding behind her simply isn't happening.

Even though I'm still a mile and a half from home, I stamp off the bus, wrap my coat around the books I'm carrying, plus the treasured composition notebook, and start the long walk back to my neighborhood.

The chill in the air has a cumulative effect. At first, only my fingers and face are cold. But by the time I've made it past two dozen fancy white houses, my entire soul is on ice.

When you leave the part of town where the rich peoples' homes huddle together, the sidewalk gives up on life. I have to walk the last three-quarters of a mile to my neighborhood in a trench at the side of the road, overflowing with crunchy weeds that used to be summer flowers and are now lank, lifeless brown stems.

Half a dozen cars pass me, none of them slowing down as they whip cold air over me.

One of them lays on the horn. A distinctly high school boy voice shouts: "You make me horn-y!"

I put my middle fingers up and just keep walking. I don't bother with the witty, cutting remarks.

(But seriously? You make me horn-y?)

I have to save my voice for an argument I might actually win.

When I get home, my parents are both at work. I use an old comb to pick the spitballs out of my hair. I do my homework. Practice Italian verb conjugations. (What's Italian for "you suck"? None of my dictionaries are helping here.) As it gets dark, I turn on all the lights in the house. When my eyes are tired and my hand is cramped and I can't imagine doing this anymore, I make dinner.

By the time my parents get home, there's a heap of pasta on the table, alongside garlic bread that I made in the toaster oven.

"I'm applying for jobs this week," I announce. "I need my bike back."

"Will anything even be open this week?" Mom asks, picking at her pasta.

Thanksgiving is coming, a holiday that most of Hawkins celebrates with massive amounts of food and zero cultural guilt. My family anti-celebrates. We don't go out. We don't visit family. We don't cheer for parades or sports teams. We eat as little as possible. It makes way more sense to me than the gluttonous alternative.

I might make fun of my parents sometimes, with their low-rise bell bottoms and their high ideals—that they've recently compromised in the name of keeping me safe. (From what? How am I safer on that bus or walking home on the side of the road?) But I know that they want the world to be better.

I don't ever want to be cynical enough to make fun of that.

"Stores are open," I say. "And people are hiring right now. They need more help for the holiday season. I intend to be right there with my résumé." Not that there's anything *on* my résumé.

I'm expecting a fight. Or at least a lengthy explanation of why I want to join the rat race instead of spending this time enriching myself. The thing is, I *do* want to enrich myself. I just need money to make it happen. They don't seem to accept that in the eighties, nothing's free. Not even becoming a better version of yourself.

"All right," Mom says, waving her fork in some kind of blessing.

I jump up from the table. "All right?"

I can see the French countryside now. And in the city, little movie theaters tucked onto side streets where they only show French films. Visions of baguettes and dark red wine dance through my head.

"At least you won't be alone in your room all the time," Mom says. They both worry about my antisocial tendencies. They don't seem to understand that the only time I feel truly all right and fully myself is when I'm alone. "But no bike. When you get a job, we'll work out some kind of schedule with the car."

My heart sinks all the way down and puddles in my feet. "You'll pick me up? Like you did from daycare?"

"Maybe you'll learn how to drive," Dad says.

"Sure," I scoff.

They've never even let me touch the wheel. Dad is always worried that I'll breathe on the car wrong and it'll break. We don't have money for anything to replace our crappy old Dodge Dart.

Maybe my parents do understand how much everything costs.

Maybe I'm the one who's just starting to get it.

HIGH SCHOOL

CHAPTER TWENTY-FIVE

NOVEMBER 22, 1983

I walk up to Melvald's General Store the next day wearing my most adult-looking outfit: black jeans (they should probably be slacks, but I don't own any) and a button-down. My home perm pegs me as a high schooler, because an actual adult would have it done at the salon. So I pulled my hair up into a chignon, but that backfired. It just looks a frizzy pom-pom attached to my head instead of the smooth French style I was going for.

As I push my back against the glass door and enter the store, I look down at the résumé in my hands. I printed ten copies on the nicest off-white paper that I could find in the school computer lab without anyone noticing what I was up to.

The truth is that most places in town don't ask for a résumé unless it's for a real job with a salary and benefits. Most people my age just walk in and ask if a store is hiring, and then sit through a mostly perfunctory interview process. A lot of it is based on whoever shows up first and whether they fit the preconceived notions of the person doing the hiring. (Kate once told me that her cousin got a job as a waitress at Hawkins Diner just by unbuttoning a single button of her shirt and putting on her best *I aim to please* smile. Which is exactly why Hawkins Diner is *not* on my list of possible employers.) I thought I would put myself ahead of the proverbial pack by writing down all the reasons someone should hire me.

I think that might have backfired, too.

My résumé is disturbingly blank.

The aisles are lined with metal shelving and stocked with a random assortment of whatever Mr. Melvald thinks that people need (a lot of canned goods and paper products, from what I can see). The store dead-ends in the pharmacy at the back, where they probably make most of their money. Pharmacists make a good hourly rate, but they need to be high school graduates with training. As far as I can tell, the people who work in the front mostly have to just show up, stock things, and not piss anybody off.

Standing at the checkout, looking an interesting combination of bored and anxious, is Mrs. Byers. Jonathan's mom.

Will's mom.

She's wearing the blue overshirt and red nametag that

constitutes a uniform. To someone who's been sweating inside a woolen marching band uniform at least twice a week for months, it looks blissfully casual. At this point, anything without a foot-tall hat that ends in a feathery plume would be an improvement.

Mrs. Byers is standing with both forearms on the counter, staring out into nothing. My dad calls that "being at loose ends." But the ends that are loose in her life are not the same ones everyone else is used to: the little frustrations, worries, annoyances.

Her son disappeared. Then he was declared dead. Then he came back. All in the space of a week. I can't imagine what any of that would feel like. (Honestly, I can't even imagine having a kid for all of that to happen to in the first place. Small people confuse me.) But I know what it's like being treated like you're the strangest person in the room—like strangeness clings to you.

I walk up to the counter. Something about knowing that Mrs. Byers is a bit like me sets me at ease. And when I'm at ease, I'm sort of a different person. I don't have the same automatic defense mechanisms.

"Hi, Mrs. Byers."

She jerks back to reality in a halting sort of way. Mrs. Byers doesn't put on a fake customer service smile, but there's a ghost of a real one under her otherwise nervous stare. "Oh. Sorry, I didn't see you there. Hi . . . ?" There's a question mark in her expression, to go with the upward tilt of her voice.

"Robin. Robin Buckley."

"Right. How can I help you, Robin?" she asks, coming around the counter. "Do you need help finding something?" Now that's she's standing right in front of me, I can see how tiny her stature truly is. I'm only fifteen and a half and I pretty much tower over her. I think she and Kate might tie for Petite Person of the Year, but Kate could still add a few inches as an upperclassman. (I get mad at myself for thinking about Kate like she's still someone in my limited friend repertoire. I can't take her off my list of people who suck, unfortunately, after she pushed me too hard to date Milton and treated me horribly when I wouldn't capitulate. I hope that she finds the note I left in her locker, though. I hope she realizes that, even if she's hung up on having a high school boyfriend, she's better off without Dash.)

Mrs. Byers is looking at me with something sad and exhausted in her eyes. Yet she doesn't look away. It takes me a second to realize that she's waiting for some kind of unavoidable comment or question about Will.

Even just, *I'm so glad he's back.*

I am—of course I am—but she doesn't need to hear that from the hundredth stranger of the day.

"I go to school with Jonathan," I say.

"Oh, really?" she asks in a husky, half-distracted voice "That's nice. I mean, I guess that makes sense. All of the teenagers in this town have to go to school somewhere, right?" I nod. And then we stand there awkwardly, two weirdos completely unsure of what to say next. Maybe bringing up her older son wasn't the best move, either.

The truth is that I don't have much else to go on. I flash on that night at Hawkins Diner with Milton. It's the only other time I can remember seeing Mrs. Byers, except in the milieu of Melvald's itself. The truth is that so many people are part of your everyday life in a small town, and you can see them hundreds of times without properly noticing them—until something shifts. I didn't notice Mrs. Byers until that night, and I wonder if I would remember it now if Will had stayed safely at home.

Would I notice Steve Harrington if *other* people didn't notice him so much?

Would I have befriended Dash and Kate and even Milton if they weren't my assigned squadmates?

And then there's the fact that I barely paid attention to Tam until this year.

My brain keeps circling back to her, like she's someone I'm supposed to know better. Like her red hair and her sudden smiles and her shameless singing are things I need on some deep level.

Mrs. Byers is staring at me with her big, dark eyes. "Do you just want to browse around? Or . . . ?" Another question mark, a little bit smaller this time. Does her face do any other punctuation?

I've been circling around the point, letting myself get distracted. The truth is, I'm afraid that this won't work, and I'll be left sitting here thinking about Steve and Tam forever. Now that Odd Squad is more or less out of my life, I've found that Tam takes up more and more of my thoughts.

I need to stay focused right now, though. "I'm here to apply for a job. I saw the hiring sign outside."

"Oh!" She looks surprised, like she didn't see the sign outside. She probably hasn't noticed a lot of the normal, everyday things around her lately—why would she, with everything that happened to Will? Suddenly I feel bad to be bothering her with something like this. But she's blinking up at me with her warm, awkward eyes and I know that I've come too far to turn back. "Well, Mr. Melvald makes all of the final hiring decisions, but I can take a look at . . . is that your résumé?"

"Yeah." I hand one over. "Thank you, Mrs. Byers."

She waves off the formality. "Oh, call me Joyce."

I blink at her. "Okay. Thanks." But I can't quite say *Joyce.*

Until I was five or six, I called my parents by their names (Richard and Melissa). But then I got to school and everybody called their parents Mom and Dad. Or Mommy and Daddy. It was one of the first times I was aware of being different from all the other kids. It was one of the first times I changed something to stop being quite so different.

"It says here that you're fluent in four languages," Mrs. Byers says in her scraped-up voice. It feels like I can hear everything she's been through, layer upon layer of hard things, pressing her down. "That's . . . not something you see a lot of around here."

"I aim to be memorable," I say, which is as close as I'll ever get to *I aim to please.*

"And you've worked as a . . . French horn player?" she asks, with a quick, quizzical glance up at me.

I got paid once to play in a wedding band: twenty dollars to stand all night in a knee-length black skirt, blaring formal wedding music and sneaking cold pop and extra pieces of wedding cake between sets.

"That's right."

"Huh. Okay. What kind of experience did it give you?" she asks with a shrug, inventing an interview question on the spot.

"The experience of thinking that I shouldn't play French horn for a living."

Mrs. Byers's eyebrows go on a journey—at first, they scrunch like she's going to laugh, then they dip down low with concern. "You might be too smart to work here, Robin. It's . . . fine. It's a job. But it's not going to change your life, you know? It's definitely not going to challenge you."

Mrs. Byers looks around at the store like she's not quite sure how she ended up here, spending so much of her life re-stocking paper products. She looks out the window at the rest of Hawkins. Is she imagining some kind of freedom beyond this place? Is Hawkins her own personal prison, too?

"I don't need a challenge," I blurt, because Mrs. Byers seems like the rare kind of adult you can be honest with. "I need a paycheck."

She nods, like she fully understands that motivation.

"Do you ever think about leaving?" I ask, on an unstop-pable wave of curiosity.

"The store?" she asks. "It's fine, really—"

"The town," I say. "Hawkins."

"People have been talking to me about fresh starts, but . . ." Her voice trails off, and I feel bad that I made her go to that place. I wasn't even thinking about Will. I was thinking about *her.* I could picture this tiny, formidable woman doing so many things besides working in this beige store in this tiny town. Wearing that comfortable but ultimately forgettable blue shirt day in and day out.

"Who is this?" Mr. Melvald asks, barging in from the back room.

"Robin Buckley. Sir." I tack that last bit on, not sure if it's making me sound formal and respectful or about five years old.

"I think we should hire her—" Mrs. Byers starts.

She barely gets through the sentence before Melvald flattens my hopes. "No high schoolers."

"What?" I ask reflexively. "Why?"

He puts up three fingers and then ticks them off in quick succession. "Don't like 'em. Don't trust 'em. Don't hire 'em."

"Is that your personal mantra?" I mutter.

Joyce is watching us now with wide eyes and a grimace. "I think that Robin could help out with the holiday shoppers—"

"Here's the thing," I say to Mr. Melvald. "I agree with you."

They both turn to me, mystified.

Mr. Melvald is clearly waiting for me to expand. "I don't particularly like or trust the people I go to school with. But you know who *they* don't trust? Adults. And not everybody in this town with general needs is over the age of forty. If you had a teenager working here, it could be good for business."

I'm just using a logic-based approach, but Mr. Melvald stares at me like I've spat on his tie. "Did you just try to strong-arm me into hiring a young hooligan so I can attract other young hooligans into my store where they can no doubt steal things, loiter, and make a general nuisance of themselves?"

"I . . ."

"Out," Mr. Melvald says, pointing toward the door.

As I leave in utter defeat, Mrs. Byers runs out after me, making the bells do their nervous little jig.

"Robin! Why don't you try the Radio Shack?" she asks. "I hear they're hiring."

Radio Shack is right next door, and I could go there now, but I really have to go home and make dinner and glare at the huge backlog of homework I've been ignoring. At least I have a lead for tomorrow, though. I feel my hopes perk up significantly.

"You're the best, Joyce."

Her eyebrows fly straight up.

Exclamation point.

HIGH SCHOOL

CHAPTER TWENTY-SIX

NOVEMBER 23, 1983

Tomorrow is Thanksgiving. Everything will be closed. Friday is the last big game of the season, and I'll be marching, marching, marching (and trying to avoid any real interaction with the three people in my squad). After that comes a big shopping weekend. Most stores will be too flooded with customers to focus on hiring. If I want to find a job before the holiday rush, it needs to happen now. And if I miss this window, there's no way I'll save up enough money for Operation Croissant by next summer. I've done the math ten different ways and it just doesn't add up.

I take a deep breath and walk into Radio Shack.

And I almost walk right back out.

It's a strange place, filled with pasty-faced men perusing electronics. Their hands caress packages like they might hold some kind of secret life-giving property. The air holds a strong whiff of metal and plastic. It's very eau de robot. Is this what the future smells like? I'm not sure I'm on board.

The person at the counter is wearing a gray T-shirt adorned with a maroon nametag. Is this what my future looks like? Color-coordinated shirts and nametags? They don't have things like this in Italy and France. Customer service isn't even a *concept* there. I'm looking forward to being snubbed by shop workers up and down the continent.

I squint to read his nametag.

Bob Newby.

"Hello, Bob," I say, cutting straight to the part where I use his first name like another grown-up would. Maybe that will help me get the job. Maybe, considering how tall and uncomfortably hair-styled I am, he won't even notice I'm a teenager at all.

"Hello there!" Bob says. This man has more than the usual amount of cheerfulness. He's short, portly, and practically glowing just from the daily joy of working at Radio Shack. It doesn't look like he's pasted the smile on for corporate reasons, though. His buoyant manner seems genuine.

"Can I talk to the manager or the owner?" I ask, looking around for someone with an air of obnoxious and probably unearned authority. I don't actually want to deal with management, but I'm not making the same mistake this time—getting off to what seems like a promising start only to get dramatically shut down by the person in charge.

"You definitely can," he says, leaning over the counter conspiratorially, "because you already are!"

My eyes widen with suspicious wonder. How can a person like this—so unspoiled by the shittiness of the world—actually exist? I can't tell if he would become my absolute favorite or if he would wear my patience down to nothing in a single shift.

"I'm looking for a job," I announce. "I heard from Joyce over at Melvald's—"

"Joyce?" Bob tugs nervously at the collar of his polo. "Mentioned *me*? Oh, that's . . . that's nice."

Okay. Not going to touch that.

"Actually, she just said the store needs some extra help. I'd love to work . . . here." I have to muscle out the last word.

"What makes you the next great Shacker?" Bob asks. Then he hastens to add, "That's not an official name for our employees, just a fun little thing I came up with."

"I know all about CoCo2, Radio Shack's new color computer," I lie through my teeth. I've literally just said everything I know about CoCo2 in one sentence.

"Oh, we love CoCo around here," Bob confirms, pointing to a corner of the store (which seems to consist mostly of nooks and corners in a way that defies normal Euclidean geometry), and a display devoted entirely to the CoCo computer line. "But we're so much more than that. Any kind of radio or electronic need? We can fill it. Morning, noon, or night? Well, we're only open until six, but you get the spirit of the thing."

"Got it. After this Friday, I can work absolutely any day. Any shift." I wince in anticipation of the next bit. "Well, I have to go to school, but any shift after that."

"Whoa! I love the go-get-'em attitude, but not so fast. What components do you need to build a simple crystal radio?" he fires off, suddenly serious and intent.

"A . . . um . . . crystal? And a radio."

"What brand walkie-talkie would you recommend to an enthusiastic amateur versus a parent looking for a kiddo's birthday gift?"

"The nicer one?"

"If a customer asks you for help and you're already with another customer on the phone, do you hang up and call back, ask the customer in the store to wait, or ask another employee for backup?"

"Can I go with D, all of the above?" I try, already knowing that I've tanked the pop quiz portion of my interview. At this point I'm dangling from a thin thread of hope. If I can make Bob laugh, maybe he'll want to keep me around.

"Hmmm." A frown, which looks entirely new to his features, settles in. "I'm afraid you don't have the right base knowledge to work here. But if you want to study up on transistors and come back in the future, I'll be here."

I don't have time for that. It's way too late to add Electronics to the list of languages I need to learn right now.

"Listen here . . . what was your name again?" Bob asks.

I perk up, thinking he might be about to change his mind. "Robin. I'm Robin."

"You'll find your place, Robin." Oh. We've reached the platitudes portion of the proceedings. I start to walk away, thinking he's done, but then he launches back into it, and I loop back around to the counter. "You'll find your place and the people who need you the most, and when you do, you'll just know. It'll fill this great big hole inside of you, this gaping spot that maybe you didn't know about until all of a sudden, it's gone. Just like that." He snaps dramatically. At this point, it feels like music should be swelling in the background. "And you're more than gainfully employed. You're . . . well, you're more or less home."

I can't imagine the place I work as a teenager being anything other than a pit stop on the road to somewhere better. And Bob Newby's motivational speeches aren't exactly the stuff of legend. Maybe I dodged a bullet with this one.

"Um. Thanks?"

I push my way back out into the late-November afternoon. The gray sidewalk is the same color as the sky. Dead leaves scud around in the wind, over the street, and into the gutters, where they stir restlessly. I watch my shoes—black patent leather, not something I would normally wear—beat a path down the side of Main Street.

My parents are planning on picking me up at the far end, down by the Hawkins Diner, in half an hour. Stores are starting to close for the night, their holiday lights adorning otherwise lifeless windows. There are handwritten signs about being closed for Thanksgiving on some doors, while others just take it for granted and flip to the looping red script of Closed signs.

I'm running out of time and running into bad weather. Flurries are coming down thick and white. "I'm not ready for this," I murmur. "So just stop it, okay?" But the sky spits on me like it's been waiting for this opportunity all year. I didn't have a coat to match my Very Adult interview outfit, just the same puffy one that I've had since eighth grade. I thought it would ruin the effect so I insisted I was warm enough without one. Now I'm shivering, and the last few résumés in my hand are getting wet from the snow and the ink is running down the pages like Tam's mascara ran down her face as she cried over Steve Harrington.

I fixed that, though.

I can fix this, too.

Across the street, the yellowish marquee bulbs of the movie theater draw me in, like a fly to honey. I wait for a car to pass—and slosh icy water onto my painstakingly chosen clothes—before crossing the street. The marquee itself gives me some relief from the snow, but inside it looks much warmer, with the red velvet benches and steaming popcorn machine.

I storm inside and stamp off snow.

"You're between shows," the twentyish girl at the ticket counter calls to me. "Want to buy a ticket for the next one?

We've got *A Christmas Story,* and *Terms of Endearment* for the late show."

I look around, feeling desperate and hopeful all at once.

"Are you hiring?" I ask on a whim.

"Are you kidding? We're always hiring. One of the concession workers just told off a customer for asking for a layer of butter between every scoop of popcorn. You can have his job. If you're any good and you stick around for more than a month, you can work your way up to cleaning the floors and ripping the ends off ticket stubs."

"Sounds glamorous," I deadpan.

"That's Hollywood for you," she deadpans right back. "You want to get started?"

"Right now?" I ask, the vague promise of a paycheck finally starting to solidify into dollars and cents.

She shrugs. "Like I said, we're playing two more shows tonight. *Terms of Endearment* is a big draw for bored moms. *A Christmas Story* brings in folks who are home for the holidays but can't stand looking directly at their family members' faces. For each show, I'm making popcorn *and* filling enormous cups with pop *and* dealing with little kids who can't decide if they want Milk Duds or Jujubes *and* taking tickets, which means a lot of pileups."

"Do you have a phone?" I ask.

"Sure thing," she says, pointing to the other end of the lobby.

I walk the parquet floor, passing posters for *The Outsiders,*

The Big Chill, Flashdance, Trading Places, Return of the Jedi, and *The Dead Zone.*

I get a slight thrill at the idea of absorbing so many movies by osmosis, just by being here every day. The single theater in Hawkins, with its reliance on big studio releases, might not play the movies that I love best—classics and foreign films and art-house cinema that we have to wait an extra year to get on video in Hawkins after the movies are released in tiny fly-speck theaters in major cities—but filmmaking draws me in, no matter what. It's a sort of language, and I love languages. This one is made up of visual symbols and subtle looks, framing choices and music cues, sharp dialogue and deep subtext. It's an orchestration of meaning and emotion. A way to say something that the world needs to hear. And even though I'm building up excitement to travel in person, this gives me a way to constantly leave Hawkins for the rest of this year without having to set a foot over the town line.

Slotting a quarter in the pay phone, I pick up the receiver on its squishy metal wire and call home. When Dad picks up, I find myself breathlessly telling him that I found a job and I can start right away. "Can you pick me up after the late show?"

I hear him sigh.

"I know it's late, but—"

"I'm proud of you, Robin," he says out of nowhere.

"Because I'm joining the rat race?" I say with a heavy dose of sarcasm.

"Because you're getting out there."

"Oh," I say, still startled by his reaction. "Yeah. It feels good."

But I can't help wondering what he'll say when *getting out there* also means *leaving on a jet plane.*

When I hang up, I turn around and find the girl from the ticket counter waiting for me, a bright-red polo gripped in one hand. With a start, I realize that she's twentyish and already in charge of hiring (and probably firing) people. Maybe I really *can* work my way up if I stick around. "My name is Keri with a *K* at the beginning, one *R* in the middle, and an *I* at the end, but I put *Carry* on my nametag because it confuses people. What do you want on yours?"

HIGH SCHOOL

CHAPTER TWENTY-SEVEN

NOVEMBER 25, 1983

By Friday, I've already worked two shifts with Keri at the movie theater and taken home a whopping forty dollars. (I make four dollars an hour, which is over minimum wage, but the need to repay my two polos and a Milky Way that I ate instead of Thanksgiving dinner chomped through my first paycheck like Pac-Man on his very urgent way to a ghost.) But even with a little bit of money put away, the idea of leaving Hawkins is becoming real.

Which makes it easier to get through one last day of marching between rounds of high school boys ritualistically knocking into each other.

I'm standing on the sidelines, wearing a uniform that has

by this point gathered an entire season's worth of sweat in the creases. Some people have theirs dry-cleaned every week, but I'm not spending a single penny of my newly garnered wages on this abomination of tassels and buttons. Did I mention the feathery hat? It's called a shako, and it makes me look like one of those horses that pull a fancy carriage. Honestly, those horses probably have more dignity. I can't wait to get out of here, away from all of this.

Though there *is* one moment today that I'm looking forward to.

We're debuting a new song (we always do a special number just for the final game of the season), and despite my best attempts at not caring about any of this, I jitter with excitement as I run over the fingering one more time.

It's a great distraction from the ever-present Odd Squad.

"Hey, Robin," Kate says for maybe the fortieth time today.

"Sorry," I say. "I'm going over something."

Kate sighs. She knows I don't want to talk to her. As far as I can tell from their flirting levels, she's still dating Dash.

"Robin?" Kate tugs at my elbow.

"Wow. Look that play," I say vacantly, pointing at the football game.

I have no idea what play they just ran. But the crowd is cheering and Steve Harrington is out on the field acting like a gleeful ass, so something must have gone well.

He seems to be really enjoying his moment. He snaps up to standing, throws the ball, does some kind of ill-advised dance. He's giving himself over to football as if his life, or at least his popularity, depends on it.

I watch the crowd love him, wildly, collectively. I can't help hating them for it. I close my eyes, mutter French verbs, and dream about a beautiful day when I'm in a place where school sports don't take on the combined fervor of battle and religion.

"Go, Hawkins!" most of the band shouts, pumping their instruments into the air.

"Whatever," Wendy DeWan mutters. "I can't believe they're even having the game this year."

"I know," Milton says.

It's a pretty common opinion among the band, and one I happen to agree with. In light of how weird this fall was, shouldn't we cancel this bacchanal and spend our time at home, glad that the little kid who recently disappeared is back? Grateful that whatever dark abyss we were all teetering on seems to have receded into the distance?

Shouldn't that be enough?

But people want to celebrate the return of normal to Hawkins. They want to throw it a parade and sprinkle it liberally with confetti. And what says "celebrate American normalcy" better than a mediocre sports team, a halfway decent marching band, and a few cheerleaders high on pep like it's the new drug of choice? What better mascot for "normal" can they find than Steve Harrington, his smile absurdly wide and his mane roughed up by the late autumn wind?

Here's the thing. I don't want to go back to normal.

Not that I want anything *bad* to happen—and definitely not to kids like Will Byers. But there's absolutely no version of Hawkins that I want to revert to. Normal was killing me, and everybody here wants to shake its hand.

I wish I could tell Milton any or all of these thoughts. Normally I would just lean over and start spewing sarcasm like a broken spigot. I would tell him about my job, too, and all the money I'm going to hoard for Operation Croissant. All the museums it will pay for to wash the taste of this travesty of a cultural experience out of our mouths. But Milton and I haven't talked in a week. It feels like the silence at the end of a record. It feels like static where my favorite broadcast used to be.

It feels like crap. And I'm getting tired of it.

But Milton's standing next to Wendy, and they actually seem to be hitting it off. She magically looks good even in her marching band uniform—even the universally unflattering shako. Milton is making her laugh. He laughs, too, his low, not-at-all-awful laugh, and I remember why we're suffering this stupid socially mandated distance. Milton is falling for Wendy. No matter how cynical I feel sometimes, I can't seem to begrudge him that.

I want Milton to be happy. Not just suffering through an adolescence in Hawkins with me.

Really, actually happy.

A whistle blows and teams head off the field—ours at a

dejected jog. No matter how well that one play went, we're losing. We're always losing.

It's the marching band's job to get the crowd excited again. A Sisyphean effort, if you ask me. Any amount of excitement we gain will be immediately lost the next time our team fumbles a touchdown or misses a field goal.

But we march out there anyway, the frigid afternoon knifing us over and over. I can feel it through my woolen outfit. The Odd Squad takes its place at the far left corner of the field for our first march. I can't remember what it's officially called (everyone in band just calls it "Sousa's a Loser"), but if Milton asked, I would bet ten of the dollars I just made that it has "America" in the title somewhere. It's jangly and jingoistic and awful.

The crowd loves it.

We play two and a half more songs like that, tracing all sorts of complex formations over the field. This whole elaborate process, which for years has made little to no sense in my brain, suddenly reminds me of the Nazca Lines in Peru. They created enormous shapes in the fields that could only be understood from the sky above. They can even be seen from space. How do I spell *HELP* in a way that any friendly aliens watching us would understand?

My legs go numb. My mellophone and I are on autopilot. The truth is that a lot of pieces have extended rests for my instrument, so for a lot of this show I'm doing my best knees-up and nothing else.

The Odd Squad sails through a formation where we make an X across the field, nearly brushing shoulders with the Sexophone Squad. (Not their actual name, of course, because Miss Genovese vetoes it every year, but it's what they call themselves anyway. For official purposes, they're known simply as *S* squad.)

Despite myself, I start to get excited.

In a few seconds, we're about to debut our new song.

Halfway through the last scheduled march, we break out of the expected formation and leave behind the Sousa. Instead of an old, pompous song, "Total Eclipse of the Heart" blares from our instruments, pouring forth from our half-frozen fingers and my mostly thawed heart. I still can't believe we're actually doing this.

It was my idea.

Half of the band creates a heart shape, while the other becomes a crescent moon, sweeping across the field and pushing the heart to the side. It works perfectly, just the way we practiced it.

People in the crowd are on their feet to get a better view. I can even see Milton's mom hoisting the family's beloved and brand-new Sony Betamovie BMC-100 onto her shoulder. It's big, chunky, and gray, and it's capturing every second of this to be remembered for the rest of time. (Or at least for as long as people use Betamax.) Milton's mom and little sister wave at the Odd Squad, like we're all still friends.

Bonded and unbreakable. An atom, like Kate always called us. It takes a lot to break an atom—it takes high-speed and high-energy particle smashing. And that's exactly what happened to us. Sophomore year (not to mention Dash's stupid, selfish face trying to kiss mine out of nowhere) smashed us apart.

"Do you hear that?" Kate shouts during one of the rare rests for the trumpets. "They love it!"

"That's because they always love it," Dash snarks at her.

Kate's smile droops, but it doesn't quite disappear. She goes back to playing as the final chorus swells.

The rest of the band is loving it nearly as much as the crowd. Earth, Woodwind, and Fire Squad is marching with a sort of energy that I haven't seen since early in the season. As we march into a new formation, I catch a glimpse of Sheena Rollins with her perfect white sneakers and white ribbons down her sectioned ponytail. She's actually *smiling*—as much as you can smile and play an oboe at the same time.

Even Miss Genovese looks happy, which is nearly unheard of.

It's tradition for the Hawkins High School band to put our raggedy, tired traditional marches aside for the last game of the season and play something new. When Miss Genovese asked for a "fresh number" to round out our repertoire and bring the house down at the final game of the season, there was only one song stuck in my head, because Tam had been singing it that morning. Because Tam was always singing it.

" 'Total Eclipse of the Heart'?" I said.

Milton shot me a look (the first in a while), and I remembered telling him that the song was Tam's favorite.

But what did that matter? Was he worried that I was becoming best friends with Tam now that I wasn't allowed to spend my afternoons parked in front of his Yamaha/MTV setup, arguing the merits of Kajagoogoo (none, in my opinion)?

I didn't pick this song because Tam has in any way replaced Milton. I just said "Total Eclipse of the Heart" out loud because I couldn't stop thinking about it. Couldn't stop thinking about her. Playing this song every day has been a way to funnel all of those stupid non-friendship feelings somewhere.

A microscopic part of me wonders if Tam's up there in the bleachers. If she's watching. If she's excited that we're playing her favorite song. Did she take this opportunity to buy a chalky hot chocolate and cheese fries from the concession booth that the Booster Club sets up? Is she impatiently waiting for the moment when Steve Harrington bursts back on the field? Did the familiar notes catch her off guard? Did she lose a little bit of her balance?

And even if she's looking at us and seeing what I hope she sees—that we're playing this song, just a little bit, because of her—would she even recognize me under this abomination of a hat? I wave the plume out of my face, but it just keeps drooping.

And then, with one final crescendo, we're done.

The crowd loses its collective mind.

Everybody is up on their feet, and I'll admit that it feels good. Not least because we upstaged the football team that we're supposed to exist solely to support.

I empty my spit valve for the last time this season, tuck it into the case, and sling the mellophone onto my back. Not that I have anywhere to go just yet. We've been released into the wilds to watch the rest of the game. Normally, I wouldn't stay—I'd bike straight home (back in the golden age of wheels and freedom), or I'd go back to Milton's and watch the Betamax footage and help set the table for dinner. Neither of those are an option anymore. So I head for the concession booth, hoping they have something I can buy that takes the smallest possible chunk out of my Europe money. I stand at the end of an abominably long line. Out of the corner of my eye, Tam's red hair is like a beacon. I turn to it, without thinking.

"That was amazing!" she's saying to Jennifer. "Didn't you love it?"

Jennifer shrugs, noncommittal to the last.

They're both gathering their orders. Craig Whitestone appears out of nowhere and puts on a horrible act of gallantry, insisting on carrying their nachos. "You liked the little show we just put on?" he asks.

"That last song," Tam says. "It's the best. Whose idea was it to play 'Total Eclipse of the Heart'?"

"Ladies, look no further," Craig drawls. "It was my idea."

Kate pushes forward from her place in the middle of the line. Even if I'm not talking to her, she's not one to let any untruth go unchallenged. "Actually, it was Robin's idea."

"Really?" Tam looks all the way to the back of the line,

like she knew exactly where I was the whole time. She gives me a skewed smile. "I didn't pin you as the Bonnie Tyler type."

(Tam pinned me? This is news.)

"I'm not," I admit. "But that song just keeps getting stuck in my head." I leave out the part where it's entirely because of her. I also leave the line, approaching the spot where Tam stands with her nachos, which she's taken back from Craig. Jennifer draws back like I have some kind of undiagnosable disease.

The game starts up again.

Steve Harrington is busy getting trounced on the football field.

I'm right here. With her.

I swipe my face one more time, to be absolutely sure there's no band-inspired spit left on it. (Dry. Thank goodness.) "Have you seen the 'Total Eclipse' music video?" I ask, thinking of the dozen times it popped up while Milton and I were watching MTV. "With her in that gauzy white dress and the guys with glowing eyes and all of the weird gymnastics?"

Tam laughs. "How embarrassing is it if I tell you I taped it? And that I watch it all the time?"

Jennifer moves her weight from one leg to the other and tugs the end of her cardigan, which is foolishly tied around her neck. Has Jennifer not gotten the message that it's nearly December? Or is slinging a sweater around your shoulders such a great status symbol that it's worth the frostbite?

"In case you haven't heard, I'm the Weirdest Girl in

Hawkins," I say. "So that really shouldn't embarrass you. Not around me."

Where did that come from?

Why did I admit how weird I am, boldly and yet in the softest voice, *right in front of Tam*?

It doesn't seem to put her off, though, because she's laughing again. And not in a mean way. "I'm always singing when I get into Click's class because when I get out of my car, whatever was in the tape deck is fresh in my head. It's like I can't stop the music from coming out or it'll just . . . dry up inside me. You *must* have heard me sing Bonnie Tyler before class."

I feel like she's calling out something that happens every day, but I don't know why. Is she trying to say that she notices how aware I am of her singing? Do I admit it? What happens if I tell the truth? What happens if I lie?

"You've got a great voice," I squeeze out.

(I chose D, all of the above.)

"Well, it's not great enough to turn *Our Town* into a musical," she says, pretending to pout.

Wow. Okay. We have in-jokes, too.

"Only Bonnie Tyler herself would be powerful enough to do that."

Tam shakes her head. "I still can't believe you played my song." She blinks at me a few times, disbelieving. Her eyes are a bright brown. Her lips are muted purple, a softer and prettier color than the fuchsia that everybody in band is obsessed with, and right when I realize I shouldn't be staring at her mouth for more than a second to clock the lipstick shade (because: that's weird) she starts to hum. The notes burst into lyrics and Tam is singing her favorite song. For me. In public. She's *total eclipsing* me right in front of the snack bar.

And then it's over, and Jennifer is dragging Tam away to the bleachers and talking about how unfortunate my hair looks because it's been under the shako all day. Tam doesn't laugh. She doesn't pile on.

She just looks back at me and shrugs.

Like she's not sure what to do with all of this *normal,* either.

CHAPTER TWENTY-EIGHT

DECEMBER 22, 1983

Nearly a month later, I'm in Miss Click's classroom waiting for a test on the Industrial Revolution to hit my desk, but my mind is wandering along the French Riviera.

And I'm imagining Tam at my side.

Mr. Hauser has asked me, more than once, if I have a travel companion in mind for Operation Croissant. I go to his classroom nearly every day now, either during lunch or free period. I mostly read while he grades tests, but sometimes we talk. Eventually, our conversations end up where my mind always goes these days. In Europe.

Or with Tam.

Or both.

My original plan was to wait for Milton, but the longer he goes without even remotely talking to me (or asking out Wendy DeWan), the more I wonder if I should give up and move along. And the closer we get to the new year, the more I want to have this figured out. It's not exactly something you can spring on someone in May and expect them to leave Hawkins with you in June. This kind of planning takes time and a certain amount of emotional precision. But Kate and Dash made a mess of everything, and weeks later I'm still scrambling to clean it up.

Maybe this is good news in disguise, though. I never would have thought of Tam as my first choice, but with the entire Odd Squad out of the running, she's suddenly at the top of my list.

And ever since Tam opened her purple lips and sang right in front of me like we were the only two people who mattered, I've been wondering if maybe she's like me. A weirdo who's been lying low—with the occasional episode of bursting into song—just waiting for the opportunity to escape.

What if I can give her that?

I've saved up over five hundred dollars since I started working at the Hawkins Theater. I'm going to pick up double shifts over the holidays. By the time school starts up in January, I should be tantalizingly close to the amount I need for my plane ticket. Then I can start saving for a second one.

The Industrial Revolution quiz is handed back by the girl in front of me, and I fill it out so quickly that I'm left with too much free time. My eyes wander over to Tam. She's wearing a white miniskirt and a yellow sweater and it's easy enough to imagine her in that same outfit, settling into a long flight with me. Walking through the Bargello. Singing in every piazza we pass through. (Maybe not riding a bike through the Italian countryside, but I'm sure she can bring some pants with her, too.)

She keeps filling out her test, slow and careful. When she's done, she takes it up to Miss Click and sets it on the finished pile, and then turns back to the class, her eyes snagging on Steve Harrington.

He's squinting at his test paper like it's written in invisible ink.

It's laughable, really, to think that a girl as smart and ambitious and talented as she is would waste all of her glances on him. (Especially after she cried over him in the bathroom and vowed to be done with him forever.) But what if she only stares at him because she thinks she's *supposed* to? What if it's part of her cover, the way that being a perfect band nerd is part of mine?

I open the Operation Croissant composition notebook and turn to a blank page.

And—in French—I let myself dream.

I write everything I can imagine us doing together. I translate every wild hope, every silly dream.

When the bell rings, Steve Harrington is still struggling his way through the Industrial Revolution. And I feel so stupid about what I've just written that I tear it out of my notebook, the paper ripping raggedly away from the center. This doesn't belong with my plans for Operation Croissant. Tam would never go to Europe with me.

(The truth is, I would never ask her. I'd be too afraid she'd say no.)

(I'd also be slightly afraid she'd say yes.)

I crumple the paper and let it drop into the trash basket on my way out. Steve is still working on his test, and Tam and her friends are straggling, probably in the hopes that she can get him alone for a second.

Even though he's still dating Nancy Wheeler.

Wow, I hate myself for caring about any of this.

I stop outside the classroom for a drink from the short, sporadically functional water fountain. My face feels flushed with the kind of embarrassment that can only come from wanting to befriend a girl way above my social station.

This must be what Victorians felt like all the time.

I sip at the measly little stream of water and splash some on my face. When I straighten up, I can see Tam and her friends gathered right outside Miss Click's classroom. They're all bending around something. A piece of paper. I've seen them do this sort of collective note-reading ritual before. It takes me a second to realize that Jessica is clutching *my* discarded paper, now uncrumpled and whole.

She's clutching it to her chest like it's a defibrillator. Like it could restart her shriveled heart.

"Who do you think sent it?" she asks. "Did you see anyone

drop it near my desk?" Her desk is right by the wastebasket. Perfectly placed for a piece of paper that missed its target and bounced onto the floor.

I do a quick, vital scan of my memory. I didn't write Tam's name anywhere on the paper, did I?

No. Jessica thinks the note was for her. And her mom is from Montreal, so *Jessica can speak French*. Oh, merde.

"It's *très* romantic," she says in a voice that's 90 percent breath. "I wonder which boy in our class knows French."

Boy? What is she talking about?

Romantic? *What is she talking about?*

My brain slams into the implications of those words. I'm not a boy, and I wasn't writing about love. Those were just daydreams. Those were *my* daydreams, and Tam should never have seen them.

I study her face.

I pick apart her reaction.

She doesn't seem to be terribly interested in the note. She bounces on her feet. "Gotta get to my next class, okay?"

She leaves Jessica there to pore over the note.

My heart sinks as Tam leaves. Why did I want her to blush raspberry pink when she heard those words? Why did part of me hope she'd understand the note was for her, the way I wanted her to guess that "Total Eclipse of the Heart" being played by the marching band was inspired by her, too?

Her red hair swishes as she disappears down the hall.

Jessica reads the note again, this time out loud, translating for her friends as she goes.

I listen to it.

And I *hear* the words this time—not from my own perspective, but from the outside. I wrote about walking hand in hand with Tam down the Champs-Élysées, picking out books for each other at Shakespeare and Company, getting dinner together and sharing dessert (because one of us orders chocolate soufflé and the other gets tarte tatin, so *of course* we have to trade bites). She tucks her head on my shoulder as we stroll at dusk, because I'm taller and we're both tired. Then we tuck away in a rented garret, watching the city lights come on as we light up inside at the thought of doing it all again tomorrow. And finally, we fall into the garret's one tiny bed together, because, well, it's a garret, people, not the Ritz.

Still. Snuggling together into one tiny bed is, objectively, romantic.

Suddenly I'm glad that Tam left for her next class, because my face is burning with the fire of a thousand suppressed blushes.

Milton told me that I'm good at solving puzzles, but I somehow didn't see this puzzle for what it was until I dropped the missing piece and someone else picked it up.

And I might be good at languages, but I've been using the wrong one to try and decode how I feel about Tam. My world is filled with the assumption, everywhere I look, that girls like boys. That girls date boys. That gay people are just a rumor about what happens in towns that *aren't* Hawkins, a segment on the news. I had no context to assume that, when I looked at Tam, I was feeling anything other than friendship. It took Jessica and her handy Rosetta Stone of boy-girl crushes to make me see this for what it truly is.

I have a crush on Tam.

I think I've had a crush on her since she walked into Miss Click's class the first day of school.

HAWKINS
HIGH SCHOOL

CHAPTER TWENTY-NINE

DECEMBER 22, 1983

I get through the rest of the day—the last one before winter break—in an utter fog, and when I come out, I'm on the other side of the big, gay woods.

I like Tam.

I like *girls.*

Weirdly enough, the thing that still bothers me about this is that I couldn't see it sooner. I couldn't see it at all. I'm supposed to be smart, and yet I wasn't doing the most basic possible math. Robin + Tam + Staring + Feelings = Enormous Crush.

That wasn't so hard, was it?

But somehow, it was.

Of course, there's the whole "I had no context to understand my feelings for what they actually are" factor. But on further examination, there's something else at play. They really might revoke my nerd card over this one. All year, I've been so certain that I understand everybody around me, but I haven't been looking at my own feelings with any kind of real scrutiny. Doesn't knowing things presuppose that you know things about *yourself*? Or at some point, does hoarding information become an excuse? It's like writing your own emotional hall pass: if I can learn three new languages, I don't have to learn whatever's going on inside my own head.

Now, thanks to the Jessicas of the world and the fact that I couldn't stop myself from daydreaming about Tam—and then discarding those daydreams as hopeless—I'm stuck with this revelation.

It doesn't help that I'm also stuck on the bus, which smells like exhaust and wet gloves and rowdy freshmen. They're hopped up on holiday excitement—they're basically still kids waiting to see what Santa will bring, only they know Santa is their middle-class dad maxing out his credit card.

Meanwhile, the metalheads in the back of the bus are extracting their stashes of pot out of the brown-taped holes in the back of the seats. They probably need it to help them get through the break.

I can't really blame them.

All of a sudden, the idea of ten days without seeing Tam feels excruciating. At the same time, I'm not sure how I'll survive our next encounter. If the monster that is Hawkins

High was a concern *before,* I can only imagine how it would react to this: a girl with a crush on another girl who only has eyes for Steve Harrington.

When the bus stops—it feels like a minor crash every time—I get out with a group of freshmen who quickly disperse to their own houses. I can't handle being in that kind of confined space for another second. The bus driver doesn't seem to notice or care that I'm always getting out at other people's stops. As long as everyone's gone by the end of the line and nobody's dead, she's done her job.

December is a prickly sort of cold, but I don't mind. The shards of wind feel like the truth that keeps hitting me—bracing and necessary. I march along the side of the road, and where the sidewalk ends, I trudge into the narrow ditch.

A few seconds later, a car pulls up beside me. I can hear it slowing, slowing, stopping. The window cranks down.

I'm done with this interaction before it's even started. Whatever lackey the monster that is Hawkins High has sent to mess with me this time, I'm not playing nice.

I have my middle fingers cocked and ready—and I turn around to find that I'm flipping off the chief of police.

"Hello there, missy." I've only seen Chief Hopper around town, never up close like this. He's wearing his khaki-colored uniform with the gold badge affixed to one side of his chest, and it's layered with a blue jacket for the winter weather. He's a big guy with floppy brown hair parted down the middle and a patented Mr. Potato Head face. He's got the same mustache and everything. It's uncanny.

"You shouldn't be walking on the side of a busy street like this," he says. "And you definitely shouldn't be pointing *that* finger at people who are trying to help you. You need a ride home?"

"No," I say automatically.

"There something wrong?" he asks, looking up and down the otherwise deserted stretch of road.

"No," I say, this time more defiantly.

There's nothing wrong with me.

Not that most people in Hawkins would agree with that assessment.

I've heard people in this town talk about "the Gays." I've heard Kate's parents hold forth on the dangers of "even one homosexual lurking in a community." That's light dinner conversation in her house and they're not the only ones in our town who feel that way. Of course, they're talking about gay men. They act like gay women don't even exist. How could they? Women *need* men, right?

"You going to see a boy?" Hopper asks. "You walking to a boy's house?" He looks around as if my paramour might be waiting to pop out from behind a tree.

"A boy's house?" I can't help it. A slightly hysterical laugh rises up. I put my hand to my mouth, press my lips together.

The chief gives me a stern look. The kind that is probably supposed to summon surrogate dad feelings, but he's more of the awkward uncle type.

"Listen, you're a girl. A *teenage* girl. It's . . . There's a lot that I don't get. I know that. Okay? I know that more than you could ever possibly understand." Underneath his blundering, I'm starting to feel like he's talking about something important. But as far as I know, he doesn't have any kids. So. That's weird. "But if you're out here because some boy told you to visit him, it's almost dark and this place can be surprisingly dangerous. You should let me drive you right back home."

"I can say conclusively that I'm not out here because of a boy."

Hopper nods. But his car doesn't budge.

Besides the inherent awkwardness of climbing into a stranger's car, I don't want to accept the ride and have my parents be home early for once only to see me arrive with the police chief. It wouldn't exactly augment their current trust levels. They think I've been taking the bus this whole time, when in reality I've been walking at least halfway home most days.

"You must have something better to do than chauffeur a teenage girl who doesn't like the smell of the bus." Though his car, even from where I'm standing, doesn't smell much better. It's syrupy sweet and slightly crisped, like the ghost of a hundred toaster waffles. I like waffles as much as the next person, but this seems excessive. "I know Hawkins is boring, but . . ."

"This town? Boring?" He pulls down a pair of aviators. They would look cool on literally anyone else. "Sweetie, you have no *idea.*"

He drives off with an unnecessary spray of gravel.

And I'm abruptly left alone to face my winter break.

HAWKINS
HIGH SCHOOL

CHAPTER THIRTY

DECEMBER 26, 1983

My parents and I had a quiet Christmas. Our tree was small and scrawny, more of a potted plant than a full-size conifer. We always pick the one that looks like it needs the most love at the Christmas tree lot (aka the parking lot outside the pizza parlor strung with festive lights and covered in stray needles).

They gave me good, thick winter socks and a new cassette player.

I gave them new pajamas and the gift of not announcing how dry our turkey dinner was. I stayed focused on the side dishes.

And Tam.

I couldn't stop thinking about her. Where the sugarplums should have been dancing, visions of kissing girls with purple lipstick spun through my head.

Now we're on to another holiday.

All morning, the driveway fills with cars, including several VW bugs, which are fairly uncommon in new-car-obsessed Hawkins. The house floods with people wearing their best peasant skirts and knitted vests.

It's Hippie Christmas.

When I was little, this was my favorite day of the year. People would hoist me on their shoulders, break out worn-in guitars, and sing folk songs at odd intervals. My parents' best friends from back in the day, Miles and Janine, are now world travelers, and they would always bring me back little pieces of wherever they went. As I got older, I stuck to the fringes of the living room, watching the adults drink suspiciously strong-smelling eggnog and reminisce in louder and louder tones (with fewer and fewer inhibitions about what they were admitting) while I kept one eye on the pack of feral children they unleashed on small-town Indiana. Some of them traveled here from places like Maine and California and Arizona. My parents have the honor of hosting every year because we live more or less in the middle.

This year starts out the same as always, but after dinner, Miles and Janine call me over and give me a glass of eggnog. (Which tastes as strong as it smells. I think I could take off my nail polish with this stuff.) They start asking my opinion about things. And when I give them, everyone listens. Even my parents.

They're treating me more or less like an adult.

Miles and Janine ask me about the future, but not in the college-obsessed way the other adults here always do. Questions like: "Robin, what do you want to do when you're finally out of that prison they call school?" or "Robin, are you going to be as wild as your parents were?"

All I want to do is blurt out my plans for Operation Croissant.

I need to start telling people the truth. I can't keep it all inside of me anymore. I can feel everything I've been fighting to hold down: How weird I am. How much I want. How much of this town I *don't* want.

"I'm going to see the world," I say. "Like you."

Miles beams, his smile given brilliant backup by the Christmas lights. Janine nods deeply.

"It's good to see more," she says.

And it feels like she's not just talking about traveling. It feels like she's talking about everything.

I would love to give the details of my travel plans. I hate holding back so much. It's not actually in my nature, and I'm just starting to realize that. I want to spill the contents of my soul, but there are so many reasons to brick it up behind sarcasm and cynicism.

For instance, if I talk about Operation Croissant, my parents will be forced to go along with it, or they'll reveal their new suburban nature to their oldest friends. They would probably pretend to be groovy with it in front of their much groovier company, only to bring the parental foot down after everyone goes home.

I don't want to deal with those eventualities. Maybe this is the true curse of being smart: it's not about being a social outcast, it's about knowing all the ways your bravery might go wrong.

I stay quiet and I sip at my eggnog.

My mind slips back to Tam.

What is she doing right now? Did she have a good Christmas? Does her family have parties and traditions where she feels both absurdly loved and infinitely out of place?

Now that I'm looking, I can't help but notice that everyone here, even in the land of *free love,* is paired up, boy-girl, boy-girl.

But sometimes my parents tell stories about people they knew. Men who loved men. Women who loved women. People who loved people, not even remotely based on whether they were men or women or anything at all.

I could be Kate, stuck with parents who virulently disapprove of what they call "the homosexual lifestyle." I could be Dash, with a family who doesn't seem to give a crap about anything but having plenty of currency, social and otherwise. As far as being a lesbian in Hawkins, I basically won the filial lottery.

I'm not afraid that my parents will have a bad reaction when I find the right time to tell them. But what about literally everyone else? What about my town, with its normality obsession, where I've never heard a single person say the word *gay* out loud like it was anything but a curse? I need to talk to someone who knows what this feels like. And as much as I love Hippie Christmas, nobody at this party will suffice.

I take the rest of my eggnog to my room and sprawl out on my bed.

And as suddenly as I figure out the truth about how I feel, I realize exactly who's been waiting all year for me to figure it out.

HIGH SCHOOL

CHAPTER THIRTY-ONE

JANUARY 3, 1984

"Mr. Hauser!" I nearly shout from the doorway of his classroom.

I ran all the way here—I only took the bus halfway to school and then I couldn't handle people writing homophobic slurs on the steamed-up winter windows. Those things always bothered me, but right now they feel like individual knives being thrust into my eyeballs. So I got off when the door accordioned open, shouldering my way past a bunch of oncoming metalheads, ignoring the confused bark of the bus driver, and I jogged the rest of the way in sleet. My lank, halfway-grown-out perm is now a hundred individual icicles.

But I made it before the bus. I made it with ten minutes to spare before first bell, and every one of those minutes is worth the fact that I'm now doubled over, panting. I've been waiting to talk to Mr. Hauser for a week, working impatiently through all my shifts at the movie theater, inching my way forward until I'm finally back in this classroom.

"Mr. Hauser, I wanted to talk to you. . . ."

My voice dies a horrible death, curled up in my throat.

Mr. Hauser is emptying out his desk.

"What's going on?" I ask with a little too much hope spiking through my voice. "Did they change your classroom?" They don't usually do that midyear, but it's the only explanation that makes sense. The only one that could possibly turn out okay.

"Oh, Robin," Mr. Hauser says.

"Don't *Oh, Robin* me," I say. "That's what adults do when they think kids are in the dark about life, and I'm not. First of all, I'm not a kid. And second of all, anything that I was unaware of before today, well . . . I'm not anymore."

He looks twitchy about whether or not anyone is listening behind me in the hallway. I walk all the way in and close the door. These things aren't perfectly soundproof, but they are heavy. And there's only one tiny window inset in each one, with little squares etched over the glass.

"So you know that I'm gay," he says quietly.

"I know that *I'm* gay," I say without any sort of volume control. "And I reverse engineered that you probably are, too."

It was right there—in the fact that he connected to me on

some level that I couldn't quite see. In the way he offered his classroom as a safe place for the days when I couldn't stand being inundated by my peers. Even in the way Dash found him creepy.

For all of his Nerds Will Rule the World rhetoric, Dash isn't really talking about the uprising of the weird and the truly left out. He means guys like him, who intend to use their brains to win women and money and all of the other things they feel entitled to. They just want to invert the jock pyramid. If Dash knew I was gay, he would be the first one to laugh at me, to set the monster of this school snapping at my heels.

I can't believe I sat next to him in Mr. Hauser's class for half the year and talked to him like we were friends. I can't believe I listened to Kate talk about how great he is in a gooey-sweet voice without pointing out that he's actually, most of the time, not a nice person at all.

I can't believe I told him about Operation Croissant.

"Well, Robin," Mr. Hauser says. "You were right. About both of us. Maybe 1984 will be a better year for the gays of Hawkins."

My eyes go so wide I can feel them stretching their outer limits. The fact that we're talking about it, that we're standing in this horror show of a high school and actually saying these words out loud (even if it's just to each other) has to be a good sign, right?

But then he shakes his head so bitterly that I know I'm wrong.

He's only being this obvious, spelling it out for me in plain terms, because it doesn't matter anymore.

"Not that I'll be in Hawkins for much longer," he says. "I really wish we had more time."

"No," I say. "We're not doing this. I just got there. I *just* figured this out and . . . you can't leave."

"My hand is being forced, I'm afraid."

I stand between Mr. Hauser and the door, crossing my arms. I'm not letting him leave without giving me more. I'm not letting him leave, *period*. "You're the best teacher in this school. And by best, I mean the only functioning teacher."

He gives a laugh, but even that sounds bittersweet. Mr. Hauser comes around the desk, and I realize that he's not wearing his usual brown suit. He's in jeans and a white T-shirt. It illuminates every bit of how young he actually is. Mr. Hauser is an adult, yes, but he's closer to my age than my parents'.

He's been using the tweed as his own camouflage.

I know what that feels like now. The desperate blending. The hope that if you keep yourself in line, nobody will notice that you're out of the ordinary. I've been doing it ever since I hit high school, without fully knowing why.

"What is going on, Mr. Hauser?" I ask.

"You might as well call me Tom," he says.

"Um. No. Thanks to your class, I know enough about foreshadowing to be aware that calling you Tom means things are about to change in a way that I won't like. I'll stick to Mr. Hauser."

"Robin, you knew about foreshadowing when you were in fourth grade. You're my best student."

"I didn't read *The Sun Also Rises,*" I admit. "I didn't even crack the spine."

Mr. Hauser raises one sandy eyebrow. "The truths are all coming out now." For a second he's back to his gruff self. This is how it's supposed to be. I'm supposed to admit things to him, and he's supposed to make me feel like it's all going to be all right.

He's supposed to tell me I'm not alone.

Instead, he sits on the edge of his vacated desk and runs both hands through his hair, messing up the neat teacherly side part. "Robin, we're not going to make it to the Shakespeare unit together, but you know what a hamartia is, don't you?"

After a second of sputtering, my brain coughs up the answer. "A tragic flaw."

"Well, I think my one great flaw is . . ." I'm afraid he's going to say being gay. Or not being able to *stop* being gay. I wince in anticipation. "I love my job."

"How could that possibly be a bad thing?" I ask.

He points to one of the chables. I perch on top of it, a mirror of how he's sitting on his desk.

It's a lesson, but he only has one student.

"Last year was my first at Hawkins High, but it wasn't my first as an English teacher. I've worked at three different high schools since I started my career. Three schools in ten years. Every time I start at a new place, I put my head down and teach. I do the best I can with the books they give me and the students who show up, and I hope . . . I hope that's enough. But, almost like clockwork, I'd get word of a teacher in a nearby district, sometimes in my own school, getting fired . . . for being like us."

The unfairness rips through me, keeping me cold even as the clanking radiators spew heat.

"So I move on. Quietly. I make sure my personal life stays out of public view."

Which, again, makes me viciously upset, to the point that I'm shaking. Mr. Hauser shouldn't have to hide like that. No one should. I wrap my arms around my middle and try to pretend it's just because I'm still covered in sleet.

"Is that what's happening right now?" I ask. "You got fired? For being—"

"Not precisely," he says. "Think of it more as seeing the future and acting accordingly. Like Cassandra, the doomed Greek prophet, except I already know nobody's going to listen or care. I've been careful in my previous situations, Robin. I could stretch things out for a few years before I needed to move on. I hoped I could do that in Hawkins, maybe stay five years, even ten. But . . . I fell in love with someone."

"In *Hawkins*?" I can't help it, that's the first question that barges into my head.

"There are gay people everywhere, Robin." Mr. Hauser can't seem to decide if he's amused with me. A smile hovers over his face, then falls. "Over holiday break, someone saw us together. We weren't being careful enough. We were out very late, walking through the quiet town under the holiday lights, holding hands." He pauses, seeming unsure if he should admit the rest. "We kissed once or twice. The happiness went to my head, I suppose." I try to imagine gruff Mr. Hauser, giddily in love. "We found an anonymous note on my car. Someone must have recognized me. It could be a parent, a student. . . . It doesn't matter, really. They threatened to tell the school board."

A chill slices me clean in two.

"There must be some way to find whoever saw you," I say. "To stop them from saying anything."

Mr. Hauser finishes filling the box on his desk with a renewed quickness. "As much as I appreciate the offer of amateur sleuthing . . . I have to do this quickly. As soon as someone breathes a word of this to the board, in a job where I work with young people every day . . . my career is over."

I think about my parents, how they taught me to stand up and shout when something is wrong. (I swear I'll never make fun of their hippie past again.) "We'll go to the school board and tell them first. We'll fight—"

"There's no doubt of the outcome, unfortunately. Not right now. Not here. And once that's on my record, there's not much chance of getting rehired. I'd have to give up the job that I love for some indefinable reason. I'd have to give up students like you."

"But you *are* giving me up," I say.

And he's leaving at the exact moment when I need him most. He's abandoning me to this place.

"You'll be all right." He revises the thought swiftly. "You'll be better than that. You'll be *Robin*."

"The Weirdest Girl in Hawkins, Indiana?" I try, with a weak smile.

There are people outside now, in the hallway, moving in droves. I've known most of these people for most of my life. But now, knowing that any of them could have left that note on Mr. Hauser's dashboard, every face fills me with fresh dread.

The first bell rings.

Mr. Hauser grabs the box he was filling with his books, his coffee mug, the few pitiful things that he's taking with him.

I stay where I am, stuck on the chable, unable to move.

My voice flies to catch him at the door. "You told me once that if it isn't running away . . . you take someone with you."

All of the composure melts off Mr. Hauser's face. I wish I hadn't asked, because I know the answer before he admits, "I have reasons to go. He has reasons to stay." He shoulders the door open and leaves me in his empty classroom with a final brusque nod. If he lets me see any more of his emotional reaction, the student-teacher relationship will disintegrate completely. Teachers can be honest in front of students in extreme circumstances, but they can't *cry*.

Mr. Hauser leaves me alone with the heater cranking into high gear and the substitute teacher bustling in like nothing even happened.

I may never know exactly who left that anonymous note

on his car, but I know exactly who to blame. I calmly walk over to the chalkboard, claim a little sliver of white chalk, and write in tall letters:

Hawkins High School is a monster.

Discuss.

HIGH SCHOOL

PART THREE

HIGH SCHOOL

CHAPTER THIRTY-TWO

MAY 7, 1984

Mr. Hauser's one-time love might have had his reasons to stay in Hawkins, but I'm more convinced than ever.

I need to get out of here.

My nights at the movie theater have become an escape from my days at school, but they're not enough. For one thing, I have to watch the same films over and over and over and over, and when a movie isn't very good to start with, the monotony is enough to make me want to scream. A horrible, heart-jolting, B-horror-movie scream. Especially when Tom Cruise's face is involved.

Then there's the fact that no matter how many movies I

watch, there's nobody like me up there on the screen. Not even a whisper of a gay person. Maybe art-house cinemas somewhere are chock-full of lesbians, but those movies don't get made in Hollywood and they don't get played in Hawkins. And TV definitely doesn't help the situation, either. If people in this town want to act like we don't exist, or we don't exist *here,* they're being given a really good excuse.

For another, the movie theater is a site of the most obvious dating rituals in town. If I have to watch one more couple nuzzling in the ticket line or acting like nobody can see them one step away from breeding in the back row of the theater, I might implode.

I try to focus on the little things.

Take tickets. Rip tickets. Make jokes with Keri about the absurdity of *Footloose.* (A town like that cannot be turned around with a few musical numbers, believe me.) Smile at Sheena Rollins, who comes in at least once a week with a bagful of knitting and quietly works on her all-white oversize sweaters while she watches a movie by herself—breaking the unsaid rule that movie theaters are only for couples and groups. Intentionally shine my flashlight in the eyes of people who are breaking rules, including the ones making babies in the back row. Shovel out popcorn.

Rake in dollars.

I now have more than enough for my plane ticket, and I'm two hundred dollars short of the second one. I still dream about asking Tam, but that's all it is—a dream. Not even a daydream anymore, because I'm too scared to air it during the daylight hours. I think about it late at night, but I've gotten farther and farther away from talking to her at school. I'm terrified that I'll slip and somehow give something away.

About liking girls.

About liking *her.*

At this point, the idea of going to Europe with Milton next summer is the only thing keeping me from a complete meltdown. Prom tickets go on sale at the end of the week, and if he hasn't asked Wendy DeWan by then, I'm going to have to intervene. Our friendship has been on hold for long enough.

Tonight the theater is showing *Sixteen Candles,* which would not be particularly exciting, except Keri told me that our regular projectionist (a twenty-whatever guy named Russ who failed out of film school and came back home to Hawkins) needs time off soon and he's going to train me.

Soon I'll be in charge of the audience's destiny.

Plus, I'll get paid double for projectionist shifts.

That will pay for *so many* breakfast pastries.

In France, chocolate croissants are de rigueur. In Italy, they have their own version, called cornetti, either plain or filled with perfect clouds of thick crème pâtissière. And in Spain, there are lots of tempting choices—lemony magdalenas, torrijas coated in cinnamon or honey, sweet breads like ensaimadas that would be perfect with a little taza de café. Not that I drink coffee. But I *could.*

I wonder what else I'll learn how to do while I'm gone. I wonder who I'll be by the time I come back.

(Although, the more I think about it, the harder the coming-back part is to imagine. Ever since Mr. Hauser left, since this place drove him away, my brain has gotten very good at blocking out the return journey.)

"Robin, are you listening?" Russ asks, getting frustrated.

"Of course," I say, only half of me in the cramped little space above the movie theater with Russ.

The other half is heading down grand avenues and cobbled alleys, wandering from museum to museum, wearing wide-leg slacks and striped shirts and maybe even a jaunty hat, who knows. Smiling at a pretty girl, hoping she'll smile back. Asking what breakfast pastries *she* prefers.

These are my new daydreams. These are the only dreams that matter. I can imagine being myself, *all* of myself, but only somewhere else.

"Robin. Seriously. We need to start the movie, and you're just standing there holding the first reel."

"Oh. Right."

Russ shows me how to thread it and get the picture to flicker to life. It seems simple enough.

As soon as the movie starts, my eyes sort of unfocus. I've already seen it three times and there are some major problems. One: Shermer, Illinois, might be made up, but John Hughes is a bit *too* precise about how awful it is to be a Midwestern teenager. The gauzy pink dress at the end cannot cancel out all the social torture that preceded it (not to mention another girl being handed off to a nerd like she's a prize he won at the arcade). Two: the whole thing is about being a girl exactly my age who, of course, longs for the perfect boy, as if there's nothing else a sixteen-year-old girl could possibly long for.

Three: Molly Ringwald's short, tousled red hair will never stop reminding me of Tam.

"Come back in a little while and change the reels," Russ says.

"Shouldn't I stay up here?"

"I can't watch you watch this movie. Your face has too many feelings on it. It's stressing me out."

"Wow. Thanks."

I run down to the snack bar, which is more or less deserted because the movie is playing. Keri is the only one there, eating Junior Mints and reading the latest *Redbook*.

"Don't you want to watch?" I ask, helping myself to my regular dinner of popcorn and soda. Keri doesn't charge me for those, because she calls them the "renewable resources" of the movie theater industry.

"Not this one," she says. "It'll only make me sad that my boyfriend is nothing like Jake. He's not even half of a Jake. He's *maybe* a quarter of a Jake." Keri might talk about her boyfriend a lot, but at least she never pushes *me* to talk about boys. "The whole thing is a big, unhelpful fantasy."

"It seems pretty on-the-nose to me," I say, looking around at our depressing town, where a prom dress is the only thing most people seem to look forward to.

"Are you kidding?" Keri scoffs. "That movie is more of

a fantasy than *Return of the Jedi,* which has magical glowing swords and warrior teddy bears."

"Wait," I say, tossing popcorn into the air, arcing it back down to my mouth. "Because Molly Ringwald is happy at the end?"

"Because she thinks that getting the guy *means* being happy at the end. I got the guy, and honestly it's not that big a deal."

Wow. I used to disdain dating in all forms, but that was only because I couldn't see who I really wanted to go out with. Now I can't imagine thinking of dating as *not that big a deal* ever again.

"Here," Keri says. "I'll spot you a Milky Way if you go do my rounds in the theater."

It's not a chocolate croissant—but I would never say no to a Milky Way.

"You got it."

I grab her flashlight and take it into the darkened theater, creeping around and making sure that nobody's got their feet up on the seat backs. Part of me sort of hopes that one day I'll find two girls in the dark, holding hands. I want to know that they're here. Mr. Hauser said there are gay people everywhere, and I know it's true, but I need to *see* it.

All I see are middle schoolers licking Milk Duds and throwing them into each other's hair. I round the corner at the front of the theater and start up the second aisle. From the screen comes the sound of fake "Chinese" music.

Oh. Right. Here's a fourth problem with this movie. The only Asian character is used as a long-running joke. I might get upset about Hollywood intentionally ignoring people like me, but turning someone's existence into a punch line is a whole different kind of awful. I think about Milton getting angsty. I get angsty on his behalf.

"This movie is messed up!" I yell. "In case you hadn't noticed!" Most people are too busy throwing popcorn at each other to care that an employee's gone rogue in the aisle.

And then a brand-new problem catches me off-balance.

There's a couple in the back row. I can see the silhouette of the hair from here: Steve Harrington. I can only see the shape of a girl leaning against his chest in the dark, but she's petite like Tam, and suddenly it feels like I've walked in on something that I really, truly don't want to see.

Then they start kissing. Right there, in the theater, exactly like they're *not* supposed to.

Do I break them up? Do I protect myself from having to see what's happening in detail?

I put up my flashlight and head back there, ready to rain all over Steve Harrington's parade. But before I can make it up the aisle, the girl runs out of the theater like she's on a mission.

Maybe she has to pee. Maybe she's fleeing the scene of a bad date.

Whatever it is, I follow her up the aisle, briefly shining my light right in Steve's eyes as I pass him.

"Hey! Watch it with that thing!" he cries.

"Watch yourself, AquaNet," I snap.

He runs a hand through his hair with a slightly self-conscious air, and I can't help but feel a tiny bit victorious.

On the other side of the lobby door, the movie instantly muffles. Keri's immersed in her *Redbook,* and the door to the ladies' restroom is flapping shut. I run over, pushing it in. I don't know why I'm doing this, really. I only know that if it's Tam, I need to be there for her.

Even if she'll never like me back.

But the girl standing in the bathroom, staring at herself in the mirror like she's completely forgotten what she looks like, isn't Tam.

It's Nancy Wheeler.

She's got a heart-shaped face that pinches down sharp at the chin, and she's so pale you'd think she was watching a much scarier movie. She's wearing an ankle-length skirt and honest-to-God pearls. My first instinct is to ask her how she got Steve Harrington to agree to see this movie in the first place. My second is to announce something quippy about her *honest-to-God pearls.*

But I don't do either, because she's crying: ragged, chunky sobs with very little control.

And even though I barely know her, I have to do *something.*

Is this my job now? To defend girls in this town from undeserving boys? Nobody else seems to be doing it.

"Hey, did your boyfriend pull something dumb back there?" I ask, crossing my arms over my official work shirt. "Because I will gleefully kick him out."

She grabs a scratchy brown paper towel and wipes her nose. "What? Steve? No." She says his name like Steve is the last thing on her mind. Like Steve is the least of her problems.

Which is . . . not what I expected at all.

"What's wrong?" I ask. I probably shouldn't pry, but I'm already here, and she's still upset, even if her tears have leaked to a stop.

"I'm just worried," Nancy says. "About my best friend."

"You mean Barb Holland?" I ask, my Barb-worship from earlier this year suddenly flooding back to me. "Did you hear from her?"

Nancy's mouth twists up tight, but she blinks hard enough to keep her tears in check. "No."

"Is she okay?"

"I don't think so," she says, her voice hollow and her eyes fixed on the mirror. Then she whips around to me. "Forget it. Forget I said anything."

And she runs out.

If Nancy hasn't heard from her, why does she sound so certain that Barb *isn't* okay? Is the silence of a best friend a sign in itself, a reason to think something terrible might have happened? For the first time since Barb vanished, I feel genuinely scared for her.

I think, against all self-regulations, about Kate. Our silence has stretched on and on, mostly because I don't want to deal with Dash, and Kate didn't immediately break up with him after I left that note in her locker. She tried to talk to me a few times—left me notes of her own, called my house—then gave up when she realized that I wasn't reading the notes or returning the calls. I don't really care about her excuses. She knows the truth about how horrible Dash was that night. And she made her choice. She picked her boyfriend over her best "girlfriend."

(Okay, *now* I understand why that word bothers me. Because Kate is a girl and she used to be my friend, but it really was a very different feeling from what I experience every time I see Tam. Or think about Tam.)

"Get it together, Buckley," I say to myself in the bathroom mirror.

I make it back to the lobby right as screams burst from the theater.

The audience starts streaming out through the double doors, everyone shouting and complaining over each other, a melee of disgruntled voices. Keri is standing in the ticket booth trying to calm everyone down. I sneak a look through the open doors into the theater itself—where the film has bubbled into a crispy black state and the movie has gone caput.

"You never came back!" Russ shouts from the open door of the projection room.

"You couldn't just change the reels yourself that one time?" I shout, incredulous.

"You're supposed to be training. It's *your* job."

"Not anymore," Keri says. "Sorry, Robin. Melting the movie is sort of a one-strike deal. You're out."

She hands me a Milky Way as my consolation prize.

I can't say I'm sorry for taking this movie out of rotation. So I just strip off my work shirt, glad that I'm wearing another layer beneath it, and toss it on the floor as I walk out.

I was *so close* to having all the money I need for Operation Croissant, but I can't keep waiting. As I emerge from the timeless cavern of the movie theater, I can nearly taste summer in the air.

It's already May.

It's time to see if Milton is in or out.

HAWKINS
HIGH SCHOOL

CHAPTER THIRTY-THREE

MAY 11, 1984

I shouldn't feel this nervous standing on Milton Bledsoe's doorstep.

But I need him to know about this plan. I needed him to know about this plan six months ago. So when I got off the bus halfway home, instead of walking to my own neighborhood, I made my way over to Milton's, one awkwardly half-jogged block of sidewalk at a time. If this were a big Hollywood movie like the kind we play at the theater, people watching me jitter and jolt as I ring the doorbell would probably wonder if I'm about to propose.

Milton opens the door, looking confused. And a little

breathless. And no tiny amount nervous. Wow, I even miss how his anxiety pinches his face.

"Hey," I say. "Can we talk?"

"Robin Buckley!" he shouts, his voice amplified like he's informing some third party that I've arrived. At first, I think his parents or his little sister might come to the door, but then Wendy DeWan appears. As if by magic. She's breathless, too, wearing pink shorts and drinking one of the Snapple Tru Root Beers that Milton's dad keeps stocked in the fridge at all times.

"Hey, Robin!" she echoes. "Do you want to hang out with us?"

"Oh! No! I mean, I didn't want to interrupt . . ." I give Milton a searching look. Because, what is going on?!

"I'll just wait in the living room, then." She gives Milton a look of her own, complete with a scalp-tingling smile. My face surges with heat. I can't tell if it's because Milton's blushing and I'm blushing by the associative property, or because Wendy is really pretty and I can't help it.

"You did it!" I whisper-shout as soon as she's gone.

Milton puts his hands in his pockets and shrugs.

I inspect his lips. They're puffy, and his rate of breathing is just now returning to normal. "Were you two making out when I rang the doorbell?" Milton looks like he might melt into embarrassed goo and spill all over the front steps. "I'm going to take that reaction as a yes."

He shakes his head at me—but he's smiling.

"And she said yes?" I ask. "About prom?"

"She rejected my prom invitation, but she came over to make out with me anyway," Milton deadpans.

I yell into the house, "Please give me a pillow so I can throw it at him!"

The truth is, I'm proud of Milton. He did what he wanted to do, even if it was extremely hard for him to work up to it, even if he had to banish a thousand anxieties. The other truth is that I'm jealous for the exact same reasons.

"Wait!" he says. "I have something for you."

He disappears for a second and then comes back with a white card laden with cursive writing. Very fancy.

"This is a ticket to prom. With my name on it. You just told me that Wendy . . ."

"She wants to be my date. She *is* my date. And maybe, possibly my girlfriend." He blushes again but forges bravely ahead. "I might have admitted that I stopped hanging out with you because people were being weird about it, and then she got a little mad that I'd ever ditch a friend like that, especially on her behalf. So I came up with a plan. She got a ticket with her friend James. And I got this one for you. Once we get there, Wendy will be my date. And you can come, too, and I can apologize for the whole thing." He holds the ticket out at arm's length. "Take it. Please."

"I have no interest in prom," I say, honestly. "I have anti-interest in prom."

I've literally never thought about going. Even as an upperclassman, I had firm plans to skip.

"But they're going to play such bad music," Milton says.

"Who else is going to make fun of it with me? Besides, if you say no, you'll always wonder what it would have been like. The absurd decorations! The taffeta dresses!"

"Yeah, but if I went, I'd have to *wear* one of those dresses." They're basically a uniform at this point. Everyone wears one—it's just a question of how puffy the sleeves are. "At least you get to wear a suit."

"My brother's old powder-blue tuxedo," he says. "You can't miss that. Right?"

He's got this hopeful smile on his face. And I believe that he missed me as much as I missed him over the last six months. But I can't go to prom for Milton. I can't subject myself to that kind of teenage torture for *anyone*. "Trust me," I say with my hand over my chest, swearing a very sincere oath. "I am not going to have a prom-shaped hole in my heart."

He sighs, finally pocketing the ticket. "Fine, but if you change your mind, your name is on the list as my date, so—"

"I have other things to plan for, actually." I take a deep breath and dive right in. "I'm going to Europe this summer."

"Wow! That's immensely cool. Are your parents taking you?"

I shake my head. Here goes.

"I was hoping you'd come with me."

"Oh . . ."

That one little sound is enough to make my hopes take a sudden swan dive into the abyss.

"I would love to do that, Robin. I really, really would. But I promised my parents I'd help out with Ellie this summer.

And Wendy . . . I mean, she's leaving for school in the fall. . . . We don't have a lot of time. . . ."

"You need to be here." Even though you hate it here.

"Yeah."

I try not to let bitterness infect my voice. "Okay. Yeah, of course. I'll find someone else." But there's literally no one I can imagine asking at this point. Not with Kate and Dash being—Kate and Dash. Not when thinking about Tam in any capacity, let alone a European escapade, makes me too nervous to breathe right. I try to stay focused on the part of this that *is* working—the part that I can control. "I've already got enough money for my plane ticket. But then I got fired from the theater for burning through *Sixteen Candles.* Literally."

"Wow, I really have missed a lot," Milton says.

I think about Tam. About everything I've figured out.

He really, really has.

HAWKINS
HIGH SCHOOL

CHAPTER THIRTY-FOUR

JUNE 8, 1984

Remember how I told Milton I would never put on a taffeta dress and go to prom?

It turns out, I was only half right.

It's Friday night and Hawkins is in the sweaty grip of prom fever. Students at school have spent all week creating dramatic social fireworks over every last detail—rides, hair-dos, corsages—counting down every minute. I've barely seen them as they buzzed around me. I've been too busy with some last-minute plans of my own.

Yesterday, I went out to Hawkins's one and only thrift store and found a secondhand dress that fits me. (Not like a glove. More like a sausage casing.) It's electric purple and so shiny that it's basically a mirror. I spent a precious eleven dollars from my Operation Croissant funds on this terrible thing.

I'm in prom uniform, which I never, ever thought I would be.

But it's all in service of my plan.

I stoop in front of the mirror on my desk, trying to shove my entire body into the little square, checking my hair (teased), my lipstick (also bright purple), and my expression (a mix of elated and terrified).

My parents think I look like this because I'm going on my first date. I didn't exactly lie to them and tell them outright that I'm going to the prom with Milton. But I didn't dissuade them from thinking it, either. I only mentioned true things. He bought me a ticket. He wants me to be there.

(Nobody asked, once, where *I* want to be.)

There's a small bag, already packed, tucked under my bed. The trick is going to be sneaking it into the car without my parents noticing. I have my learner's permit now, and Dad gave me a few hesitant lessons right after my sixteenth birthday, but I'm not going to drop their car off and leave for Chicago. It's too much like what happened with Barb—her car abandoned outside that party.

I have to believe she made it out. That she's living a defiantly great life far, far away from here. The alternative is too upsetting. If Barb didn't run away, that means Hawkins just . . . swallowed her up somehow. That the monster I've been fighting all year got hold of her and didn't let go.

I shake off a shiver.

To suit my chosen cover story, I'm going to let my parents drive me to prom (which would be humiliating to anyone who actually cared about the dance, but in my case it's a practical choice). I'll wait until they clear the parking lot, swap my high heels for sneakers, walk to the train station half a mile away, and catch the late train into Chicago. I should reach the airport just in time to buy a ticket for the red-eye that leaves at midnight. The Midwest will be dark and docile as I rise above it, finally leaving this place behind.

Eight hours later, I'll land in Paris.

It's wild, really. If you can afford it, you can shrug off your entire existence like an old sweater. You can change your life in a single night.

I decided to move my plans up right after I found out about Milton and Wendy, aka as soon as I realized that I was truly on my own. On the one hand, I didn't have anyone to take with me, after all of the time I spent waiting for Milton to be allowed to speak to me again. On the other, I had plenty of money to travel on my own.

The freedom was dizzying and slightly vertiginously scary. I wonder if this is what it will feel like to take off in the plane tonight.

I know that Mr. Hauser wanted me to travel with a friend, that he thinks I should share this experience with someone. He doesn't want me to be lonely, but he should understand more than anyone else: sometimes you have to leave town on your own terms. The best I can do is go before this feeling gets any worse. Every day since Tam's friends unfolded that letter, the itch to leave has grown bigger and bigger, slowly taking over every bit of my skin.

It's not like I'll be missing that much by leaving early, anyway. The last two weeks of school are a bad joke without a punchline, sprawling out longer and longer as we learn nothing from our checked-out teachers and the brick oven of the building gets hotter in five-degree increments.

And I'm only a sophomore, which is good news for once. I'll get in trouble for missing those two weeks, maybe, but it won't really matter in the long run.

But the second I think about the *long run* in Hawkins, I feel sick.

Maybe I won't come home at all.

I don't want my parents to worry too much. I'm going to call them from the airport, and I'll send them a postcard from every single place I go. Maybe I'll send Milton and Wendy one, too.

I check my bag again. Passport, two changes of clothes, a few granola bars, a book for the plane. The Polaroid I took of myself the day I decided to go to Europe. (I look so much older now. Were those really *my* squirrel cheeks?) My composition notebook with all of the plans I've gathered over the course of a year, with one page ripped out. A page that changed the whole story.

As I come out of the bedroom, my parents swarm, which I wasn't really expecting. Dad's even got his own camera out, the proper Kodak, and he's snapping shots of me waddling around in my dress.

"You look beautiful," my mom croons. "Just beautiful, Robin." She can't really like this outfit, can she? "Your soul is really shining right now."

Ah. That makes sense. Thinking about leaving is enough to make my soul do delighted backflips.

Dad sighs. I hold my breath, afraid he's going to say something about how fast I've grown up. I'm not sure I could handle that right now. If they get emotional, I'm going to get emotional, even if their emotions are based on something completely false (like my prom date) or completely bizarre (like this dress). Still, I'm afraid that if we all start crying right now, I'm going to burst a seam, literally or metaphorically, and everything I haven't told them is going to spill out.

But Dad just sniffles a little and says, "Ready to go, Robin?"

"I've been ready since the first day of school," I say. "Wait, I just need to grab something." I don't think I can get away without them seeing my bag, so I have to commit to my first actual lie. "It's for after the prom, just a change of clothes for hanging out at Milton's house."

I snatch up the bag, running like a streak of purple lightning across the house, into the garage. "All right! I'm ready!"

The doorbell rings sharply. Who is that?

"Oh, hello . . ." I hear my mom's voice waft from the living room.

What's going on? Did somebody figure out what I'm doing and come here to stop me? Did they get hold of my composition notebook, somehow, and read it? No, it's nestled safe in my bag. I've checked the contents three times. But maybe someone picked it up and read it and now they're here. . . .

I walk into the living room, only to find Milton and Wendy framed in the front door, the blue almost-summer evening behind them. They're both dressed to the nines, and then multiply that by another nine. I would never have guessed that someone could look *good* in a powder-blue tuxedo, but Milton is making it happen. Instead of his normal nerd-standard hair, he's done it up in a sort of wall, like an abstract sculpture, similar to some of his favorite New Wave artists but also completely his own. Wendy's dress is silver and shining, with a full skirt and capped sleeves. Her hair is curly and piled high, topped with a silver lace headband that would make Madonna cry.

Milton clears his throat. "I'm here to pick you up. Throw on something nice and—" He actually seems to notice me for the first time since I entered the room. "Whoa."

"Whoa," Wendy agrees.

Even her friend James, who's hovering on the steps behind them, adds his own faint "whoa" in the background.

I can't tell if it's a good reaction or just a shocked one. I know that this is the style everyone seems to like right now, but I can't help feeling that I look like a grape Popsicle with big dreams.

Milton shakes his head, like I might be a mirage. "I thought you said you weren't coming."

"You told us Milton couldn't pick you up," Mom says,

squinting me like she's seeing me through a haze, like she can't quite get a clear picture.

"I offered," Milton starts, "but Robin told me—"

I give him a look that means *stop talking, you're about to ruin the secret plan I've been working on for a year.*

Dad comes in from the garage with my bag open. He sets it down on the table, my things spilling out.

"Young lady, what is this all about?" he asks.

In my entire life, I've never been *young lady*-ed. It makes my throat close up. My parents are onto me.

Mom sifts through the contents of the bag. Clothes, food, passport. "This doesn't look like what you bring to spend the night at a friend's prom party. Milton, are your parents hosting a party?"

"No," he says as Wendy elbows him in the side.

She saw the look.

"Are you going somewhere after prom? A hotel? Why do you need a passport?" My mom's questions gather in speed and intensity.

My dad turns the bag upside down, dumps the rest of it on the table. The wad of money that I tucked at the very bottom drops out, sitting right there on the kitchen table, looking enormous.

"What in the world do you need that much money for, Robin?" Mom asks.

"Is it for drugs?" Dad follows up quickly.

"Are you kidding me?" I ask. "I spend half of my time

in the room next to yours and the other half at school! You would know if I do drugs!"

"I don't know, Robin," Mom mumbles, looking at the spilled contents of my bag. "It feels like there's a lot that you're not telling us. . . ."

Okay, fair.

"Are you getting my daughter in trouble?" Dad asks, rounding on Milton.

Now I'm laughing uncontrollably, my emotions swinging everywhere. Because seriously—Milton?

"My boyfriend could get someone in trouble if he wanted to," Wendy announces in his support.

"Boyfriend?" Dad repeats, still trying to work this out, his puzzle pieces hopelessly jumbled. "So you two aren't . . . ?"

"It must be some *other* boy that she's meeting with a packed bag," Mom says. "A boy who she has a reason to be hiding." She goes into some kind of nervous parental fugue state, pacing all over the living room in a frenzy, running her hands down her long hair. "I knew that I'd rub off on her. I knew it. I did all kinds of stupid things when I was younger, and I got in trouble with all sorts of boys and—"

"I really need everyone to stop assuming that everything is about a boy," I say quietly.

"You'll have to give us another explanation, then," Dad says, sitting down like that somehow makes his point final.

This is *not* how I'm going to tell them I like girls. Absolutely not. Even in the midst of a disaster, I'm not going to sully that feeling.

So I rip open the rest of my secrets and pour them out on top of everything else they just found. "You think I'm meeting a boy in secret to pay for a mountain of drugs, and then . . . running them over the border with my middle school passport? I'm planning on going to *Europe*! Without any of you!"

When the dust settles, there's a thick layer of uncomfortable silence.

"We should probably get going," Milton says. "We're going to be late. . . ."

He backs off the front steps, into the shadows. Wendy mouths the word *sorry* and then spins to follow him.

The door bangs shut, leaving me alone with my parents.

I grab my bag, clutching it to me as if I can somehow salvage my plans. But they're strewn around me with everything I so meticulously packed.

"Whatever the truth is, we'll figure it out. Until then, you're not leaving the house," Dad says. He holds up the thick collection of bills, the ones that I painstakingly collected, shift by shift. "And we're confiscating *this* until we know what's going on."

"You don't believe in grounding me," I remind them.

Mom and Dad exchange a look of worrisome solidarity.

Mom points to my room. "When you start acting like Robin Buckley again," Dad says, "you're no longer grounded."

HIGH SCHOOL

CHAPTER THIRTY-FIVE

JUNE 8, 1984

Those words linger long after I've slammed my bedroom door.

When I start acting like Robin Buckley again, I can leave.

What does that even mean?

I pummel my empty travel bag onto the bed, and it flips around, releasing something that survived the Big Purge of Robin's Dreams.

My Polaroid flutters to the bed.

The girl in that photo has a gleam in her eye. She *wants* to be a rebel—and she thinks she's ready. She believes it's as simple as getting on an airplane and waking up somewhere new. Now, with that plan in tatters all around me, I can see that even her so-called rebellion is just another partial lie.

She's hiding from the truth. Always hiding.

Because she knows that leaving for a few weeks and coming back isn't going to change everything. But she's gotten so good at conveniently not noticing the parts of herself that might be inconvenient to everybody else. And she's so encumbered by all the camouflage that I think she can't even see some of it anymore.

Something in my brain has snapped, and I can see every little bit.

The things I did to keep myself safer, smaller, quieter. Because I know how different I really am. I know that letting it all out is committing to a life where I fight the monsters of normality every single day.

And doing it alone.

As it turns out, my rebellion is not going to be as easy as saving up some money and packing a suitcase.

It's going to start with stripping down every bit of self-deception and facing the truth:

I'm not sure I've been entirely myself for years.

I sit down at my desk and pop Italian tape 4, side 1, "Landscapes and Vistas," out of my new Walkman. I scan my pitiful music collection. The only new cassette I've bought this year so far is by Queen—which is funny, because I didn't particularly like Queen until I heard a new song playing at the record store a few months ago.

I spent a few of my precious Europe dollars on this tape on a complete whim.

All because I'd heard Milton's voice in my head: What *do* you like?

I pop it in and fast-forward, the player making that high-pitched scribbling noise, until I reach the song that I bought the cassette for.

"I Want to Break Free" fills the space between my ears, floods my brain with the anthem that I need.

I've been acting like the only true rebellion would be breaking free from Hawkins—but what if it means breaking free from all of this hiding? What if people had to deal with who I really am on a daily basis? Maybe it's not safe for me to stand up in the middle of the cafeteria and declare that I want to kiss girls (starting with Tam). But that doesn't mean that I have to suppress my whole personality. It won't be easy to be publicly weird and utterly alone, but it's so much harder to keep going like this.

I might not be able to be honest about who I like, but I'm going to be honest about absolutely everything else.

Starting with this dress.

I take the scissors out of my desk drawer, and I hack off the entire train, all the way to my thighs. I cut into the tight (and yet somehow puffy) sleeves until there's only a fringe of wild purple fabric. I make stars out of the shiny purple left-overs, then I cut up the black shirt I wore to all my interviews and create a backing for the stars so they'll stand out. I glue them straight onto the dress while I'm wearing it.

It feels so good that I keep going. I pick up the scissors

again, take hold of a teased tentacle of hair, and start hacking off the perm that's been haunting me all year. There are so many dead follicles that I have to keep moving closer and closer to the scalp. The cut hair itches my skin, and I keep swatting it off. When I'm done, I have about three inches of dark blond hair left, a short mane that makes me look like an untamed lion. The carpet is covered in the last sad remnants of my attempt to fit in, to fool the monster of Hawkins High into ignoring me. Let it try to mess with me now.

I almost can't wait to get back to school—to see the shock on everyone's faces. I can't wait to shoulder past them, not caring a single bit.

This isn't Operation Croissant anymore.

This is Operation Robin.

And there's more work to do. I scrub off my makeup with a scrap of the shredded dress, watching as the blue eyeshadow, hot-pink cheeks, and purple lips disappear. Then I replace them with a storm of gray eyeshadow and black eyeliner. I reach into my desk and find pots of nail polish, most of them gifts from Kate, who kept deciding what she thought I'd look good in. I fling turquoise and magenta and candy pink over my shoulder, landing on the shag carpet with thuds like little bombs going off. I don't see anything dark enough—until I notice a Sharpie.

With my nails scribbled black, I stack a few mismatched bangles on my wrists.

I'm all dressed up with somewhere pretty obvious to go.

I throw on a pair of black sneakers and the men's suit

jacket still hanging in my closet from my Annie Lennox costume.

I check myself in the mirror one more time. I look like a nerd *and* a rebel—some kind of hybrid that Hawkins has never seen before. This wasn't the rebellion I planned on, but maybe it's the right one. It turns out I didn't need to go to Europe to be brave enough to stop being afraid of what everybody else thinks. That power was waiting for me the whole time.

My new look doesn't feel complete yet. Something's missing.

Oh, right.

My middle fingers shoot up.

"The accessory every girl truly needs," I say.

I pick up the Polaroid camera and take a new picture of myself, leaving it on my pillow for my parents to find whenever they check in on me. I shake it a few times, but I don't wait for it to fully develop.

I'm already gone.

HIGH SCHOOL

CHAPTER THIRTY-SIX

JUNE 8, 1984

Leaving the house while grounded by two parents who have no real idea how to crack down on a wild teenager is easier than it should be.

I feel bad for them.

(Not *that* bad. I mean, I was planning to be on a train to Chicago right now, and then a plane to Paris, and now all I'm doing is crossing Hawkins. I'm not even disobeying the orders that were laid down earlier. Not really. My dad said that when I'm acting like Robin again, I'm free to go, and I've never felt more Robin than I do right now.)

My first-floor bedroom window opens into the backyard. All I have to do is quietly remove the bug screen, hop out without ripping my newly shortened dress right up the middle, and crouch-run to the garage, pulling up the door by the metal handle. I keep it slow and quiet, only banging a little bit right as it hits the top.

"Crap." I pause, but all I hear are the crickets going crazy, trying to find each other in the dark. Apparently, they know it's prom night, too.

I creep inside, my eyes adjusting to the garage gloom. Even months after the return of boring, safe Hawkins, where no kids or teenagers mysteriously go missing, my bike is still trussed up with a padlock. After three futile tries at guessing the combination (and an uncomfortable flash of what it would feel like to ride a bike in this now-minidress), I notice Dad's car keys hanging on the pegboard, right out in the open.

"I guess it's time to drive."

I pluck the keys off the hook, get in the car, and jolt the seat backward so I fit more or less comfortably. My legs don't seem to be compatible with the amount of space available, but I get my sneakers flat on the pedals and decide that cramped knees will just have to be okay. I've never done this on my own before, but from the few short lessons Dad gave me, at least I know the standard motions.

I push the key in and turn it, wincing as the engine coughs and wakes up about as audibly as Dad on a Monday morning.

Then I creep in reverse, haltingly, and when I hit the end of the driveway, I take a deep breath. This is the tricky part. I have to pass right in front of our house and hope my parents are too busy arguing about me to realize that I'm sneaking down the street right in front of the living room window.

I release my breath as I make it to the end of the street. Now, even if they notice I'm gone, they won't be able to catch up easily. This is their only car, and I can't really imagine them running all the way to Hawkins High.

I smash the gearshift as I leave my neighborhood behind, speeding up to reach prom before everyone gets too deep into the party punch to notice I'm even there. I'm not wasting this night on wasted jocks.

I want everyone to see that I'm still here—that I've always been here, and I've always been weird, and I'm not hiding it for anybody's comfort ever again.

But first I have to survive my first solo drive. The Dodge Dart is not exactly a luxury automobile, but I feel like we're in this together as we glide through the quiet neighborhoods of Hawkins. Everyone is turning in for the night—or waiting with a light on in the living room until an errant teenager comes back from prom and a night of mostly sanctioned stupid choices.

Booze and prom-night sex might seem rebellious to some kids in Hawkins, but honestly it sounds pretty unimaginative to me as I roar onto school grounds in my hacked-up prom dress, ready to fight my way into the belly of the high school beast and shake everything up.

Who knows.

Maybe I'll even ask Tam to dance.

As I pull into the parking lot, it feels official.

"I made it," I whisper. "I really made it."

There's a sense of freedom and relief that I'm not sure even touching down in Paris could parallel. I laugh and put one fist up in victory—which is when I lose control of the heavy wheel. It pulls suddenly to the left, and I crunch into a parked car. A really nice one, too: a red Maserati. I back my car away, but it's pretty simple to see which pieces got crunched together.

The Dodge Dart is now smoking from under the crunched hood, and it's all I can do to get it to limp over to an empty parking space near the back of the lot. Of course, I haven't worked on parking, and now my previous confidence is just as smashed up as my parents' only car. I smack the bumper of a mini-truck on the way in, then overcorrect and grate the side of my car against some sporty coupe with a T-top.

"Those things are dumb anyway," I mutter to myself as I finally settle into the parking spot on a severe diagonal.

I get out of the car, pulling down the bottom hem of my dress and then shooting the cuffs of my jacket. I'm here now, and there's literally no turning back, because my getaway car is a smoking hunk of useless metal.

I should be nervous, but I just let out a shocked laugh.

The funny thing is, nothing can touch the joy pumping through me right now. Joy—and a bit of wild disbelief that *I'm actually doing this.*

I stride toward the school.

It's time to introduce everyone to rebel Robin.

CHAPTER THIRTY-SEVEN

JUNE 8, 1984

My first interaction with the prom committee is not promising.

"You can't come in," a blond sophomore named Claire insists. She's wearing an emerald-green parade float as a dress and seems pretty put out about being stuck at the desk with me instead of inside, dancing the night away.

I never thought I'd want to be here tonight—but I *do* have an official invitation. I've seen the ticket in person. I'm no longer ignoring the gift of Wendy's wanting to put things right and Milton coughing up thirty bucks to get me in that door.

"I'm on the list," I say firmly.

She checks it. I can see my name upside down, listed as Milton Bledsoe's date.

"See?" I ask, a little too smugly.

"What I see is someone who's breaking the dress code in about seventy different ways," she retorts.

"Besides," says her tablemate, Shannon, whose peach satin getup is even shinier than her extensive orthodontia. (Talk about camouflage. Shannon is no stranger to surviving the vicious halls of Hawkins High, and I feel a fleck of pity.) "Milton came in an hour ago and you weren't with him, so you don't actually qualify as his date."

Okay, pity revoked.

Claire shoots Shannon a look—like she can't decide if she's pissed that her shutdown got interrupted or grudgingly glad that Shannon made an actual point.

"Fine. I never wanted a date, anyway. The ticket's paid in full, and the committee has my name *right there.*" I tap the list so they can't pretend to not see it. "So . . ."

"You can't go in there *stag,*" Claire says with a horrified gasp. "It's the number one rule of prom." I wouldn't be surprised if she clutched her chest, fainted, and could only be revived by smelling salts. At this point, any kind of social throwback would make sense to me. Sometimes it seems like the rules for these kinds of events were written in the Stone Age—they're so outdated. I wonder if teenagers in twenty years will still be barred from their proms because they don't have an opposite-sex partner to make their presence palatable.

I wonder if we'll ever evolve.

"I thought the number one rule is that you treasure this night for the rest of your life," I say. "I hope you treasure the memory of that table. But I'm going inside."

I try to walk past them, and a few adults materialize out of nowhere.

Chaperones.

Oh, crap. These are the parents and teachers in Hawkins who have nothing better to do than sacrifice an entire weekend of their adult lives on the altar of teen socializing. They're far more likely to stop me than Shannon and Claire, whose power to admit or deny people was mostly symbolic. And one of them is the gym teacher, so I can't outrun him, even if he's in dress shoes and I'm in worn-in sneakers.

God, he's even wearing his whistle with his suit.

One of the parents crosses her arms, and I can't help feeling she's been waiting since her *own* prom to lord over someone else's. "No date, showed up late . . . inappropriate attire . . ."

"You'll have to go home, sweetie," the gym teacher concludes.

"Sweetie?" I mutter, seething with the grossness of it all.

"Go on," the mom chaperone says. "Now."

"I can't," I say, honestly. The Dodge Dart is still emitting a faint stream of smoke out there in the darkness of the parking lot. And I really don't think I can walk all the way home in this dress.

The gym teacher squints at me like I'm the smallest line on the school nurse's eye exam chart. "Is that . . . *Buckley*?"

I flick my eyebrows up in a quiet challenge. "Yep."

"What are you doing here?" he asks.

"I'm here to promenade."

Students, teachers, chaperones, all stare at me blankly.

"Prom is descended from the more antiquated term *promenade,* the part of a ball where everyone walks around, couple by couple, to show off how fancy they can be to whoever is the most important in the room, further cementing status and creating a stratified class system that persists to this day, only we pick our king and queen based on the designation of hotness instead of the divine right to rule. Doesn't anyone else think it's weird that our country threw off monarchy only to keep reenacting it, but this time in a sweaty gym?"

They keep staring at me. If it's possible, their expressions get blanker.

"Have you been drinking?" the self-important mom chaperone finally asks. "We can't admit anyone who's been drinking."

"Another strike," Claire adds, like keeping me out of prom is her life's new, fervent mission.

"Alcohol doesn't make you better at etymology," I point out as one of the chaperones sniffs my breath.

"You show up looking like a deviant straight out of some godless music video and talking like I don't even know what. . . ." She stops when another teenager shows up in a reflective vest, shoots a suspicious glare at me, and then whispers directly into the ear of the mom-perone. It feels like we're back in the second grade and someone's tattling on me.

"My parking monitor tells me that we have some reports of cars being dinged up by a new arrival."

"Parking monitor?" I nearly snort.

"Do you drive a Dodge Dart?" the boy asks.

"That is not my car," I say, which is technically true. It's my parents' car.

The mom-perone squints at me, unconvinced. "We have the Hawkins police on radio for the night, and we're supposed to call if anyone is out of line."

"You're an inch away, Buckley," the gym teacher adds, as if he doesn't get enough of talking like that during the school week.

I grit my teeth and weigh my choices.

I can hear the static on the line as mom-perone fires up the walkie-talkie that, if I'm supposed to take her word, will get Chief Hopper to personally kick me out of prom (and give me that awkward ride home that I've already avoided once).

"Thanks," I say, turning my back on them.

"Wait!" Shannon cries, sounding suddenly desperate for my validation now that they've rejected me. "For what?"

"Reminding me how much this place sucks."

I walk away. But that doesn't mean I'm done here.

Most people, if they had just hit three parked cars and then failed to crash prom, would give up. But it's not a real rebellion if you turn around and go home at the first (or second or third) sign of trouble.

I'm not leaving.

I'm doubling down.

I walk around the side of the building, headed over toward the band room. It probably looks like I'm off to lick my wounds—but I have an idea. There are three soundproofed practice rooms so that students can blow into and whack at their respective instruments without anyone's ears having to suffer. (Also, so people can make out after school without anyone's eyes having to suffer.) During school hours, Miss Genovese keeps one of the windows forever cracked so, in case of absolute nicotine emergencies, she can smoke in practice room three, dispersing the evidence before it sets off the alarms.

And—because I'm lucky or the janitors are lazy at the end of the school year or both—it's still open.

I nudge it up an inch at a time, then hook my leg over the side of the window and execute a full body roll, landing on the hard floor. It smells like sheet music and old cigarettes in here. I roll over, feeling the entire side of my body that's already turning into one long bruise. "Always a warm welcome, Hawkins High."

CHAPTER THIRTY-EIGHT

JUNE 8, 1984

I stand at the cracked door of the music room, trying to determine the best path to the gym. Up the busy senior hall, which will take me there directly? Or do I choose sophomore hall, which should be much quieter but will add time and distance to my sprint? I might have made it within the walls of the high school, but I have to crash prom and show the Hawkins High monster that I'm not going to live in fear forever, or my entire rebellion so far was a lot of sound and fury and fashion choices signifying nothing. (All right, that's not true. My anti-makeover made me feel so much better that it would have been worth it even if I just sat at home forever.)

I edge forward. There's the undeniable fact that Tam is in

that gym, and I want to see her. I want *her* to see *me,* without all of my camouflage.

While I calculate my route, I notice Mr. Hauser's classroom door standing open down the hall, and for a second I forget that he's not still here.

That he'll never be here again.

Would he be proud of what I'm doing tonight? Would he warn me against it—tell me to lie low until graduation and then make a break for it, find greener and more open-minded pastures where I can be myself without all this trouble?

I think about all the things that he tried to teach me this year. I think about "The Lottery" and *Lord of the Flies.*

But what I finally land on is my botched audition for *Our Town.*

The words I couldn't say without losing my breath, because they were so true that they lodged in my chest. They were so true they hurt.

"Oh, earth, you're too wonderful for anybody to realize you," I whisper. Like a mantra. I'll never say it on a stage in front of the whole school like Mr. Hauser wanted, but I understand it better than he could imagine.

I wanted to leave this place so I could see the world—and experience every weird and wonderful thing it has to offer. I *still* want that. But I got so caught up in the idea of somewhere else that it stopped being a way to make things better, and it became an excuse to completely ignore my life.

Emily was floating through her life—more of a ghost

when she was alive than after she died—when she woke up to everything she'd been missing.

I'm not going to let that happen.

I'm not going to sleepwalk up until the moment I leave Hawkins. I'm going to throw myself into things, headfirst. I'm going to make it into that gym and claim my place, no matter who doesn't like it.

The thump of a new song starts in the gym, a synth-laden eighties heartbeat, a siren song luring me forward.

It's time to run the gauntlet.

I go slowly down senior hall at first, sticking to the shadows. But some of those shadows are littered with people: crying girls, drunk friends making the most of a flask, unhappy couples, *much* too happy couples. And in the tiny window of a classroom door, two boys standing close to each other, so close it looks like they're dancing, even though they leave a little space. But I see their hands twine together.

We're here. We're everywhere.

"Robin?" someone shouts as I speed up. I've been spotted, and now all I can do is run. "What are you doing here?"

"Robin, what are you *wearing*?"

People are laughing. I can feel the monster breathing on the back of my neck, snapping at my heels.

"Stop right there, Miss Buckley!" shouts the mom-perone.

"Hey! Back here! Now!" That gravelly command was definitely issued by Chief Hopper.

Rounding the corner, I pass the concessions that line the

hallway outside the gym. About a dozen people are mingling and grazing on platters of cookies and chips and trying to figure out exactly how spiked the punch is.

"Robin!" The sound of my name echoes down the hall. Dash is the one shouting it now.

I need to slow him—and all of my detractors—down. So I make a *tiny* detour, barreling into the table that holds about seventy gallons of (judging by the smell, extremely spiked) punch. It pours out in a cascade and I leap forward, avoiding the worst of the spill as everyone else screams and gets their prom attire coated in sticky, chemical sugar.

The big double doors of the gym are in sight now. Is Tammy Thompson already dancing? What will she think when she sees me burst in, wild and reckless and trailed by local law enforcement?

What will she say when I tell her how I feel?

No more time for hypotheticals.

I throw the double doors open. The prom greets me with wild synthesizers—and the exact nightmare of crepe paper and laser lights that I anticipated. I'm on a small balcony above the dance floor (read: gym floor), which means that beneath me is a sea of students in their best suits and most voluminous dresses.

"Hey, Tam," I whisper under my breath, practicing for the big moment. "Do you want to dance?"

"You're on *my* dance card tonight, Buckley," Dash says, grabbing me by the elbow. He looks like he's gunning for prom king in his obscenely expensive suit, even though he's just a sophomore prom committee volunteer.

"Let me go, Dash," I grit out.

"The adults are going around the long way, which means I get to do the honors myself," he says. He tugs me toward the door.

"Keep your hands on me for one more second and I'll announce that you're a cheating jerkwad to every girl in school," I say coolly.

He backs off, hands in the air.

"Still using that brain of yours, I see," he says with a dismissive smirk.

"What, you thought that I would lose IQ points when I turned down your slobbery advances?"

"I think nerds will never rule the world if we act like you do," he scoffs. "You *could* be great, but you'd rather waste your time on being bizarre and different, as if it makes you special."

I shake my head and it feels amazing, frankly, to not have the perm follow my movement like a bad-smelling pet. "I *am* different, Dash," I say, and I mean it in the best possible way. "Just like Mr. Hauser is different." Dash's face goes a whiter shade of pale than usual. "I don't care how smart you think you are—you don't get to decide who belongs in Hawkins and who doesn't. I might be trying to leave, and when I do, it will be on my own terms." I look him up and down, decoding him once and for all. "You think you're so much better than the jocks and the popular kids, but all you want to do is invert the social pyramid. As if it's somehow better to use your brains to get the money, the girls, the big win. All that talk about nerds ruling the world was never really because you wanted us to change things. You just want to come out on top *and* look like the underdog while you're doing it."

We have a small audience now—the students on the balcony who've heard my voice rising in pitch and intensity as I sling truth after truth.

"That's it . . . ," Dash says, grabbing for my arm again.

Just as I dodge away, Dash lets out a horrible howl and withdraws.

It takes me a moment to realize that Kate has descended on him in a whirlwind of midnight-blue taffeta, stomping the spiked heel of her white prom shoes straight into his soft leather loafers.

She does it again. And again. "Stop!" Dash cries.

"Not until you get away from Robin . . ." She stomps again. "And stay away!"

Another flurry of stomps.

Dash backs off toward the double doors he came in through. "What kind of demon is possessing you, Kate?"

"One with the common sense I've completely ignored all year," she growls.

Dash shakes his head like he's tossing off this entire situation. "The chaperones and Hopper will take care of both of you."

"Are you seriously still talking?" Kate asks, taking her shoe off and wielding it in her hand like a weapon.

Dash turns and runs out of the doors, straight back into the spiked punch explosion. He skids and goes down hard.

I hear people laughing as the doors slam back shut.

I don't have a lot of time before someone else catches up to me—but I have to ask Kate something important. "Did you really just smash your prom date's foot for me?"

"Date?" Kate mutters as she hops on one foot in her pantyhose, wedging her shoe back on. "I broke up with Dash *months* ago." She looks up at me, eyes wide and sincere. "I tried to tell you, Robin. That note you left fell to the bottom of my locker . . . but when I finally found it, I confronted him. That ass admitted he's been cheating on me with not one but two student council underlings. He said he didn't really care about them, though, so we could stay together! Do you want to know the worst part?"

"That's not the worst part?" I ask, eyebrows sky-high.

"He kept cherry-picking quotes from famous philosophers to make it sound excusable. 'He who thinks great thoughts often makes great errors.' That's Heidegger." Kate shudders. "Obviously, I dumped his ass."

"Here's a special quote just for Dash. 'He who fights with monsters might take care lest he thereby become a monster.'" I smirk in the direction of his dramatic, floundering exit. "That's Nietzsche."

"Robin, I've been wanting to say this forever. . . . Can I say it now?" Kate looks up at me, her dark eyes so nervously certain that I'm going to shut her down.

"Yeah. Of course."

"I'm really sorry I pushed you. To date Milton. To date anybody. It was unfair and selfish and . . . it just plain sucked. And I swear this is not an excuse, but I worried I would lose you as a friend if our lives started pulling us in different directions. But then I went ahead and lost you anyway."

"Wow. Thank you for saying all of that." She hug-bombs me, and I pat her head—finding her hair extra-crimped. It makes me miss all the time we spent together. But that doesn't mean we're going back to who we used to be.

"Wait, so do you accept my apology?" she asks, drawing back. She still needs all the data.

"I do. And I should apologize, too. All year I've been acting like crushes are stupid and I'm above it all. Let's just say that I know what it's like to . . . feel some really overwhelming feelings."

I worry that Kate is going to immediately push for details that I'm not ready to give, but she just says, "Speaking of that . . . ," and drags me over to meet her date—a junior from the debate team. I can tell in a single glance she likes him better than she ever liked Dash.

And suddenly my head is filled with visions of Tam.

Dash might be wrong about a lot of things, but the chaperones and Chief Hopper will catch up to me any minute. It doesn't take *that* long to run around the gym to the entrance on the far side.

I have to find her. Now.

CHAPTER THIRTY-NINE

JUNE 8, 1984

I detach myself from Kate's new social group and sweep a look at the dance below. I'm looking for red hair, anything that will let me know where Tam is. I can't see her from up here—it's time to throw myself into the fray.

I run down the stairs from the balcony to the dance floor. I'm in the thick of it now, surrounded by dancing groups and couples. I catch sight of Jessica and Jennifer in nearly matching sky-blue dresses, but no Tam. I wonder if she's hovering near Steve Harrington or standing alone and waiting for someone to ask her to dance. . . .

And then Cyndi Lauper starts to play.

Not one of the obvious singles—"Time After Time" or "Girls Just Want to Have Fun"—but another song that I recognize from the first sparkling notes.

"All Through the Night."

On my next sweep around the room, my eyes stick on Milton over by the DJ's massive stack of speakers. He's smiling right at me. And in an instant, I forgive him for coming over to my house tonight. For messing up Operation Croissant. He didn't know I was planning to leave tonight. I should have told him more. I should have told him that he was my best friend—back when that was true.

Right now, we're just ex-friends grinning at each other like total doofuses while Milton pretends to play the synthesizer part of the song on an air Yamaha.

"Did you request this?" I shout across the dance floor.

"I told you I'd be a good prom date," he shouts in response.

"You're not really my type," I say with a nose wrinkle. "But I want to start hanging out again. You know, if you can pencil me in."

"MTV and buckeyes?" he asks, raising his eyebrows hopefully.

"Only if you let me try the theremin."

He cocks his head, pretending to think about it. "I think that can be arranged."

And then the crowd parts around a couple, and I catch the copper glow of her hair. The pink froth of her dress.

Tam has gone full Molly Ringwald for prom night.

My heart gives a single, faint scratch as I see her arms loop around a boy's neck.

"Oh," I say, and my heart sinks all the way into my dress-code-inappropriate sneakers.

Tam's out there already. She wasn't waiting for me to show up and ask her to dance. She wasn't holding the same unnamed hope inside of her all year.

"Oh," I say again.

Like there's a glitch in the space-time continuum. Like I don't know how to move past this moment.

My lips press together, my eyes pricking with stupid tears.

"Craig Whitestone, though?" I ask, realizing all at once who Tam is paired off with. Our crummy drummer—the one who lied and said *he* picked Tam's favorite song for our marching band's final number of the season. For all the pining she did, the boy she's with on prom night isn't even Steve Harrington.

I guess Tam and I were both hopeless in our crushes. Maybe that's the biggest thing we had in common.

And because I can't keep staring at her without the tears having their way, I glance around and find Steve Harrington and Nancy Wheeler sitting on the bleachers, ignoring both each other and their glasses of punch. They both look strangely lonely and a little scared.

Like they know there are monsters in Hawkins, too.

I shake off that thought and go back to Tam.

Tammy. She was never Tam, except in my head.

She's absolutely glowing. Which is kind of strange

because, well, she's dancing with *Craig Whitestone.* But she really does look happy. He's got his hands splayed awkwardly on her waist, his gaze on her lips like a laser. Her lipstick is dark pink, and it makes for such a contrast with her hair, which is freshly trimmed and redder than ever, redder than a broken heart.

The floor fills with couples as the song reaches its first chorus.

I have to laugh, because all night I've been telling myself I'm wildly different from everyone in this room, but the truth is I'd love to have someone to dance with. I'd give anything for a group of friends I fit with—which will probably be *much* harder to find now that I'll never force myself to fit in again. But I still want to be seen and accepted and liked.

It turns out there is something normal lurking in my soul, after all.

"Um, what are you laughing about, Robin?" Wendy asks as she and Milton dance by me, swaying deeply.

"Will you accept Vicious, Delicious Irony?" I ask.

Milton tilts his head, considering. "Good band name."

I eye the door. Nobody's coming for me—yet.

But this might be my last chance.

"I want to dance," I admit.

"This *is* your song," Milton agrees over the dulcet tones of Cyndi Lauper.

It's time to claim my crown as the Weirdest Girl in Hawkins, Indiana.

I felt unsure when Mr. Hauser first dubbed me with such

a dubious title, but now I'm ready to claim it. How do you crown yourself, though? When you're not prom queen, just some weirdo who busted into the gym with half of the prom committee hot on her heels?

I slip off my sneakers and step onto the dance floor, letting the music swell over me and seal me off in a world where it doesn't matter if people are giving me weird looks for spinning myself in circles, closing my eyes, moving in ways that nobody else here would dare to move as they follow the boring, laid-out steps, and I carve out my own space on the floor.

Or maybe it does matter. I proudly accept those looks.

"Hey, Robin," comes a voice from behind me. A voice that I don't recognize—but somehow feels familiar.

I turn around and find Sheena Rollins standing in front of me in a white dress (*gown* would actually be closer to the right word) that makes her look like a princess in the most medieval sense of the word. There are vines trailing up and down a corset-laced top and a flowing skirt that trails behind her for several feet. I feel certain she sewed the whole thing herself, which is so perfectly different and utterly cool. Her white-blond hair falls straight and unpermed all the way down her back, and she's wearing a gold circlet on her head. Forget prom queen: Sheena brought her own crown.

"Do you want to dance?" Her voice is lower-pitched than I expect, but not weak or whispery at all. Sheena Rollins sounds like she knows exactly what she's saying and precisely what she wants.

"Um. I really, absolutely do."

She takes my hand and we move deeper onto the dance floor. We get a few looks, but I really don't care. I know we can't sway close like all of the fused boy-girl couples. That would get us kicked out by every chaperone in the gym—aka every chaperone who isn't already chasing me. But that sway-dance doesn't look very exciting, anyway. Instead, I grab Sheena's hands and we fly all over the dance floor, weaving between couples, unstoppable. We dance like the girls at the roller rink. Like we're having too much fun to stand still.

We make it to the center of the dance floor.

"I never thought you'd come to prom," I admit as we circle each other, twirling and laughing.

"That's okay," Sheena says with a secret, satisfied smile. "I don't let what people think get in my way."

She spins me, and I spin her. My hand rushes over her waist as I pull her back in. Then she dips me, which is pretty hilarious because I'm at least five inches taller. She looks down at me and beams. I don't know what this dance means to her—if it's just a prom-night whim or something else—but I know what it means to me.

It's my first dance with a girl. And it won't be my last.

Sheena and I bring our hands together and put them palm to palm between us right as the song ends. Right before the *entire* prom committee, half the chaperones, and a red-faced Chief Hopper in full beige regalia slam through the gym doors.

I grab my shoes—no time to put them back on—and run barefoot for the locker rooms and the back door beyond it.

“Robin?” Milton yells. “Are you leaving already?”

“Gotta run!” I shout right before I hit the locker room door, greeted by the ever-lingering smell of gym socks. The red Exit sign glows, beckoning me onward. Sliding on the tiled floor, I make a break for fresh air and my final escape.

I broke into prom. Now it’s time to break free.

HIGH SCHOOL

EPILOGUE

JUNE 7, 1985

If you'd told me a year ago that I would be taking a summer job at an ice cream parlor in Hawkins instead of traveling the world, my heart would have plummeted straight through the center of the earth.

But all the money I saved for Operation Croissant barely covered the (not one, not two, not three but *four*) cars I messed up on prom night—including the used-car lot purchase of another Dodge Dart to replace the one I totaled. My parents forgave me eventually, but I don't think they'll be teaching me how to drive anytime soon.

The silver lining was that my parents said I could have a bike again, and even gifted me one sans flower decals and the dead remains of streamers for my seventeenth birthday. Yes, I've crossed the edge of seventeen.

No, my life isn't nearly as epic as that song makes it sound.

But I'm only getting started.

I spent junior year making everyone at school uncomfortable with my sarcasm and sartorial choices. Even the band nerds didn't know what to do with me. Odd Squad is officially a thing of the past—Miss Genovese decided to mix it up and grouped me with three random new trumpet players—but Milton and I get together occasionally and watch MTV as he plays his Yamaha and fills me in on how Wendy's doing at college. Kate is still with her debate club boyfriend; their relationship seems both adversarial and adorable. Sheena Rollins and I talked a few times after prom. It turns out she's not particularly shy, but few people at Hawkins High merit her precious words. We didn't have the chance to get very close, though; she graduated early, got into a prestigious fashion design program, and left Hawkins without looking back. I can't exactly fault her for that. Tammy Thompson and Craig Whitestone didn't last (shocking, I know), but I've never really hoped she might run, heartbroken, into my arms.

So that's progress.

Oh, and I actually tried out for the fall play, a student-directed production of *Macbeth,* and got up onstage in a cloak to play a witch on a blasted heath, in a move that felt suspiciously close to typecasting. (Joke's on them: I loved every minute I spent cackling.) On closing night, Mr. Hauser was right there in the middle of the audience—sitting next to a very nice-looking man who he introduced after the show as Charles. Mr. Hauser got a new job teaching English in a small town in Illinois, and I've only got one more year before I can pack up and leave this place for good.

I'm going to need a new source of income for that.

Now that I've faced down the monster that is Hawkins High and lived to snark another day, a food service job seems fairly benign. Even if it's at the shrine to newness and money that is Starcourt Mall.

I show up on my first day of training as the mall is just opening, its white concourses already filled with people who are far too eager to spend their time and paychecks here. The food court pumps the smell of hot dogs everywhere. Everything is bright and synthetic and bizarre, an over-lit alternate universe.

Right there, past the Claire's and the Waldenbooks and the Sam Goody, waiting in all its sugary glory, is Scoops Ahoy. It's a little early for ice cream, so I expect to walk in and find the place empty, with the exception of the manager who hired me.

But there's one other person sitting in a booth. I see his hair towering over the top before I see the rest of him.

"No," I whisper. "It can't be."

I keep walking to find Steve Harrington sitting with his arm thrown over the vinyl back of a booth.

"What is he doing here?" I ask the zero people in Scoops Ahoy. I guess I'll have to speak to Steve directly. "What are *you* doing here?"

"It's a free country," he says, nearly knocking me over with the force of the cliché. Then he scans me up and down with a lazy sort of consideration. "Hey, do I know you from school or something?"

"Oh my God," I mutter. "The depths of your ignorance are astounding."

I walk behind the ice cream counter, through the staff room behind it, to the employees-only bathroom, where I don my Scoops Ahoy outfit for the first time. The white collar and puffed sleeves on the striped shirt are a little much, but I'll admit that I sort of like the vest and the high-waisted shorts. The hat . . . well . . . the hat is an indignity that my head will just have to get used to.

I affix the red nametag to my vest.

I'm Robin.

I might get you a waffle cone with double chocolate sprinkles, but I don't have to be happy about it.

That's how I ended up at Scoops—when I worked my way through the mall, most of my interviews were even more disastrous than the ones I had on Main Street at Melvald's and Radio Shack. (RIP, Bob Newby.)

Despite my work experience at the movie theater, my new insistence on being an unrepentant and wholly honest version of myself all the time didn't go over so well at the Gap (I wasn't enthusiastic enough about folding T-shirts), the food court (I wouldn't smile on command), and the new portrait studio where people pose for soft-focus photos (I wouldn't make *other* people smile on command). Here at Scoops Ahoy, they only seemed to care that I show up consistently and clean the ice cream scoops between every customer.

Done and done.

I check myself in the little mirror, the dark eye makeup and black nails and mismatched bracelets that are now part of my everyday look clashing with the Scoops Ahoy costume in a way that I find most pleasing.

I leave the employee bathroom behind to find the staff room is no longer empty.

"Robin, we have a possible new hire that I want to get your take on," says my manager, a thirty-something guy named Ned who has escaped the sailor outfit but still has to wear navy-blue slacks with white piping and a tie with ice cream on it. He flips some papers on a clipboard. "His name is Steve . . . Harrin—"

"Here are seven reasons why *no,*" I spit out. "He's unreliable, he's self-centered, he shows up late for literally everything and then acts like he's doing everyone a favor when he finally jock-waltzes through the door, he's going to flirt with every girl who comes in until they turn the color of raspberry ripple, and he'll eat ice cream morning, noon, and night."

"I see what you're saying," Ned wheedles. "But I wonder if it's still worth hiring him because of his . . . assets."

I cross my arms, preemptively unimpressed. "Are you talking about his hair?"

Ned shakes his head like he's not proud of himself, but he doesn't switch course. "Do you know how many girls will come in and order ice cream just to be near hair like that?

Believe me, I did not have hair like that when I was younger, so I can do the math."

"Wait, did you hire *me* for my hair?" I ask sarcastically, twisting the ends like I'm showing off my tresses. It's grown out since I hacked it unceremoniously on prom night. Now it touches my shoulders, naturally wavy, dark blond or light brown depending on who you ask. It's nowhere near the height of fashion. It's a non-style, an in-between color.

It's mine, and I love it.

Ned scoffs and buries his face in his clipboard. "I hired you because you're a responsible young adult. That's why you're going to be in charge of him."

Hmmm. At first blush, working with Steve Harrington all summer seems like a punishment for some horrible crime in a past life. But being *in charge* of Steve Harrington all summer?

That's something I could potentially get used to.

"All right," I say. "Hire him. He'll get bored and quit by Fourth of July."

"Welcome aboard the Scoops Ahoy ship, Steve!" Ned says as he parades out of the staff room.

I follow him, arms crossed, still wary.

What did I just agree to?

"Do I have to wear *that*?" Steve asks, pointing to my jaunty, if completely cheesy, outfit.

I've lived through so much since the beginning of sophomore year. Even though I heard that he and Nancy Wheeler broke up in the most bitter fashion, I get the feeling that Steve Harrington still needs an education in having things *not* turn out the way he wants them. Maybe I can give him a crash course.

I make a disgusted noise in the back of my throat. "Are you going to be this much of a prima donna about everything?" I ask. "Because this place gets really busy."

"I'm nothing like Madonna, so that doesn't even make sense," he says with a sudden frown.

Oh. I really like making him frown.

"You're going to be fine with the monotony of scooping ice cream for entitled adults and whining, sticky children all summer? What happens when one of your many friends and admirers comes in and you wish you were out there having fun instead of in here slinging another U.S.S. Butterscotch?"

His frown morphs slightly into a stubborn look. "I can handle it."

"Sure you can, rocket man," I fire back.

He runs one hand through his hair—not preening. This is a purely defensive move.

"I do know you, don't I?" he says, squinting as Ned fills out the rest of the paperwork to make this scenario official.

"No," I say. "You really, really don't."

Steve Harrington barely recognizes me, even though I spent an entire year of my life thinking about him (and Tammy Thompson). But even if he did recognize me from school, I'm so much more than anybody at Hawkins High knows.

"Click's class!" he shouts, and then makes a V for victory over his head. "We were in the same history class. Or don't *you* remember?"

"I remember everything, Steve," I say sharply. I want to keep him on his toes.

"All right, you two. It's going to be a sweet, sweet summer!" Ned says, pulling another corporate catchphrase out of his ass. "Steve, let's get you into Scoops gear right away."

"Yippee," he mutters as Ned disappears into the back.

"Hey, look, if we're going to be working together this summer, let's call a truce, okay?" Steve extends a hand to shake. "I don't know why you don't like me, but I'm a pretty okay guy."

It flashes through my head that it's possible—infinitesimally possible—that there's more to Steve Harrington than I know about. That the look I saw on his face on prom night was more than a passing cloud in his sunny, perfect life.

Then he gives the smarmiest smile I've ever seen. Is *this* how he charms people? It looks even worse up close.

"Steve," I say sweetly.

He moves a few inches closer—so used to the instant affection of girls that he's ridiculously easy to lure in. He has no idea what he's walking into here. I shake his hand and whisper, "We might be coworkers, but there is no universe in which you and I become friends."

He frowns again, deeper this time. "Well, this is going to be fun."

Ned reemerges with another employee uniform. Two minutes later, Steve is standing in front of me, fully made over. It's the fashion show of a lifetime, really. His sailor shorts are much too tight, and the hat sits on top of his hair like a tiny lifeboat about to capsize. (I take it back. I love these hats.)

I laugh so hard I almost cry.

"That's . . . just . . . wow."

"Thanks for really upping my self-esteem here."

"Can you do a spin?" I ask, curling into the fetal position in the booth as I cackle.

Steve throws the hat on the floor.

Ned looks flustered, picking it up and dusting it off.

"Let's start you both on sundae construction, okay?" he asks.

Part of me is almost glad that I stayed in Hawkins long enough to see the great Steve Harrington working at Scoops Ahoy. Maybe things are turning upside down again, the world slowly righting itself. Maybe life will be different soon. Now that I've been fully myself for a year, I know there's no going back. As it turns out, being a loner suits me beautifully. But there are times when I crash hard into the hope of finding my people. Friends who would stick with me through anything. A girl I can have a *less* hopeless crush on.

There are adventures waiting for me. I know it.

But first, I have to get through a very strange summer.

I pull out the last thing in my bag—my Polaroid camera—and take another picture for my collection. It flashes, then makes that intense click as the white paper rolls out from the front. Steve lunges to grab the photo, but I get it first and start to vigorously shake it.

As it slowly develops, my smile spreads.

I'm framed in the front, smirking, while Steve sulks behind me in his sailor suit.

"Oh, this is perfect."

"No," he says. "Destroy that, right now."

"Sorry," I say, pocketing the photo in my oversize shorts. "I need souvenirs."

He rolls his eyes and crosses his arms, acting like the overgrown child that he is. "Are you going to be like this all summer . . ." He squints at my nametag. "*Robin*?"

"Oh, Steve," I say sweetly. "I'm just getting started."

HAWKINS
HIGH SCHOOL

ACKNOWLEDGMENTS

Sara Crowe, without that conversation we had in the coffee shop, this book would not exist.

Ann Dávila Cardinal, without that conversation we had outside a different coffee shop, this story might not have found its way.

Kristen Simmons, your margin notes and marching-band expertise are everything. Hopper and I love you.

Cory, thank you for watching *Stranger Things* with me. (Even the scary parts.)

Mav, I promise we can watch it together! Soon!

Sasha Henriques, working with you is an absolute delight, and you guided this story in all the best ways.

Netflix and the *Stranger Things* team, you gave me the chance to tell the origin story of an unforgettable nerd who showed up in a sailor hat and captured all of our hearts—and I will never forget it.

Maya Hawke, you are an icon. Thank you for Robin.

Winona Ryder, thank you for every bit of strange-girl greatness you've brought to every stage of my life.

Last but not least, thank you to the enthusiastic strangers who saw me at New York Comic Con back in 2016 and shouted "Eleven!"—even though I hadn't seen the show yet and wasn't wearing a costume. (Apparently, I looked like a grown-up version of El circa season one.) Without you, I might not have started this journey. Plus, Eleven is an absolute badass, so I take it as the highest compliment.

IF YOU LOVED READING ROBIN'S STORY, GET TO KNOW ANOTHER *STRANGER THINGS* FAN FAVORITE CHARACTER IN

AVAILABLE NOW! TURN THE PAGE FOR AN EXCERPT.

Find more *Stranger Things* books at ReadStrangerThings.com.

PROLOGUE

The floor of the San Diego bus station was mostly cigarette butts. A million years ago, the building had probably been fancy, like Grand Central or those huge places you see in movies. But now it just looked gray all over, like a warehouse full of crumpled band flyers and winos.

It was almost midnight, but the lobby was crowded. Next to me, a wall of storage lockers ran all the way down to the end. One of the lockers was leaking a little, like something had spilled inside and was dripping out onto the floor. It was sticking to my shoes.

There were vending machines on the other side of the lobby, and there was a bar over in the corner, where a bunch of skinny, stubbly men sat smoking into ashtrays, hunched over their beers like goblins. The smoke made the air look hazy and weird.

I hurried along, close to the lockers, keeping my chin down and trying not to look obvious. Back at my house, when I'd imagined this scene, I'd been pretty sure I'd be able to blend into the crowd, no problem. But now that I was here, it was harder than I'd pictured. I'd been counting on the chaos and the size to cover me. It was a *bus* station, after all. I didn't figure I'd be the only one here who was still too young to drive.

On my street or at school, I was easy to overlook—twelve years old and average height, average shape and face and clothes. Average everything except for my hair, which was long and red and the brightest thing about me. I yanked it into a ponytail and tried to walk like I knew where I was going. I should have brought a hat.

Over at the ticket windows, a couple of older girls in green eyeshadow and rubber miniskirts were arguing with the guy behind the glass. Their hair was teased up so high it looked like cotton candy.

"C'mon, man," said one of them. She was shaking her purse upside down on the window ledge, counting out quarters. "Can't you cut me a break? I'm barely short. Only a buck fifty."

The guy looked sarcastic and bored in his ratty Hawaiian shirt. "Does this look like a charity? No fare, no ticket."

I reached into the pocket of my warm-up jacket and ran my fingers over my own ticket. Economy from San Diego to LA. I'd paid for it with a twenty from my mom's jewelry box and the guy had barely looked at me.

I walked faster, sticking close to the wall with my skateboard under my arm. For a second, I thought how badass it would be to set it down and go zooming between the benches. But I didn't. One wrong move and even a bunch of late-night dirtbags were going to notice I wasn't supposed to be here.

I was almost to the end of the lobby when a nervous ripple went through the crowd behind me. I turned around. Two guys in tan uniforms were standing by the vending machines, looking out over the sea of faces. Even from across the station, I could catch the glint of their badges. Cops.

The tall one had fast, pale eyes and long, skinny arms like a spider. He was pacing up and down between the benches in that way cops always do. It's a slow, official walk that says *I might be a creepy string bean, but I'm the one with the badge and the gun.* It reminded me of my stepdad.

If I could get to the end of the lobby, I could slip out to the depot where the buses pulled up. I'd slide into the crowd and disappear.

The scuzzy guys at the bar hunched lower over their beers. One of them mashed out his cigarette, then gave the cops a long, nasty stare and spit on the floor between his feet. The girls at the ticket window had stopped arguing with the cashier. They were acting really interested in their press-on nails, but looked plenty nervous about Officer String Bean. Maybe they had the same kind of stepdads I did.

The cops waded out into the middle of the lobby and were squinting around the bus station like they were looking for something. A lost kid, maybe. A bunch of delinquents up to no good.

Or a runaway.

I ducked my head and got ready to blend in. I was just about to step out into the terminal when someone cleared his throat and a big, heavy hand closed around my arm. I turned and looked up into the looming face of a third cop.

He smiled a bored, flat smile, all teeth. "Maxine Mayfield? I'm going to need you to come with me." His face was hard and craggy, and he looked like he'd said the same thing to different kids about a hundred times. "You've got people at home worried sick about you."

CHAPTER ONE

The sky was so low it seemed to be sitting right on top of downtown Hawkins. The world whipped past me as I clattered along the sidewalk. I skated faster, listening to the wheels whispering on concrete, then thudding over the cracks. It was a chilly afternoon, and the cold made my ears hurt. It had been chilly every day since we'd rolled into town three days ago.

I kept looking up, expecting to see the bright sky of San Diego. But here, everything was pale and gray, and even when it wasn't overcast, the sky looked colorless. Hawkins, Indiana: home of low gray clouds and quilted jackets and winter.

Home of . . . me.

Main Street was all tricked out for Halloween, with storefronts full of grinning pumpkins. Fake spiderwebs and paper skeletons were taped in the windows of the supermarket. All down the block, lampposts were wrapped in black-and-orange streamers fluttering in the wind.

I'd spent the afternoon at the Palace Arcade, playing *Dig Dug* until I ran out of quarters. Because my mom didn't like me wasting money on video games, back home in California I'd mostly only gotten to play when I'd been with my dad. He'd take me to the bowling alley with him, or sometimes the laundry, which had *Pac-Man* and *Galaga*. And I sometimes hung out at the Joy Town Arcade at the mall, even though it was a total rip-off and full of metalheads in ratty jeans and leather jackets. They had *Pole Position,* though, which was better than any other racing game and had a steering wheel like you were actually driving.

The arcade in Hawkins was a big, low-roofed building with neon signs in the windows and a bright yellow awning (but under the colored lights and the paint, it was just aluminum siding). They had *Dragon's Lair* and *Donkey Kong,* and *Dig Dug,* which was my best game.

I'd been hanging out there all afternoon, running up the score on *Dig Dug,* but after I entered my name in the number-one spot and I didn't have any more quarters, I started to feel antsy, like I needed to move, so I left the arcade and skated downtown to take a tour of Hawkins.

I pushed myself faster, rattling past a diner and a hardware store, a Radio Shack, a movie theater. The theater was small, like it might only have one screen, but the front was glitzy and old-fashioned, with a big marquee that stuck out like a battleship covered in lights.

The only time I really liked to sit still was at the movies. The newest poster out front was for *The Terminator,* but I'd already seen it. The story was pretty good. This killer robot who looks like Arnold Schwarzenegger travels back in time from the future to kill this waitress named Sarah Connor. At first she just seems kind of normal, but she turns out to be a total badass. I liked it, even though it wasn't a real monster movie, but something about it also made me feel weirdly disappointed. None of the women I knew were anything like Sarah Connor.

I was zipping past the pawn shop now—past a furniture store, past a pizza place with a red-and-green-striped awning—when something small and dark darted across the sidewalk in front of me. In the gray afternoon light, it looked like a cat, and I just had time to think how weird that was, how you'd never see a cat in downtown San Diego, before my feet went out from under me.

I was used to wiping out, but still, that split second of a fall was always disorienting. When I lost my balance, it felt like the whole world had flipped over and skidded out from under me. I hit the ground so hard I felt the thump in my teeth.

I'd been skating since forever—since my best friend, Nate Walker, and his brother Silas took a trip to Venice Beach with their parents when we were in the third grade and came back all jazzed up on stories about the Z-Boys and the skate shops in Dogtown. I'd been skating since the day I found out about grip tape and Madrid boards and rode down Sunset Hill for the first time and learned what it felt like to go so fast your heart raced and your eyes watered.

The sidewalk was cold. For a second, I lay flat on my stomach, with a thudding hollow in my chest and pain zinging up my arms. My elbow had punched through the sleeve of my sweater and the palms of my hands felt raw and electric. The cat was long gone.

I had rolled over and was trying to sit up when a thin, dark-haired woman came hurrying out of one of the stores. It was almost as surprising as a cat in the business district. No one in California would have come running out just to see if I was okay, but this was Indiana. My mom had said that people would be nicer here.

The woman was already kneeling next to me on the concrete with big, nervous eyes. I was bleeding a little where my elbow had gone through my sleeve. My ears were ringing.

She leaned close, looking worried. "Oh, your arm, that must hurt." Then she looked up, staring into my face. "Do you scare easily?"

I just stared back. *No,* I wanted to say, and that was true in all kinds of ways. I wasn't scared of spiders or dogs. I could walk along the boardwalk alone in the dark or skateboard in the wash in flood season and never worry that a murderer was going to jump out at me or that a sudden deluge of water would come rushing down to drown me. And when my mom and my stepdad said we were moving to Indiana, I packed some socks and underwear and two pairs of jeans in my backpack and headed for the bus station alone to escape to LA. It was a total trip to ask a stranger if they got scared. Scared of *what*?

For a second I just sat in the middle of the sidewalk with my elbow stinging and my palms raw and gritty, squinting at her. "What?"

She reached out to brush gravel off my hands. Hers were thinner and tanner than mine, with dry, cracked knuckles and bitten fingernails. Next to them, mine looked pale, covered in freckles.

She was watching me in a quick, nervous way, like I was the one acting weird. "I just wondered if you scar easily. Sometimes fair skin does. You should put Bactine on that to keep it from getting infected."

"Oh." I shook my head. The palms of my hands still felt like they were full of tiny sparks. "No. I mean, I don't think so."

She leaned closer and was about to say something else when suddenly her eyes got even bigger and she froze. We both looked up as the air was split by the roar of an engine.

A swimming-pool-blue Camaro came bombing through the stoplight at Oak Street and snarled up to the curb. The woman whipped around to see what the trouble was, but I already knew.

My stepbrother, Billy, was leaning back in the driver's seat with his hand draped lazily on the wheel. I could hear the blare of his music through the closed windows.

Even from the sidewalk, I could see the light glinting off Billy's earring. He was watching me in the flat, empty way he always did—heavy-lidded, like I made him so bored he could barely stand it—but under that was a glittering edge of something dangerous. When he looked at me like that, my face wanted to flush bright red or crumple. I was used to how he looked at me, like I was something he wanted to scrape off him, but it always seemed worse when he did it in front of someone else—like this nice, nervous woman. She looked like someone's mom.

I scrubbed my stinging hands on the thighs of my jeans before bending down to get my board.

He let his head flop back, his mouth open. After a second, he leaned across the seat and rolled down the window.

The stereo thumped louder, Quiet Riot pounding out into the chilly air. "Get in."

• • •

Once, for two weeks back in April, I thought that Camaro was the coolest thing I'd ever seen. It had a long, hungry body like a shark, all sleek painted panels and sharp angles. It was the kind of car you could rob a bank in.

Billy Hargrove was fast and hard-edged, like the car. He had a faded denim jacket and a face like a movie star.

Back then, he wasn't Billy yet, just this hazy idea I had about what my life was going to be like. His dad, Neil, was going to marry my mom, and when we all moved in together, Billy was going to be my brother. I was excited to have a family again.

After the divorce, my dad had hightailed it to LA, so I mostly only saw him on second-rate holidays, or when he was down in San Diego for work and my mom couldn't think up a reason not to let me.

My mom was still around, of course, but in a thin, floaty way that was hard to get a hold on. She'd always been a little blurry around the edges, but once my dad was out of the picture, it got worse. It was kind of tragic how easily she disappeared into the personality of every guy she dated.

There was Donnie, who was on disability for his back and couldn't bend down to take out the trash. He made us Bisquick pancakes on the weekends and told terrible jokes, and then one day he ran off with a waitress from IHOP.

After Donnie, there was Vic from St. Louis, and Gus with one green eye and one blue one, and Ivan, who picked his teeth with a folding knife.

Neil was different. He drove a tan Ford pickup and his shirts were ironed and his mustache made him look like some kind of army sergeant or park ranger. And he wanted to marry my mom.

The other guys had been losers, but they were temporary losers, so I never really minded them. Some of them were goofy or friendly or funny, but after a while, the bad stuff always piled up. They were behind on their rent, or they'd total their cars, or they'd get drunk and wind up in county.

They always left, and if they didn't, my mom kicked them out. I wasn't heartbroken. Even the best ones were kind of embarrassing. None of them were cool like my dad, but mostly they were okay. Some of them were even nice.

Like I said, Neil was different.

She met him at the bank. She was a teller there, sitting behind a smudgy window, handing out deposit slips and giving lollipops to little kids. Neil was a guard, standing all day by the double doors. He said she looked like Sleeping Beauty sitting there behind the glass, or like an old-timey painting in a frame. The way he said it, the idea was supposed to sound romantic, but I couldn't see how. Sleeping Beauty was in a coma. Paintings in frames weren't interesting or exciting—they were just stuck there.

The first time she had him over for dinner, he brought flowers. None of the other ones had ever brought flowers. He told her the meat loaf was the best meat loaf he'd ever had, and she smiled and blushed and glanced sideways at him. I was glad she'd stopped crying over her last boyfriend—a carpet salesman with a comb-over and a wife he hadn't told her about.

A few weeks before school let out for the summer, Neil asked my mom to marry him. He bought her a ring and she gave him the extra key to the house. He showed up when he felt like it, bringing flowers or getting rid of throw pillows and pictures he didn't like, but he didn't come over after ten and he never spent the night. He was too much of a gentleman for that—*old-fashioned,* he said. He liked clean counters and family dinners. The little gold engagement ring made her happier than I'd seen her in a long time, and I tried to be happy for her.

Neil had told us he had a son in high school, but that was all he said about him. I figured he would be some preppie football type, or else maybe a younger copy of Neil. I wasn't picturing Billy.

The night we finally met him, Neil took us out to Fort Fun, which was a go-kart track near my house where the surf rats went with their girlfriends to eat funnel cakes and play air hockey and Skee-Ball. It was the kind of place that guys like Neil would never be caught dead in. Later, I figured out that he was trying to make us think he was fun.

Billy was late. Neil didn't say anything, but I could tell he was mad. He tried to act like everything was fine, but his fingers left dents in his foam Coke cup. My mom fidgeted with a paper napkin while we waited, wadding it up and then tearing it into little squares.

I pretended that maybe it was all a big scam and Neil didn't even have a son. It was the kind of thing that was always happening in horror movies—the guy made up a whole fake life and told everyone about his perfect house and his perfect family, but actually he lived in a basement, eating cats or something.

I didn't really think it was the truth, but I imagined it anyway, because it was better than watching him glare out at the parking lot every two minutes and then smile tightly at my mom.

The three of us were working our way through a game of mini golf when Billy finally showed up. We were on the tenth hole, standing in front of a painted windmill the size of a garden shed and trying to get the ball past the turning sails.

When the Camaro roared into the parking lot, the engine was so loud that everyone turned to look. He got out, letting the door slam shut behind him. He had on his jean jacket and engineer boots, and raddest of all, he had an earring. Some of the older boys at school wore boots and jean jackets, but none of them had an earring. With his mop of sprayed hair and his open shirt, he looked like the metalheads at the mall, or David Lee Roth or someone else famous.

He came over to us, cutting straight through the mini-golf course.

He stepped over a big plastic turtle and onto the fake green turf.

Neil watched with the tight, sour look he always did when something wasn't up to his standards. "You're late."

Billy just shrugged. He didn't look at his dad.

"Say hello to Maxine."

I wanted to tell Billy that wasn't my name—I hated when people called me Maxine—but I didn't. It wouldn't have mattered. Neil always called me that, no matter how many times I told him to stop.

Billy gave me this slow, cool nod, like we already knew each other, and I smiled, holding my putter by its sweaty rubber handle. I was thinking how much cooler this was going to make me. How jealous Nate and Silas would be. I was getting a brother, and it was going to change my life.

Later, the two of us hung out by the Skee-Ball stalls while Neil and my mom walked down along the boardwalk together. It was getting kind of annoying, how they were always all gooey at each other, but I fed quarters into the slot and tried to ignore it. She seemed really happy.

Skee-Ball was on a raised concrete deck above the go-kart track. From the railing, you could look down and watch the cars go zooming around in a figure eight.

Billy leaned his elbows on the railing with his hands hanging loose and casual in front of him and a cigarette balanced between his fingers. "Susan seems like a real buzzkill."

I shrugged. She was fussy and nervous and could be no fun sometimes, but she was my mom.

Billy looked out over the track. His eyelashes were long, like a girl's, and I saw for the first time how heavy his eyelids were. That was the thing that I would come to learn about Billy, though—he never really looked awake, except . . . sometimes. Sometimes his face went suddenly alert, and then you had no idea what he was going to do or what was going to happen next.

"So. Maxine." He said my name like some kind of joke. Like it wasn't really my name.

I tucked my hair behind my ears and tossed a ball into the corner cup for a hundred points. The machine under the coin slot whirred and spit out a paper chain of tickets. "Don't call me that. It's Max or nothing."

Billy glanced back at me. His face was slack. Then he smiled a sleepy smile. "Well. You've got a real mouth on you."

I shrugged. It wasn't the first time I'd heard that. "Only when people piss me off."

He laughed, and it was low and gravelly. "Mad Max. All right, then."

Out in the parking lot, the Camaro was sitting under a streetlight, so blue it looked like a creature from another world. Some kind of monster. I wanted to touch it.

Billy had turned away again. He was leaning on the rail with the cigarette in his hand, watching the go-karts as they zoomed along the tire-lined track.

I sent the last ball clunking into the one-hundred cup and took my tickets. "You want to race?"

Billy snorted and took a drag off the cigarette. "Why would I want to screw around with some little go-kart when I know how to drive?"

"I know how to drive too," I said, even though it wasn't exactly true. My dad had taught me how to use the clutch once in the parking lot at Jack in the Box.

Billy didn't even blink. He tipped his head back and blew out a plume of smoke. "Sure you do," he said. He looked blank and bored under the flashing neon lights, but he sounded almost friendly.

"I *do.* As soon as I'm sixteen, I'm going to get a Barracuda and drive all the way up the coast."

"A 'Cuda, huh? That's a lot of horsepower for a little kid."

"So? I can handle it. I bet I could even drive your car."

Billy stepped closer and leaned down so he was staring right into my face. He smelled sharp and dangerous, like hair stuff and cigarettes. He was still smiling.

"Max," he said in a sly, singsong voice. "If you think you're getting anywhere near my car, you are extremely mistaken." But he was smiling when he said it. He laughed again, pinching the end of his cigarette and tossing it away. His eyes were bright.

And I'd figured it was all a big goof, because it was just how guys like that talked. The slackers and the lowlifes my dad knew—all the ones who hung out at the Black Door Lounge down the street from his apartment in East

Hollywood. When they made jokes about Sam Mayfield's daredevil daughter or teased me about boys, they were only playing.

Billy was looming over me, studying my face. "You're just a kid," he said again. "But I guess even kids can tell a bitchin' ride when they see one, right?"

"Sure," I said.

And I'd actually been dumb enough to believe that this was the start of something good. That the Hargroves were here to make everything better—or at least okay. That this was family.